PENGUIN METRO READS
WORLD'S BEST BOYFRIEND

Durjoy Datta was born in New Delhi, India, and completed a degree in engineering and business management before embarking on a writing career. His first book—*Of Course I Love You*—was published when he was twenty-one years old and was an instant bestseller. His successive novels—*Now That You're Rich*; *She Broke Up, I Didn't!*; *Oh Yes, I'm Single!*; *You Were My Crush*; *If It's Not Forever*; *Till the Last Breath . . .*; *Someone Like You*; *Hold My Hand*; *When Only Love Remains*—have also found prominence on various bestseller lists, making him one of the highest-selling authors in India.

Durjoy also has to his credit two television shows, *Sadda Haq* (Channel V) and *Veera* (Star Plus), both of which have done exceedingly well on Indian television.

Durjoy lives in New Delhi, loves dogs and is an active CrossFitter. For more updates, you can follow him on Facebook (www.facebook. com/durjoydatta1) or Twitter (@durjoydatta).

DURJOY DATTA

World's ~~Worst~~ BEST Boyfriend

Penguin
metro reads

PENGUIN METRO READS
Published by the Penguin Group
Penguin Books India Pvt. Ltd, 7th Floor, Infinity Tower C, DLF Cyber City,
Gurgaon 122 002, Haryana, India
Penguin Group (USA) Inc., 375 Hudson Street, New York, New York 10014, USA
Penguin Group (Canada), 90 Eglinton Avenue East, Suite 700, Toronto,
Ontario, M4P 2Y3, Canada
Penguin Books Ltd, 80 Strand, London WC2R 0RL, England
Penguin Ireland, 25 St Stephen's Green, Dublin 2, Ireland (a division of
Penguin Books Ltd)
Penguin Group (Australia), 707 Collins Street, Melbourne, Victoria 3008, Australia
Penguin Group (NZ), 67 Apollo Drive, Rosedale, Auckland 0632, New Zealand
Penguin Books (South Africa) (Pty) Ltd, Block D, Rosebank Office Park,
181 Jan Smuts Avenue, Parktown North, Johannesburg 2193, South Africa

Penguin Books Ltd, Registered Offices: 80 Strand, London WC2R 0RL, England

First published in Penguin Metro Reads by Penguin Books India 2015

ISBN 9780143424635

Typeset in Bembo by Manipal Digital Systems, Manipal
Printed at Replika Press Pvt. Ltd, India

A PENGUIN RANDOM HOUSE COMPANY

World's ~~Worst~~ BEST Boyfriend

1

Twelve-year-old Dhruv sat crying in one corner of the playground, plucking at the grass, watching the other kids play at the far end. It had been a couple of months since he first started avoiding them. His friends often talked about how his dad and mom were separating and they would ask questions to which he had no answers.

'Do they fight?' 'Don't you try to stop them?' 'Will you leave us?' 'Will you stay with your mom or your dad?' 'Is your mom marrying again?' 'Is your dad?'

Their curiosity was legitimate. No one knew of such a case in their middle-class neighbourhood. Divorces, even in television soaps, were cause for much distress. Families were meant to stay together till the end of time.

School was a nightmare. He would have stopped attending if not for his mom. She taught in the same school—chemistry and maths for eighth and ninth standards—so skipping school wasn't an option at all.

Things had gone downhill so slowly that he didn't notice anything in the beginning. It was like Tetris on slow rewind. He thought other kids were going through the same crisis. For the past few months, there were rumours of his mother having a torrid, Mills-and-Boon-esque affair with the principal, who also owned the school and three other branches. The seniors would often cook up stories about his mother and the principal locking themselves in his room for hours. Dhruv would innocently ask, 'Why would they lock themselves in?' The seniors would affect a boisterous, evil laugh. He would ask again, 'Tell me, why would they lock themselves in? Tell me?' He would try hitting them and they would push him away. He would then lock himself in a bathroom stall for three straight periods.

Today morning, between the third and the fourth periods, when he was hiding in the bathroom, he overheard two seniors talk outside.

'I can't believe Namrata ma'am is banging that oldie. She's quite something, isn't she? Very perky breasts for thirty-five,' said a senior, probably in the ninth grade.

'Dude. We should totally check out the CCTV footage. Imagine her naked on top of that man! Did I tell you? That guy in the other class? Ramit? That bastard dropped a pencil and Namrata ma'am picked it up. She totally bent over and showed everything. He tried clicking a picture but it came out totally blurred.'

'Should we repeat it in her class tomorrow?'

They laughed. Dhruv heard the taps run. The boys left the washroom.

*

Dhruv returned home in a sullen mood.

'Why are you not eating, Dhruv?' his mother asked, ladling another spoonful of rice, then cradling his face in her palms and kissing it. She was a good cook. Despite the toxic environment, Dad always ate quietly, concentrating on every morsel.

'I don't feel like eating.'

'You didn't eat your lunch too. Is there something wrong? Someone troubling you? Should I talk to your class teacher?' Mom asked, making little rice balls.

'I don't feel like eating, Mumma,' snapped Dhruv, pushing her hand away.

'What's the problem, Dhruv?'

'IT'S NOTHING! THERE'S NO PROBLEM, MUMMA. LEAVE ME ALONE!' His mother retreated in shock. Dhruv had never shouted at her. They were always on the same team. And then he spoke. 'Don't pick up pencils from the ground tomorrow.'

'Why?'

'Because I am asking you not to, Mumma!'

'But why?'

'JUST LIKE THAT!'

'What's the matter with you, Dhruv?'

'THE SCHOOL WANTS TO SEE YOU NAKED. THEY WANT TO SEE THE CCTV FOOTAGE OF YOU IN THE PRINCIPAL'S ROOM WITH THE PRINCIPAL.' Dhruv pushed the plate away and ran to his room. His father looked up from his plate, his eyes burning embers. For the next three hours, he heard Dad and Mom shout at each other in the next room, things breaking. He blamed himself for opening his mouth and cried into his pillow. Later that evening, he sneaked out of the house through the window.

*

It had been three hours he had been missing from home and no one had come looking for him. The other kids had gone home. He wandered the streets alone hoping that his parents, exhausted from all the shouting, would find him gone and come looking for him.

He had wandered to the E block of their apartment complex. This part had the cramped flats—little stinking one-bedroom apartments with flaky wall paint and wet clothes hanging from clotheslines in balconies. As he aimlessly looked on, he saw a family stroll out from the lobby, giggling and laughing. A middle-aged couple, much like Mom and Dad, and two kids. The younger of the two seemed to be around his age and she was staring at her sandals which flopped and made a clapping sound as she walked. Her skin was brown and white in patches, like a dalmatian, but she was smiling. Dhruv felt envy rip him apart.

2

Aranya did not like Mango Madness, she liked Orange. Orange was one colour, unlike the yellow-and-white-striped Mango Madness.

'There's no Orange,' said the mother.

'Cola?'

'No Cola.'

'Vanilla?'

'No Vanilla, just have Mango Madness. It's good. Your brother likes it,' said the mother and shoved the ice lolly in her palm. She knew better than to fight her brother's choice—he was her parents' favourite child.

She would have rather stayed home and watched *Evil Dead* for the thirty-third time on her brother's computer, a second-hand

AMD 1.2 GB Thunderbird Athlon, with 320 MB SDRAM, SoundBlaster Live sound card, a CD drive with a 12 GB hard disk.

She was making a list of her favourite movies in her head while her parents talked about the next loan instalment and lamented about the rising prices of onions, potatoes, lentils, ladies' fingers, brinjals, textiles, cable subscription, electricity, petrol, water, and even bribery rates! In her list, *Evil Dead*, *The Texas Chainsaw Massacre* and *The Blair Witch Project* were the top three horror movies of all time.

'What do you want to watch these for? They are all so scary,' her mother would ask whenever she wanted a new VCD.

'They are not scary at all,' she would protest. But they would all go by her brother's pedestrian choice of movies.

'Let your brother choose,' her father would say.

'Is it because I'm this way?' she would snap, pointing at the skin on her arms. Back then she was gradually beginning to realize there was something off about her. She knew she was different. She was yet to find out that the world treated the different with hatred.

'No,' her mother would lie.

Generalized vitiligo was one of the first phrases Aranya had learnt to write down. It's what her prescriptions had said. It's a disease with no certain cause. It causes the skin pigment cells to die resulting in patchy, sensitive skin. Since people can't pronounce the scientific term, they often use the Hindi words *safedi* and *fulwari*.

It started showing up when she was only two. For a little kid it wasn't much of a bother, in fact it was a delight. 'Hey! I have two skin colours. I'm fair and I'm tanned. So cool!' she used to say.

The condition slowly worsened as her entire body went light pink and white in patches. The 'condition' didn't matter a lot to her, at least not till she turned nine. She thought it was just something people had, like short height, or a bad nose, or a shitty attitude, a brain less smart, or pointy ears.

Now she knew that pointy ears would have been better.

As she grew taller and wider and bigger, the patches swelled in size like an ink dot on an inflated balloon. Soon she was a 'freak' in school.

'Don't touch her or you will get the same disease. Don't share pencils with her. Don't use the washroom she uses,' warned the ignorant parents of her classmates. Even her own brother wouldn't share a towel with her.

She grew up without friends.

While they licked on their ice creams that night, she could feel someone's eyes on her, not for the first time. Her skin often attracted a lot of unwanted attention. People would look at her and then look away, repulsed. She had learned to forgive.

She turned to see a boy staring at her. After a few moments of indecisiveness, the boy started to laugh at her, at first slowly, and then out loud, pointing fingers and such. Aranya's face flushed, her ears burned. Her mother put an arm around her and shouted at the boy, 'There's nothing to see here,' as if she were a policeman at a scene of a grisly accident.

The boy laughed some more and ran away. The brother sucked on his ice cream like nothing out of the ordinary had happened. Aranya stared at her hands—olive brown like tanned Brazilian models in patches, and pale white like the women in the fairness cream ads; two perfect complexions like spilled paint cans on a floor. She was a shade card.

'He didn't have to laugh. Why did he laugh?' Aranya asked her brother, who was playing Doom on the computer later that night.

'Because you're different.'

Her brother picked up the CD cover of *Chucky* and threw it at her.

'I'm like this?' snapped Aranya, still hoping it was a joke.

'Not really, but you get the idea. You should get used to it.'

Aranya stared at the monstrous face on the cover of the CD. After her brother went off to sleep, she spent the night on the Internet searching for what being different really meant. Sameer woke up the next morning with a slip of paper with her sister's beautiful handwriting on it:

'Sameer bhaiya, you're shorter in height than the national average of seventeen-year-olds in the country. Your BMI is lower than the accepted healthy ratio. Your scores in Hindi and social science have been way below your school average. So, I am left thinking that what does different really mean?'

The note was passed on to their mother who would have slapped her had it not been for Aranya's scholarship interview for the new school. Without the scholarship, Aranya would have to miss a year and try again the following year, a chance her financially strapped family didn't want to take. Luckily for them and for Aranya, the interview went well. In two weeks from then Aranya would join her new classmates, a patch-faced orc amongst fair, and dark, and lovely little kids.

3

Aranya loved the smell of books, new and old, she loved to scribble, take notes, memorize and recite, and feel a little smarter the next day. And unlike at home, it was where girls are believed, respected, loved and cared for, sometimes even more than the boys. Boys were seen as the inconvenience they really are.

'Where's VI A?' asked Aranya to a group of seniors milling about in the corridor, discussing skirt lengths and pubic hair.

'Why do you want to know?' asked one of them.

Aranya had received two double promotions, once when she was in LKG and once in the first standard, making her the youngest in her class.

'I'm a new student.'

The senior who now seemed to have noticed her patchy skin, pointed in the direction of the class, and looked away from her as if staring any longer would give him the disease as well.

'It's not contagious!' said Aranya sharply and made her way to the class.

Her new classmates welcomed her with sideways glances and scared whispers. She sat alone on the first bench. The kids on the second bench leaned away from her. Some covered their noses. A few minutes later, the teacher walked in and the class settled down. A few kids still looked at her, cringed, but that was okay. She felt worse about her brother throwing that CD at her than the behaviour of these kids.

The teacher noticed Aranya sitting alone, smiled extra benevolently and said, 'If you need anything, my staffroom is on the fourth floor.'

People often thought Aranya had special needs because of her condition.

'Ma'am, except for school picnics, which I would like to be excused from since I get sunburnt if I expose myself to too much of the outdoors, I think I would be able to manage myself. Thank you though for the help, Ma'am. It was too kind of you,' clarified Aranya with her gap-toothed smile. The teacher smiled back, asked her to sit down and welcomed her again.

'Open to page no. 33. And all of you who don't have the books can go outside the class,' said the teacher.

She had started reading from the book when a boy at the door interrupted her. 'Good morning, Ma'am, may I come in?'

'Dhruv? You're late again. I can't let you in,' said the teacher. Dhruv, without protest, took two steps backwards, leaned against the wall and stood there.

Aranya wondered where she had seen him before. She turned back to ask the two scared kids who held their breaths about the boy. 'You can breathe. My disease isn't contagious.'

One of the girls let up. 'Dhruv. He's the son of one of our teachers. He has failed twice. He keeps picking up fights with seniors.'

'Why?'

'They say things about his mom.'

'What things?' asked Aranya.

'Dirty things.' Aranya drew a blank. 'That her mother gets naked with the principal in his room,' whispered the girl.

Aranya gasped. 'What? Why would anyone say that? That's horrible!' said Aranya. She saw Dhruv shift in his place. He looked inside and caught Aranya staring at him. She recognized him now. He was the boy who had pointed fingers and laughed at her that night. The pity in Aranya's heart melted away.

Maybe he deserved it.

4

Dhruv woke up early that morning to shouts and screams, and sounds of things breaking. He stumbled out of the room and saw his mother dragging out two suitcases. His father was throwing things which landed near her feet and shouting incessantly, 'Take this! Take this! Take this, too! Go away and don't ever come back!' he shouted, his voice breaking, his eyes full of tears. He had never seen his father so disturbed before. Mom dragged the suitcases out of the house but Dad kept on shouting. The next-door neighbour peeked through the grille door.

Tears streamed down Dhruv's face, his feet felt bolted to the ground. He wanted to scream but his throat ran dry. 'Take me!' He wanted to shout. He could hear the suitcases tumble down the stairwell. He ran after his mother but Dad caught hold of him.

'She doesn't want you,' he said.

'NEITHER DO YOU!' He broke free from his father's embrace and ran behind his mother. She hadn't even bothered to wake him up before leaving.

'MUMMA! WHERE ARE YOU GOING? WHERE ARE YOU GOING?' shouted Dhruv and ran into Mom's arms as she lifted him up; he was crying, slamming both fists into her shoulders.

'You woke up? I'm so sorry. I'm so . . . so . . . sorry, Dhruv. I didn't mean for this to happen. I will come and get you. I promise I will come and get you.' She bent down and kissed him all over his face.

'WHEN! WHEN! WHEN!' cried Dhruv, his mouth open, the words barely audible.

Mom took his face in her palms and wiped away his tears. She tried to walk away but Dhruv latched on.

'We will come and get you,' said a man's voice and Dhruv felt an unknown touch ruffle his hair. 'There's nothing to worry about now.' Dhruv lifted his head to see the principal of his school staring down at him, smiling. So it was true.

His mother was leaving him and Dad for the principal.

'SIR!' gasped Dhruv.

His mother clutched the principal's hand. Dhruv felt the insides of his stomach turn to mush and rise up his food pipe.

'Mumma! NO!'

'Dhruv, you have to understand. I'm not happy in this house,' said Mom and bent down to talk to him. Not happy? What did she mean? She wasn't happy with Dhruv? What had he done? What?

She tried holding him in her arms but Dhruv fought free. 'Everything is going to be alright, Dhruv.'

'You're lying. YOU ARE LYING! NOTHING IS GOING TO BE ALRIGHT.'

'Trust me, Dhruv.'

'YOU'RE LYING. LYING. LYING. LYING.'

'Listen to your mother, Dhruv,' the principal said sternly.

'SHUT UP! SHUT UP! You took my mom away,' bawled Dhruv and kicked the principal on his shin and ran towards the stairs of his house and then into the arms of his father who had already poured himself a drink.

'I'm never going back to her. I'm never going back to her,' cried Dhruv.

'You don't have to.'

5

'We will be together now,' said his father to Dhruv after he won Dhruv's custody.

Soon after, his father had to break into his fixed and recurring deposits to cope with the expenses of his alcohol problem. He wasn't doing a good job of bringing Dhruv up, either. Dhruv missed Mom like he missed a limb. In her absence he felt a constant nagging pain. She would come to see him every week, and then every alternate week, and then once a month.

'Why are you being so difficult?' Mom would ask on the monthly visits.

'Because you're not my mother any more.' Dhruv would pretend to watch *Duck Tales* and *Swat Cats*. Mom would switch off the television and he would snatch the remote from her. 'The remote is not yours any more!'

During these monthly visits, Dhruv's father would go missing and Mom would spend most of the time cleaning the house of empty soda and whisky bottles. And when Dad returned, it would end with a verbal duel between his parents about who had been the worse parent.

'Both of you!' Dhruv would shout from behind a locked door.

Mom would leave behind a toy, a hand-held video game, a CD player which Dad would smash and throw out with the trash. Dhruv did not mind. Sometimes Dhruv and his father would break those toys together.

The divorce proceedings and the custody battle were tedious and robbed Dhruv's father of most of his savings, and a good part of his mind. Dhruv had to leave school.

'If you don't send him to school, I'm going to take you to court,' Dhruv's mother threatened his father.

So Dhruv was put back in the school, no fee charged.

The first day was horrendous. Dhruv put up with the sniggering without breaking down. He walked the corridors like nothing had happened. His mother, now freshly married, looked more beautiful than before, even younger. She was made the vice principal of the school.

Dhruv would never leave his class. During lunch breaks, he would go to the end of the class and sit down on the floor, hidden from his mother's prying eyes. Sometimes his mother would keep lunch wrapped in an aluminium foil on his desk.

'What are you doing down there?' asked a girl one day while Dhruv fiddled with a fountain pen, shirt stained with little blue spots of Chelpark ink. Dhruv looked up to see the girl from his colony, the dalmatian, the one with the spotted skin, looking at him. 'Do you want to share my lunch?'

Dhruv shook his head.

'You won't get it if you touch me or share my food. Didn't you get the flyer that was never distributed?'

'I didn't say no because of that,' lied Dhruv.

Dhruv was hungry. His father would not wake up in time to help him get ready for school, or prepare lunch, or even drop him to the bus stop. He would, though, kiss him on his forehead every day at least once as they rushed to get dressed. 'I love you, and we are happy together,' his father would assert like a universal truth. But Dhruv wanted a lunch box and a clean uniform, too.

'Why do you sit here every day?'

'My mother is a teacher in the school and she comes looking for me with a lunch box. I sit here and wait for her to leave.'

'Where's the lunch box then?'

'I don't take it. She waits and she takes it back.'

The girl starts to laugh.

'What?'

'It reminds me of a ghost-woman from a Bollywood movie who wears a white saree and roams about with a candle in her hand.'

Dhruv frowned. 'She's not a ghost.'

'I'm sorry. I'm really sorry. I don't know why I said that,' the girl said. Dhruv went back to taking the pen apart. 'I heard your story. I don't see why anyone should talk about it. If you were in the US, you would be in the majority. Divorce rates are 54.8 per cent there.'

'How do you know that?'

'I have a computer at home. AMD 1.2 GB Thunderbird Athlon computer with 320 MB SDRAM, SoundBlaster Live Value, CD drive and a 12 GB hard disk. It's actually my brother's but I can use it after he's done. He only watches porn.'

'Porn?'

'It's just biology in action. Nothing something you would be interested in till you're thirteen.'

Dhruv's eyes widened. 'Can I see your computer? Do you have Wolfestien on it?'

'No,' Aranya lied. Dhruv's shoulders drooped.

'My parents are very strict,' she said. 'And no friends are allowed at my place. We have to serve them Coca-Cola if they come and Mom says it's expensive. Sometimes, my mother adds water to those glasses. No one can tell the difference.' Aranya continued, 'But you should tell people about the 54.8 per cent. They should talk about something else.'

6

Aranya and Dhruv would spend the lunch break together, sitting in the class, sharing lunches. Dhruv had played FLAMES using her name and his, and despite the result, he had decided she would be his wife. He would protect her from the world. They would always share their lunches. He had vowed he would never let her shirt stain with ink spots. And the day he grows up to be a senior, he would hunt every last student in the school who had hurt Aranya and punch them in the nose.

To twelve-year-old Dhruv, she was the most beautiful girl in the whole wide world and he would love her fiercely till the end of time.

By now Dhruv had learned to make his lunch—four slices of bread generously spread with pineapple jam. They would sit on the last bench the entire day and write little messages for each other on the desk. The class called them the weird couple. They ignored them. Dhruv finally realized what his mother meant when she told him, 'Everything would be alright.'

During the lunch break, they would wait for the students to leave and draw each other on the blackboard. Dhruv would draw her with big hands and big eyes, and she would draw him with big ears. Together, they would draw little hearts at the edges. They would also draw a little house they would live in when they grew up. It would have a lot of big windows and two computers.

'What's that?' asked Aranya pointing to a patch on Dhruv's shirt.

'Dad vomited again this morning. It smelled really bad so I mopped it up. I couldn't get this out,' said Dhruv, rubbing his hand over the stain. 'Also, I found this is the mail today morning.'

Aranya took the envelope in his hand and tore it along the fold. Aranya and Dhruv read it together. It was a letter warning Dhruv's father of his extended absence in office.

'He might lose his job,' said Aranya.

'People who work in the government don't lose their jobs,' said Dhruv from previous knowledge. 'What does your father do?'

'He is in construction. When people buy a new flat and they have to break a wall or two, redo the plumbing and the wiring, they call my father. He lost the thumb of his left hand. He can't hold things in his left hand any more. I think that's why he's constantly angry.'

Dhruv laughed at this and then apologized, not sure if it was a joke. 'At least he doesn't smell bad like my father does.'

'At least your dad loves you. Papa loves only my brother,' muttered Aranya.

'At least you're together.' Aranya smiled weakly. 'What did the new doctor say?' he asked Aranya.

She shook her head. 'Same thing. It's incurable, non-contagious. It picks its victim at random. Quite unfair too if you ask me. You can touch me though, you're totally safe.'

Dhruv touched her skin. He didn't die or feel woozy like the kids in their class had prophesied. 'Will you always be like this?'

Aranya nodded. 'That's why my parents hate me for it. Mom says I wouldn't make a pretty bride and I will live with them for the rest of my life.'

'You can come live with me then. In our little house.'

'Why would I live with you?' asked Aranya and smiled.

'I will make you breakfast every day for the rest of your life,' answered Dhruv, his face flushed red like those little cartoons on greeting cards. 'But you have to promise not to leave.'

'I promise.'

'Promise?'

'Promise.'

Twelve-year-old Dhruv held her hand. Their hands sweated, but neither of them wanted to let go. From then on, he would hold her hand whenever he got the chance to. 'I love you,' they would say and blush furiously and hold each other's hands tighter. It was them against the world, they had decided, forever and for always. Dhruv would always be Aranya's first love.

Not because he was a boy and she loved him but because he was the first one who chose to love her.

Usually people would go to great lengths to avoid her touch. Dhruv, too, had been scared but he knew what the word non-contagious meant. However, as it turned out, he was soon to use it against her. The girl he had fallen in love with, the girl who loved him back, the girl who had promised him a forever, the girl who was supposed to make everything alright simply because she was happy being with him.

The girl who'd now lied . . .

7

There was pin-drop silence in the room. On one side of the shiny mahogany table sat the school committee and the teacher who had caught the two of them in the storeroom, and on the other side sat Dhruv and Aranya with their parents.

'Do you have any explanation for what happened today?' asked the principal.

Dhruv stared at his Converse shoes, their laces frayed, the little aluminium rings that had held them ripped away from their place. He pressed his toes down, hoping to crack the earth and descend into Middle Earth, maybe. Outside the room he could hear people talk about the alleged kiss between Dhruv and Aranya.

'How could he do it?' 'She's so ugly.' 'Won't he fall sick, too?' 'Will his skin become like hers?' 'Why would he do it?' 'Who in his right mind would do so?' 'Why?' 'Why?' 'Why?'

Aranya had been slapped twice by her parents. Her mother was crying and begging in front of the principal, blaming Dhruv. 'My daughter is a scholarship student. She couldn't have done it. She couldn't have done it. IT'S HIM!'

The others in the room looked at Dhruv for it seemed like a valid argument. Dhruv trained his eyes on Aranya who had started to cry. He grabbed the paperweight on the principal's table. He didn't know what to do with it exactly but hurling it in the direction of whoever made Aranya cry would be a start.

'Tell them, tell them that the boy did everything! WHY ARE YOU QUIET! TELL THEM EVERYTHING!' shouted Aranya's mother.

The head of the committee spoke. 'This incident is the first for our school and we will take their silence as an admission of guilt. We will have to expel both the kids from our school. We have a zero-tolerance policy. I hope you understand.'

Just as he finished his sentence, a thunderous slap landed square on Aranya's face. Her father who had been grumbling in silence got up, grabbed Aranya by her hair and shook her violently. Dhruv cradled the paperweight in his hands, imagining it lodged inside her father's skull.

'Calm down, Sir. Calm down,' the head said. 'We are very sorry for this.'

'Please Sir, please reconsider,' said the mother. 'She's a scholarship student. If you expel her, none of the other schools will take her. Please understand. We can't afford her education if you turn us away.'

'I'm sorry, Ma'am. My hands are tied.'

'LOOK! What you did? LOOK!' bellowed the father and slapped Aranya again. Her ruffled hair stuck to her wet face. 'Is there anything you can do that doesn't bring shame and humiliation to us? ANYTHING? ANYTHING!'

Aranya wiped her tears and muttered something no one could hear.

'What did you say?' asked the father. 'What?' Her father leaned near her mouth and slapped her again. Dhruv gripped the paperweight tighter. 'SAY IT LOUDER.'

'The boy did it,' mumbled Aranya.

'What?' asked the head of the committee.

Aranya wiped the tears off her face, looked straight at the head and spoke fluently, her voice strong, her story precise and straight. 'Dhruv took me to that room. He had promised to help me with the course material. I had been struggling since I missed the earlier classes. But once there, he asked me to kiss him. I refused. But then he told me that his mother knows the principal well and if I didn't kiss him, he would make sure I would fail the examinations. I had no choice but to kiss him and that's what you saw. It wasn't my fault.'

The calm on her face reminded Dhruv of his mother's radiant face when she had left with the principal. He thought of what his father had once said, 'Women. They lie.'

8

Dhruv felt a little dizzy at first and then felt the rage rise inside him. He wanted to say that she was lying but words escaped him. And before he could open his mouth, Aranya's father charged at him and boxed his face and he saw the floor rush towards him. He blacked out for a few seconds, his hand unclenched and the paperweight rolled out of his hands. He woke up to see the peon pulling Aranya's father away from him.

'*Bhenchod! Bhenchod!*' shouted Aranya's father. 'What did you expect out of a boy whose mother sleeps around? Your school is vile! The teachers, the principal, everyone! I will sue the entire school!'

Dhruv's mother's ears burned. Her face looked like she had been slapped.

'There's no need to talk like that. We are trying to handle it here,' the head remarked.

Dhruv was made to sit on a chair as the committee members tried to restrain Aranya's father. Dhruv's father sat slumped in his chair, ashamed.

'Is that the truth?' the head asked Aranya.

Aranya nodded.

'Do you have something to say, Dhruv?' asked the head. Dhruv looked at Aranya but Aranya was staring at the wall ahead of her. He repeated. 'Do you have anything to say, Dhruv?'

Dhruv's father held his hand and asked if he had anything to say. His mother tried holding the other but he broke free. His mother asked, 'Did you really say that, Dhruv?

Outside, more students had gathered having listened to the commotion inside. Dhruv got up from his seat and walked towards the door. He started to count until ten in his head. If she looked at him, he would forgive her, or otherwise he would take her down with him . . . one . . . two . . . six . . . seven . . . eight . . . nine . . . nine and a half . . . nine three by fourth . . . ten.

'Is that the entire story?' asked Dhruv looking towards Aranya.

Aranya didn't answer.

'Whatever she said is true.' He opened the door and found fifty students staring back at him. 'I took her to the room. Not because I wanted to kiss her but because I had a bet with all these students standing here. They said Aranya's disease is just on the exposed skin whereas I said,' Dhruv chuckled and laughed, as Aranya stared back at him, 'it's on her entire body. So in the room, I made her take off all her clothes and damn, it's on her entire body. She's the ugliest thing I have ever seen in my entire life. Heaven forbid anyone has to see what I saw today! She belongs to a zoo, not here!'

The committee gasped.

'DHRUV!' shouted Dhruv's mother. Aranya looked on; Dhruv could see the life drain out of her eyes.

'And why did I kiss her?' Dhruv threw his hands in the air and twirled, making a big show of it. 'I had told them that her disease was non-contagious! And no one believed me. So I decided I would show them by kissing her and remaining the way I am—normal. So, I'm sorry. It's all entirely my fault. The girl is not to be blamed,' said Dhruv, trying his hardest to not cry.

'Dhruv, you need to stay quiet,' said Dhruv's mother, rushing up to him.

Dhruv whispered back, 'How is she different from you? All of you are the same, ugly or beautiful. All of you lie. Dad was right.'

'HE'S LYING!' cried Aranya, but Dhruv shrugged.

'Then what's the story, Aranya?' said Dhruv.

'. . .'

'Welcome to the world, beautiful,' said Dhruv, pointing to the sea of kids who looked at Aranya, who felt naked and betrayed, ugly and abandoned, stuck in the school for the next six years. Dhruv walked past everyone. He found the paperweight rolling about, picked it up, and walked out of the school, crying.

Dhruv was expelled immediately. He and his father shifted to a cheaper apartment on the outskirts of the city, and Aranya spent the remainder of her school life at the fringes, being known as the ugliest girl ever!

9

Six years later . . . Dhruv, eighteen, sat in his ex-girlfriend's house, staring at his dirty Converse shoes, worn beyond their years, a fake tear streaking down his face. He could barely suppress the chuckle that threatened to escape any moment.

No words had been exchanged for the last twenty minutes. Satvika's father was furious, his face paralysed, lower lip quivering, his frail heart giving up. 'It can't be true. My daughter can't do that,' her father muttered under his breath.

'I'm afraid she did, Sir. We did it here. In the bedrooms. On the balcony. Even on the kitchen slab, I'm afraid. I'm extremely sorry to tell you this. I never intended to. But I hope you understand what position I am in.'

Rajat, the girl's brother, wanted to box Dhruv in his face. Satvika's mother, whom he had seen in pictures earlier, looked suicidal at the news of her daughter no longer being a virgin. What could be worse for an Indian mother than knowing that her eighteen-year-old daughter had had premartial sex on the kitchen slab and enjoyed it?

Dhruv chose his words carefully to make himself the victim. 'She was my world. I really loved Satvika, Sir. If I had thought she would leave me I would have never done it. Here. Nor in the bedrooms. Nor on the balcony, or on the kitchen slab. I really thought she was serious about me. God knows I was . . . in love and she . . . sh . . . she . . . she cheated on me, in the same house with another boy!' said Dhruv, as his voice trembled and he broke down in little sobs.

He should try theatre sometime.

Dhruv had narrated the length of his rather sexual relationship with Satvika in as much detail as her parents could digest, without them wanting to set Satvika, and then themselves, on fire.

He told her parents they had been dating for the past two months, right from the time Satvika had taken admission at a local institute to prepare for the engineering entrance examinations. He ran through the rest of the story quickly, only highlighting the portions he thought were most damaging to Satvika's life thereafter.

They say, the day you fall in love changes your life, but they are wrong. It's actually the day your ex-boyfriend walks through the door and tells your parents about you being a nymphomaniac that really does you in.

Dhruv sounded genuine in his shame. Tears flowed out abundantly and ceaselessly from his sorry eyes, erasing any doubt, firmly planting the belief that their daughter was some kind of depraved girl, a pervert who used their bedroom and their kitchen for her misdemeanours.

By the time Dhruv was finished, he had made sure Satvika's parents were only slightly milder than the Talibans, that they would make sure Satvika suffered a fate worse than death. Okay, that might be an exaggeration, but not by much.

Satvika was called to the drawing room. She stood by the side of her mother, teary-eyed, her hair a mess, and her skin pale like a corpse. Dhruv smiled, seeing her pained and defeated, staring at a shackled life. *You deserve it, bitch! You should have thought about this before you let Karan take my place.*

'Is it true?' they asked her. Satvika had no answer to give them because nothing of what Dhruv had said was untrue. They were indeed dating and he was in love with her for a brief period of time, and yes, they had made out, in her parents' bedroom, in the stairs of the empty malls they went to, in the washrooms of coffee shops, and it was good, not great, at least good enough to keep the relationship going. But slowly and predictably, distance had crept in and Dhruv, in anger, had told her to fuck off from his life.

She did, quite literally, and decided to go out for a harmless movie date with a below-average boy, Karan.

Dhruv would have probably forgiven her for this slight had she not lied about it. 'I was at home with Mom,' she had said, and all hell broke loose. She had lied and for that she needed to be punished, abandoned and tortured for life.

Dhruv was asked to leave. He had just turned on the bike's ignition, a second-hand, weathered Enfield, when he heard what sounded like a dying animal's shriek.

'WHY! WHY DID YOU DO THIS? You said you loved me!' Satvika waved and howled frantically from her balcony.

'I hate women as much as I love them. Didn't I tell you that?'

'But—'

'And because you fucked him!' shouted Dhruv, putting on his helmet.

'I—'

'And you lied. I loved you and you fucking lied to me.'

'You never loved me! And we had broken up, Dhruv!' defended Satvika.

'My women don't sleep with other men. My women don't lie to me. They fucking stand by me no matter what or I destroy them,' bellowed Dhruv, the vein on his temple now throbbing, as Satvika's brother started to drag her inside the house.

Her eyes still searched for an answer, and Dhruv being the gentleman he was, responded by waving his middle finger, and drove away.

10

No matter how strong she was, how many books on feminism she had read, she still felt the need to be desired, missed, loved, talked, objectified, fantasized about and masturbated to, and she hated herself for it.

She dimmed the lights of her room and of her laptop before she clicked the 'Video call' on her Skype account. She switched on 'Show video' to check if her face or any part of her body was in any way recognizable. Not that anyone would want to see her body. Saying she was fat was an understatement. She weighed 73kg and was barely 5'3" and it constantly weighed on her head. For years she had been battling with her issues with weight.

Sameer, the boy on the other side of the video call, had first met her in an interschool debating competition about five years back. He had been talking to Aranya, on and off, for the past few months, and he showered her with a lot of attention, and it wasn't friendly attention, it was sexy, overbearing, dirty, sweaty attention.

SAMEER

Hey, I can't see you. Switch on the lights.

ARANYA

I can't. My parents are outside. Make do with this.:*

SAMEER

Oh! A kiss! The night just got very interesting! I think I just got turned on.

ARANYA

Show me.

Aranya's heart throbbed with nervous energy, a tingly sensation took over. Sameer's ex-girlfriend was tall, slender and reasonably fashionable, the kind who took selfies in changing rooms and labelled them #ugly. Aranya wanted to shove her own Polaroid in front of the ex's face and shout, 'You self-serving lowlife, this is ugly, not you!'

To think she had turned on that girl's ex-boyfriend was a cause for celebration.

The boy teased Aranya a little, gyrating and thrusting his pelvis into the camera like an octogenarian on his first yoga class. Slowly, the guy took off his shirt, and then slipped out of his trackpants. His torso was sufficiently ripped and shaved but his legs were Amazonian-level hairy. He asked Aranya if she wanted him to take his briefs off and before Aranya could type, he started. He slipped them off slowly. Not that the suspense was killing Aranya really.

Aranya squinted as Sameer proudly took his semi-hard king-prawn-like member in his palm and started flapping it around, stroking it, pointing it towards the web camera.

SAMEER

Do you like this? You do, don't you?

It was hilarious. Sameer kept stroking it till it was hard. Then he took his hands off it, placed them behind his head, and moved his penis back and forth like it was a party trick. By this time, Aranya was disgusted enough to change tabs. She watched a compilation of cute puppy videos on YouTube, and realized how easy life is for little puppies. No one says, hey, look, that's a hideous puppy.

And though the moving images of a crooked dick on her laptop made her feel sick and queasy, she felt desirable for a change. At least someone in the world would give her a second look, want her, in whichever way it might be.

SAMEER

I want to see you naked.

'No, you don't, jerk! Even I don't want to see myself naked,' thought Aranya.

She then told him that her parents were knocking on the door.

ARANYA

OH MY GOD! THEY ARE HERE . . .

I HAVE TO GO!

She signed out. It wasn't the first time Aranya had done this. She closed her laptop and gently tapped her head on it, cursing herself, almost in tears. *Why? Why does she do this?*

Her begging for validation from a complete stranger wasn't too different from her classmates wanting their pictures to be liked and commented on. And if she had a face worth a second look, probably twenty likes on a selfie would have sufficed her need for acceptance as well.

Aranya stood in front of the mirror, turned her head from side to side, inspected herself, found herself crying and with the same schizophrenic, self-pitying argument running in her head again.

Why do you do this? Why? You don't need validation from others to tell me how beautiful you are. A hard-on in the pants of a boy you barely know isn't appreciation.

But I'm not beautiful. Look at me! I'm ugly and fat and undesirable.

You're not ugly! Looks aren't the only thing.

No, I'm ugly! Look at the other girls from school, their thin, shapely legs, and their perfect complexions. They are the ones who get stared at, not me, no matter what I do. Look at my skin! No one will ever look beyond that. I'm fat and I'm ugly.

Shut up. It doesn't matter. At least you're not dumb like the other girls. You're a national-level debater. No one can touch you there. You're funny and you're smart.

But all that makes me a boy, not a beautiful, desirable girl, and that's what I'm trying to say. Why do you think I was leading that guy on to strip? Wanting to know if I can turn him on? Wanting to know if I can turn *anyone* on? Because it makes me feel good, it makes me feel wanted.

So do you feel better now?

No. I don't know.

Then don't do it again.

I might.

There will be someone.

There won't be anyone. Do you want me to remind you what happened the last time there was someone? He called me the ugliest girl in the world.

Forget him. It's been a century since then.

Feels like yesterday.

Shut up.

Shut up.

She deleted Sameer from her Skype list and texted him that her parents got to know about their little escapade and they would get him jailed if he ever tried to contact her again. She pulled the blanket over herself and lay there staring at the trophies she had won in the past few years, thinking of all the moments she had decimated her fellow competitors, mostly boys, razed them to the ground, insulting them and questioning their intelligence, and yet here she was, wishing that she would be fairer, more beautiful, skinnier—she would trade all the trophies, all the little and massive victories over those boys, for just one of them to come to her and tell her that she's beautiful.

Ashamed at her regressive thoughts, she blamed fairy tales, nice boyfriends, happy endings, red hearts with arrows through them, and she said, 'Fuck you, fuck you, boys! I don't need you,' and closed her eyes and saw the boy who was the first person ever to call her ugly, a burden she'd carried all these years. The boy she loved. The boy named Dhruv.

She bore no guilt about what had happened years ago, about the lie she said to save herself from her parents and a life full of misery. It was a desperate attempt of a young ostracized girl at self-preservation. What could she have done? Dhruv should have got that. Instead he hit back like a coward and single-handedly wrecked her life. He was the first one to tell the world she was ugly, unwanted, repulsive. It was he who had sown the seeds of self-doubt that had torn her apart for years now. He snatched away what little normalcy she had hoped for from life. She wished he were dead now, or at least as unhappy as she was with her life. She hated him with all her might.

11

Dhruv regretted his decision of riding the damned motorcycle to Delhi Technological University (DTU), the college he had gotten through. Still about fifty kilometres to go, the rotting piece of shit had broken down twice. He stepped into a dhaba while the mechanic refilled the coolant.

'*Ek chai, bina chini!*' Dhruv shouted asking for a cup of tea without sugar.

Earlier, Dhruv had filled his shaker with three scoops of 100 per cent whey protein, two scoops of glutamine, three scoops Amino and two scoops of BCAAs, topped it with water and shook it till a little bit of the froth had dribbled out. It smelled like shit but it was essential for rapid muscle growth, and to help him break out of the plateau he had hit with the overhead and the bench press.

A couple of houseflies started to hover around the dirty bandage on his right hand. He needed a new dressing for that wound. He leaned back into his chair and smiled thinking of how he had smashed Karan's face while the latter tried to run away from him, crawling on all fours, of the sweet sound of his nose crushing against his knuckles. But that's how Dhruv operated. People needed to be punished and left with scars that would remain for a lifetime. What had really cracked Dhruv up was when Karan staggered to his feet and threw a rock at Dhruv who caught it with his right hand, and used the same to break Karan's nose. Dhruv still thought he let him off easy.

Karan had admitted to kissing his ex-girlfriend and had the gall to say, 'But you had broken up with her!' Seconds later Dhruv's fist crashed into his ribs, snapping them like dry twigs.

'You need to ask me before taking my things,' Dhruv had whispered in his ear.

A serving boy came with the tea. It was the sweetest fucking thing he had ever tasted and he spat it out.

'Fuck.'

Before Dhruv could have called out to the boy and given him a mouthful, he was already serving a meal to a girl who sat at another corner of the dhaba with her back towards him. Dhruv gargled with the tea instead, not wanting any extra calories in his bloodstream, and spat it out, making sure the cashier noticed it. '*Cheeni thi*' (It had sugar), remarked Dhruv. A small round steel plate with the bill reached his table.

Dhruv got up from his chair, picked his tattered backpack and slung it over his shoulder. He walked to his bike, paid the mechanic, and kick-started it to life. The waiter scurried to Dhruv's table to collect the money for the tea and found just a bloodied bandage. Dhruv was gone.

12

Aranya noticed how pale the waiter's face was after that boy, whose face looked familiar, drove away on his motorcycle leaving behind a bloodied bandage. She burped.

'The food was good,' she told the waiter. Frankly, she wasn't an authority on food. Everything bathed in oil, sprinkled with cheese, dipped in sugar syrup tasted good to her. She hadn't had sex but it couldn't be better than a creamy bowl of pasta.

She caught the bus that would take her to DTU, her home for the next four years away from her tyrannical parents. It would be a new start for her and she would not be ignored and taken lightly there, she had decided. Unlike school, she would rule the college with an iron fist.

The bus dropped her off at the gate of her new college, from where she walked to her hostel, her home for the next four years. She signed the register, submitted photocopies of her existence and shifted into her barren, prison-like room.

Before long she unpacked, changed, threw her clothes inside the cupboard, arranged her books, put bedspreads, and flopped on the bed, thinking about her first day in engineering college—where she would be the cause of disappointment to a lot of expectant guys. 'Screw them,' she thought.

She was dreaming soon.

'Come out!' the voices shouted outside. She woke up with a start . . .

'Come out!' the voices shouted again.

Ten minutes later, she was standing with fellow students from the first year in front of a motley group of seniors, boys, uncles pretending to be boys, and a smattering of girls.

Things had changed quite a lot for Aranya since primary school. No one mentioned the story of the naked, diseased girl any more but the repulsion towards her disease remained. Her condition was always a looming shadow over her associations with people. She knew it was always at the back of everyone's minds, like it was on hers.

'Introduce yourselves,' said a fat senior whose gut was far bigger than Aranya's.

The girls started to rattle off their names, the name of the schools they were from, and some went as far as to tell them their hobbies which were as boring as their faces. Aranya could almost feel the insults flying at her. Obviously, she would be picked out and ridiculed and shamed for her weight and how she looked, but she was ready for it. She wouldn't live on the fringes of the college like she did in school.

'What's your name, fatso?' asked the senior in the front row.

'Your mother is a fatso!' snapped Aranya, putting her ruthless, debating face on. The boy clearly hurt looked left and right, hoping someone would back him up and when no one did, he said, 'You don't talk like that to a senior.'

'Why not? My seniors sit around in boxer shorts and harass their juniors, shame them for their body and their face.'

'I didn't even say anything about your face. And I'm not harassing anyone!'

'You're fucking rude! You—'

'Your mother's rude,' said Aranya.

'Fuck off,' said the boy.

'I wish I could say that back to you but that would only mean a waste of moisturizer and tissue paper.'

The boy looked at his classmates for support, but they were too busy giggling, memorizing the repartees to use them somewhere else. 'You will be dealt with later. None of the seniors will ever help you. Never! You screwed with the wrong person.'

'You're ragging me. That's like a criminal offence. Why do you think none of your friends here are backing you up? Because they know I'm just the kind of person who will report it and they are right.'

'I . . . I . . . was just asking for an introduction.'

How sweet. So here's one for you. I'm Aranya Gupta. Triple scholar gown holder in school. NTSE and JSTSE silver medallist. AIEEE rank 13, with the highest in mathematics and physics. I'm a national-level debater with a 53–1 career record, and I can recite the periodic table backwards while beating your ass in table tennis.'

'. . .'

'Now come again? You were saying that none of the seniors would help me? What makes you think I would need their help?' asked Aranya.

Having been smacked in the face by Aranya's thick CV, the senior stuttered insults which no one took seriously. Victorious, she walked away.

13

Dhruv had been in a little fight last night. The seniors had come knocking at his door and he had asked them to fuck off. They hadn't taken the affront lightly and barged into his room. The matter was settled when they roughed up Dhruv, who in turn smashed a table lamp on one of the senior's heads. They had to rush the senior to the hospital.

Groggily and with one eye barely open he looked at the timetable on his phone. He was already late for the first class— advanced physics. It took him another twenty minutes to get out of bed, brush, and find the motivation to reach his first class at DTU, the college he had always thought of as giving him the metaphorical freedom from the house he had grown up in.

Still in his shorts and flip-flops, his right palm bandaged, and with a deep gash on his forehead from last night which had needed medical attention, he walked through the corridors looking for his class.

Mr Tripathi, fifty-three, dressed in brown trousers, a faded white shirt and chappals, was teaching the first-year electrical engineering students. In a desperate bid to leave a good first impression, their eyes were glued to the old man, nodding furiously like bobbleheads, pens whirling on paper, writing every word like it was holy.

Dhruv knocked at the door. The class turned to look at him. It was a class full of hopeful and hopeless, virgin young men, and predominantly average-looking women, who would drag themselves unquestioningly through four years of engineering to get one of those million little enviable cubicles where their life energies will be slowly sucked out of them.

'May I come in?' he asked.

'Should we allow latecomers?' Prof. Tripathi asked the class. The students shook their heads.

'What is wrong with you?' said Dhruv to the class who pretended they hadn't heard him.

'You're late,' said the professor.

'I hope I haven't missed much.'

'You're not dressed appropriately for class.'

'Sir, I was hoping the first class would be a sort of informal introductory session where we would get to know each other better. So I thought it was better I dressed up for the occasion. I picked these shorts carefully. And hi! I'm Dhruv.'

The professor looked at him, unimpressed.

'Do you think it's a joke?' asked the professor.

'I'm hoping it is.'

The professor looked at him, blank-faced. 'Get in,' he grumbled.

The professor started to teach them about fusion. Dhruv sat there, looking at the five girls in the class, calculating the number of beers he would need to find the urge to sleep with them.

The first three were identical. Skinny, dark, spectacled, flat hair tied tightly into a pony, four beer stuff. One of them was fair and being the racist bastard he was, he pegged her at two beers and sufficiently dim lighting.

The last one was a little hard to place in the heirarchy. She had her back towards him. She was furiously scribbling notes, unmindful of boys nearby, or him, or even the professor. From where he was sitting he could see her head strictly followed the chalk like she was controlling it, telekinesis–type strange shit. If she turned out to be fair he would forgive her plumpness and give her a good beer rating.

But then she turned.

Dhruv's mouth went dry. The girl had patchy skin, white and brown at places, and she immediately reminded him of someone . . .

She had seen him too. For the rest of the period, she kept stealing glances at him, and he played his little game of catching her mid–glance, holding the stare . . .

And then it struck him. It was her. The girl who'd lied and broken his heart into a million little pieces . . .

14

Aranya wrote furiously in her register, the nib of her pen making an angry noise against the paper, to avoid looking at the gorgeous boy. She had noticed his roving, sleepy eyes over the occupants of the first two benches, evaluating them, and then turning towards her. She found herself thinking why the face looked so familiar and, more importantly, why did she feel an inherent hatred towards it. She reminded herself of the task at hand—be a pet student of every professor, secure the scholarships, get a project under the famed Dr Raghuvir, get a plush, overpaying job abroad, and have a great fucking life. Possibly a liposuction as well.

'Sir? It should be three neutrons, shouldn't it? Or is it four?' asked Aranya, acting confused, chewing her pen.

She had noticed the mistake right when Mr Tripathi made it. But she waited for a perfectly timed moment to point it out, her voice modulated to make her sound like a curious, dedicated, unsure student.

Prof. Tripathi noticed the mistake. 'Oh yes, thanks for pointing that out! At least someone is paying attention.' Tripathi smiled and Aranya smiled back. Mutual admiration was the first step towards a healthy and fruitful relationship.

The professor continued to teach nuclear physics to a bored class till the clock struck nine-thirty. Tripathi dictated the names of a few reference books and the serial numbers of the questions they had to finish before the next class.

'I need someone to volunteer as a class representative,' Tripathi said, wrapping up the class. Many hands went up.

Sir, I'm willing to be the volunteer. I'm your best choice. I will be a good student and will always be by your side. You can trust me. In moments of despair when you feel like your best days as a college professor are over, I will stand up and tell you how you changed my life as a professor.

Aranya could have said this but she gingerly raised her hand and kept her mouth shut.

'What's your name?'

'Sir, Aranya,' she mumbled softly.

'Aranya is your class representative. All of you will report to her from now on,' said Prof. Tripathi. Aranya offered to help the professor carry his books back to the staffroom. He turned her down nicely. 'Take care. You're a nice, quiet girl. Have a voice and don't be afraid to talk back. The seniors can be quite a handful.'

Aranya barely kept from laughing.

Prof. Tripathi left and Aranya revelled in her newfound power over the other students. Seeing someone else in a superior position had never been Aranya's idea of fun. She hadn't had much say in what nature doled out to her—the dead melanin cells, the low metabolic rate, her vile parents, a devil for a brother—so she had decided to control the outcome of everything else.

The students had started filtering out. Awkward first conversations had grown into fulsome banters and groups of students made their way to the canteen, forging new friendships and enmities. Aranya did not move out. Instead, she corrected her notes, underlining important equations, dog-earing pages in her books before she forgot. The boy was still in the class, picking at the wound in his palm, looking in her direction. *Why wouldn't he go? Why was he looking? Was he mocking her? Was he disgusted?*

By the time she finished colour coding her notes, the class was empty. The boy was still there, feet propped up on the desk, playing on his phone, little beeps filling the space around him, a murderous smirk on his face. Just as she passed him, he said, 'Nice move.'

'Excuse me?' said Aranya, her guard up.

He looked up from his game. He was playing Temple Run with his phone held sideways. She was a pro at the game but she could see that he was at a stage Aranya hadn't reached yet.

'You lied.'

'I don't quite follow you.'

'You spotted that mistake as soon as he wrote it. You were sure about the error but you acted like you weren't. You lied to get that position. Or maybe the professor just pitied you for the way you look.'

'You have a problem with me being the class representative? Why didn't you raise your hand?' asked Aranya, steeling herself.

'Not really. I just wanted to point it out. Also, I heard about the little incident you had with the senior last evening. Hurled quite a few insults, didn't you?'

'What is it to you?'

'Why did you do that? Were you making up for this?' asked Dhruv and pointed at the pink part of the skin on her hand. His eyes felt like spiders on her skin. Her ears burned. The bastard was smiling.

'I have no idea what you're talking about. I need to go,' Aranya said and started to walk away from him.

'I'm an astrologer too, you know,' said the boy from behind. 'And right now, you're going to go into your room, fire up Temple Run and try to beat my record, which by the way is Level 123 with the phone held sideways. But you already saw that, didn't you?'

'I have never played Temple Run.'

15

Half an hour had gone by and she was sitting on the toilet pot, jumping over derelict bridges, collecting gold coins, all while holding her phone sideways. It was tougher than she had imagined it would be and it was making her restless, even angry. *How could she not be better than him?* She took little breaks to wipe the sweat off her palms, the tears off her face, and then breathed slowly and calmed herself down, and tried again.

Two more hours passed by. Her fingers had started to hurt by now. For the first time in eight years she missed a class. She took out her timetable. It was organic chemistry by Prof. Mitra, the dean of the college. She put a reminder on her phone to meet him in his staffroom, apologize profusely and tell him how big a fan she was of his work on—whatever the hell he did his PhD in.

She stretched her fingers. Her eyes were burning. Another hour passed by in a flash. She was hungry now.

'You can't be beaten,' she told herself, cracked her knuckles and started tapping again. It had started to sink in that she would probably not beat the boy's record—her first defeat in years. Another half an hour and the battery of her phone died.

'NO! NO! NO! NO! NO!' she shouted at the phone and slapped it against her palm. She left the cubicle and washed her face. She whispered to herself, 'You're good. Let it go. It's okay.' She put her phone into the bag and walked out of the washroom.

'So I'm presuming that you spent the last few hours trying to beat my record?'

She turned to see Dhruv sitting on the stairs, smiling his strange, creepy, lovely smile. 'Look. I don't care about your score, okay? I am good at a million things that you're not good at. You're probably just some Temple Run junkie whose fingers will fall off some day. I have better things to do. So just leave me alone.'

'Why does defeat bother you so much?' asked the guy, texting on his phone.

'IT DOESN'T!'

'Clearly.'

'So what if I want to win everything? What's wrong with it?' She stepped closer to Dhruv.

Dhruv kept his phone in his pocket, stood up, and stepped closer to her. 'With that kind of temper, I wonder how you won your debates. Calm down, Aranya.'

'YOU DON'T TELL ME TO CALM DOWN. You called me ugly, and questioned my selection as the class representative. Why the hell shouldn't I try to beat your score and make you feel second best and not good enough for anyone?'

'Second best? Not being good enough for anyone? I think you're talking about yourself here. But I feel I will get to know more of you as we spend more time together.'

'Why would I do that?' asked Aranya.

'Because I'm Dhruv Roy. You might remember playing a hand in expelling me from school by lying in front of the committee. Remember me? The boy whose mom left him? The last desk? Lunches shared together? Your face tells me you do now. Good! It's good to see you again. I didn't expect you here either. I was as shocked as you are.' He took her hand and shook it. 'You're still pretty ugly, Aranya. I'm glad you have spent the last eight years making up for it. Debating, studies, scholarships, projects? Even TT? I'm impressed! But what about your face? What will you do about that? That will always be the first thing people look at. That's never going to change, Aranya.'

'Why are you here?'

'What can I say? It's fate. But now that you are here too, I'm sure it will be fun.'

16

Aranya had been cautious enough to stay out of Dhruv's cross hairs. He had let her be for now but she knew, sooner or later, he would mess with her.

Some seniors had tried to induct Dhruv into their groups, most of them rogue seniors who assumed Dhruv would be like them—a weed-smoking, chronic-masturbating, porn-loving, counter-strike champion, but Dhruv was yet to be infected with the responsibilities of keeping a friendship going.

That night he was sitting at the edge of the roof of the boy's hostel, his legs dangling precariously from its edge. It was too calm. He hadn't been in a fight in days and it was getting to him. The match in the parking lot of the hostel had ended with collar-grabbing and shouts of madarchod, madarchod.

All of a sudden Dhruv heard the door of the roof being banged open and a tall, lanky boy stumbled out of the staircase. From the corner of his eye, Dhruv saw him peeing off the roof, one hand raised over his head waving a peace sign.

The boy started to sing an old Hindi song, grossly out of tune. Dhruv heard the voice coming towards him and he rolled his eyes readying himself for another drawling conversation, another attempt at an induction into a circle of dull men.

The boy wobbled and sat next to Dhruv. He started to talk, his voice a low slur. 'It's hilarious.'

'. . .'

'Ask me what is hilarious.'

'. . .'

'To drench the world with your sperm and your piss and watch them walk by calmly with a sense of purpose.' He laughed.

'Why the fuck would you do that?'

'Why the fuck would I do what?'

'Piss and come on people?' asked Dhruv for the boy who stank like a municipal dumpster was the first remotely interesting person he had met in this otherwise dull college.

'It's because the world is great and it's disgusting at the same time. Imagine the beautiful Himalayas, c'mon imagine them, yes, that's more like it, pine trees, white snow, that sort of shit, nature's marvel, beautiful enough to make you jizz in your pants, and then there will be little kids spoiling it all by clicking selfies and giggling which would make you fucking mad and then you will pee all over those little annoying kids.'

'That's the most incoherent shit I have heard in a while.'

'I should write this stuff down. It's gold.'

Dhruv waved a middle finger in his face.

'Oh wait! You're the boy who got into that scuffle with the seniors, right?' Dhruv nodded. 'Respect. By the way, I'm Sanchit.' He thrust his hand forward. Dhruv didn't shake it. 'Don't worry, I use my left hand.'

'Looks like you use your face.'

'Aha. Sarcasm. A dying art I must say. Where did you learn it? *Gossip Girl*? *Pretty little liars*? *90210*? You look the type.' Sanchit chuckled, retracting his hand.

Dhruv looked away.

'I like how you have got the whole angry young man thing going about. Very 80s but still very cool.'

'You would know the 80s. Now fuck off.'

'Your vocabulary is painfully limited. Your parents should have smacked you with a dictionary.'

Dhruv waved his middle finger again.

'Dude, the anger, the brooding eyes, the mysterious aura around you, the veiny, big arms, the sarcasm, it's like you're trying to woo me. And if you had the boobies, I would totally go for you. In fact that's one of my long-standing fantasies. I love a girl with muscles. Don't raise your eyebrows like that.'

'. . .'

'That's hypocritical and sexist. You can be ripped and a girl can't you? I can loan you some FBB porn. It's epic. You must try it. You will realize how dirty you're in your head.'

'FBB?'

'Female Bodybuilding.'

'Gross.'

'What? Do you not like the female form? Or do you feel emasculated in front of a beautiful, muscular woman who has bigger traps than yours?'

'I wouldn't give a shit.'

'Check it out,' said Sanchit and fired up a video on his phone of a female bodybuilder stripping naked.

'That's the most disgusting thing I have ever seen in my entire life.'

'And you're still looking,' pointed out Sanchit and Dhruv tore his eyes off the woman. 'Female bodybuilding porn is a metaphor for the world we live in. It's beautiful with all its imperfections, even though the imperfections are born out of its quest to be perfect.'

'How drunk are you?' asked Dhruv.

'That's not a question. The real question is, do you want to pee on the world?'

And just like that, they were peeing on the world, and they weren't even high, and they weren't even friends.

17

Traditionally, Freshers' Day at Delhi Technological University was more of an awkward ice-breaker between overenthusiastic senior boys and naive junior girls.

'Fuck this, this isn't the Freshers' our college is known for,' said Sanchit, horrified.

'And what is it known for?' asked Dhruv, his eyes fixed on Aranya.

'Freshers' Day is supposed to be a comedy of errors, not this. It's when everything is fuck-all. The juniors come together and prepare horribly synchronized dance routines, someone sings woefully out of tune, an unfunny fat person mimics professors, a boy in a *gunjee* does a solo dance performance ripped off from a Step Up movie without the dexterity or the awesomeness, etc. A few girls would vomit all over themselves, a junior would be bashed up by seniors, an odd senior would get a lucky blowjob behind the flex posters, and a handful of students would be expelled,' said an exasperated Sanchit. 'They are breaking the tradition, damn it!'

At the helm of operations of this year's party was that psychotic bitch, Aranya. She had cruised her way into the cultural fest organizing team, the IEEE, the debating team, and had turned out to be a professional ass-licker. Aranya was running the machinery with military-like discipline.

'This is so fucking corporate!' complained Sanchit. They were sitting outside the single-storey structure where the first-year students were organizing the Freshers' Day with a seriousness you associate with finding a cure for cancer. Things were clearly tense.

'The girls had to go through rigorous auditions before they could make it to the dance routine. The group has only five girls now. Imagine! Last year there were fifteen, most of them with big titties,' continued Sanchit.

'Is there any time you don't objectify women?'

'I objectify men, too. Don't think I have not noticed your bulge.'

'You're fucking incorrigible.'

'Don't you want to say something? This is our heritage. Fucked-up Freshers' parties is our forte! Our college's rich history is embellished with screwed-up dance routines, lights falling on people's heads, girls tripping over heels, comics being booed off stage, music performances going awry, professors losing their shit! Who likes perfect people? We shouldn't stand for this. This is not IIT. We are the fucking upholders of average!' exhorted Sanchit.

'As much as I would like to help you to run this institution to the ground, Sanchit, I have no reason to.'

'You have no reason to? It's that girl, Aranya, who's running this place like fucking Fort Knox. I thought you hated that girl. Grow some balls and help me screw this up!'

'I hate you too. So what do I do about it?'

'You love me, man. You man-love me,' said Sanchit and wrapped his arm around Dhruv's shoulder.

'Take your arms away before I rip them off and shove them up your ass. That's the only man-love you will get from me.'

At a distance, Dhruv saw Aranya with her little black transponder hanging from her back pocket, a headset wrapped around her dopey little face, going about business like she was born for it; a little too self-assured for Dhruv's liking. As if that incident which scarred him for life had no bearing on hers.

She had grown up to be just the kind of girl who would ignore calls when she's working or out with her own heterosexual group, the girl who puts her happiness before her boyfriend's, who would harp on and on about feminism, the kind of girl who would lie without blinking, the girl who would break your heart and be absolutely alright eight years later while the boy's heart still trembles with the thought of holding her hand.

Dhruv had every reason to see her crumble to ash.

They were now sitting at the windowsill, looking inside.

'For heaven's sake! They have hired a choreographer this time. Just imagine everyone in sync. Disgusting,' exclaimed Sanchit.

The choreographer, along with his girl partner, pirouetted effortlessly on the dance floor and expected the students to follow suit. Aranya wasn't a part of the dance troupe but she stood in a corner with a writing board and spat instructions to the dancers. No one was spared from her caustic tongue.

'Stop acting like you have elephantiasis! Move those feet! Do it like he does!'

'Namita? Are you pregnant? Then why are you so scared in the lift? The boy will not drop you and kill your unborn child!'

'Anamika? Are you trying to get pregnant? I have no problems with you fucking every boy in the college but you can't do it on the dance floor. Dance, don't grind. I don't want professors to think we are vulgar. Be sensuous, not vulgar.'

Dhruv laughed at this and the voice carried to the inside of the dance room and everyone looked in his direction.

'What's so funny?'

'You, teaching people on how to be sensuous,' said Dhruv. 'Aren't you made of stone?'

'You should have said diamond or cubic boron nitride or carbon nitride, the top three hardest materials. But wait! Oh yes, you're not smart enough. I remember you being thrown out of the school because of it. And before you go into reminding me about that childish story of when we were eight. GET OVER IT!' snapped Aranya.

'I wasn't thrown out—'

Aranya shot back, 'Fuck off, Dhruv, don't make me throw you out of here as well. Don't make me call Prof. Mitra.' She turned towards her troupe who looked confused. 'What are you looking at? Can we do it again from the top, please? Music?' continued Aranya without batting an eyelid. 'And this time we will do it without thinking there are chimps peering inside to observe human behaviour.'

Sanchit goaded him to answer back, but Dhruv walked away from the hall, his eyes narrowed in anger.

After Dhruv had been expelled from his mother's school, he had been made to drudge through hours of therapy and counselling sessions from huge-bosomed women with soft, fake voices. 'Get over the girl,' the counsellors would say. Sometimes he would understand. But usually he would say *never* and ask the counsellor to piss off.

But the girl he had refused to move on from had moved on.

Dhruv walked around in circles, looking for something.

'What are you looking for?' asked Sanchit.

He found the perfect rock, picked it up and aimed it at the glass window. He imagined throwing it, the glass shattering, the students stepping on it and bleeding, little pieces of glass jutting out of their feet, and the Freshers' dance being cancelled.

The bitch deserved it.

He swung his arm and aimed, but Sanchit stopped him midway.

'Dude. I should do it. The authorities can't do shit even if they catch me. You're a lowly junior, and moreover, I deserve this. I need to be the hero here and destroy the fucking perfect Freshers' Day. Let me have. This is my moment and I'm hard just thinking about it.'

Dhruv handed over the rock to him and walked away from the building. Sanchit threw the rock and it went over, missing the target by a mile.

The dance practice went on as planned.

18

Today was another gem in Aranya's growing repertoire of achievements—the Freshers' Day at DTU.

The professors were nodding appreciatively at the fine balance of fun and sensibility, the precision of the start and end times of the events, and the smell of the fresh bouquets in their hands.

The dance routine was in two parts, the first part was on the stage, pretty average mundane stuff, perfectly timed to bore people into a lull before the second group sprang up from the audience, a bit like a flash mob, and danced like their life depended on it. The collective gasps of the audience warmed Aranya's heart, her brilliance taking even her by surprise.

'I hope you're enjoying it,' Aranya asked Prof. Mitra, the dean, who told her that he was proud of her.

'Where's Prof. Raghuvir?'

'How would I know? Check the staffroom,' Prof. Mitra shrugged as if not wanting to answer.

Aranya hadn't seen him anywhere in college yet. He was like the yeti or the Loch Ness monster—a legend. Before she had joined DTU, she had thought he would be all over the place—lecturing, researching ground-breaking ideas, patenting stuff, being handsome—but he was turning out to be quite a recluse. Truth be told, ever since Aranya cleared the entrance, she had been waiting to meet Prof. Raghuvir. She even had cut-outs of him in a physics book back in her hostel. She was a fan of his long flowing hair, the roundish spectacles he sported in all those newspaper clippings and his strikingly boyish looks.

'Hope you enjoy the evening,' Aranya said and went backstage to see if everything was in order.

Aranya saw Sanchit's swearing and booing in the crowd as he attempted unsuccessfully to rile up the crowd. She had hired three professional bouncers to tackle anyone who misbehaved but she waved them down when they asked her if she wanted them to remove Sanchit. 'Let him be and soak in the perfection,' Aranya said.

After the events were over, it was time to choose the Mister and Miss Fresher of the day. The forms had been pored over by Prof. Mitra, a couple of unimportant professors and one fourth-year student. Aranya had initially wanted Prof. Raghuvir to be on the panel but he was unavailable.

Ten girls and ten boys were asked to step up on the stage and answer questions before they could show off any particular talent.

Dhruv was the seventh.

Her palms grew sweaty and she had half a mind to ask the bouncers to get him off the stage immediately, but she knew Dhruv—the drama queen, wouldn't take it lying down.

This wasn't the time to lose her bearings. One slip and he would break her. She had maintained the facade of being unaffected around him. She had to maintain that. He had destroyed her life once. It wasn't going to happen again.

Dhruv was the next one up for the panellists' question and Aranya was already breathing a little heavy, wishing he would drop dead, which was more probable than him behaving himself.

'So, Dhruv?' asked Prof. Mitra, mentally patting himself for his insightful questions. 'What do you think is more important—looks or what's deep within?'

Dhruv looked in the direction of Aranya. She felt her breath get stuck in her throat.

19

Dhruv took a few seconds to collect his thoughts. Then he held the microphone close to his mouth and started to speak.

'Respected Sir, and other professors in the audience, I am glad you asked this question because not only do I have very strong views about the same but also because it's a pertinent one in this age. Objectification of both men and women is rampant, be it in television, movies or books. Beauty is defined by shades on a plastic strip, for both women and men, and by inches on a tape. Is that what we have become? Are we not the most conscious beings in the universe? Then why, I ask you, the boys and girls in the audience, then why, why would we always turn our heads when a gorgeous boy or a girl walks by, and not when a studious, ambitious, maybe average-looking girl does?' Dhruv's eye picked out Aranya from the crowd, and she flushed, not knowing whether to be impressed or be angry. She had been looking at the projector lights, wishing them to crash on his head, but now she was listening to him.

'Should we not look around us and try to see behind what's obvious?' His gaze now caught hers and she couldn't look away.

'Should we not appreciate what's in front of us? If we were blind, we would have been better off for we could have seen things more clearly, for what they are. The girls I see in the crowd,' he pointed out to every girl in the crowd and smiled at them, 'every one of them is beautiful to me.' He flashed an honest smile. 'Every one of them, and so much so, that if I had to fall in love with someone right now, standing here, I would fall in love with every one of them.' He brought his arm to his heart and bowed; the girls sighed and so did Aranya and made a mental note to overdose on sleeping pills and die for doing so. 'Every one of you is beautiful!' He walked to the front of the stage, addressing the crowd now. 'You're beautiful. So are you. And so are you,' he pointed to the bench of his professors and teachers. Suddenly he was Oprah. 'And so are you, Miss Aranya!'

Aranya blushed, her body exploded with warmth. 'Fuck you, Aranya, get it together,' she told herself.

And with one last gesture of holding his arms wide open, he said, 'ALL OF US ARE BEAUTIFUL!'

The crowd exploded in applause and Aranya swore she saw a couple of girls cry and mutter, 'I'm beautiful.' The girls lost it like it was a fucking Taylor Swift song.

Prof. Mitra clapped followed by the rest of the bench. Quite some time passed before the crowd settled down again, still filled up to the brim with an honest man's moving words. Dhruv was still smiling at the crowd, and at the girls. Aranya stood there, confused, almost a little angry.

'Is there anything else that you want to ask?' asked Prof. Mitra to the panel, but the professors shook their heads. 'Is there anything you want to say, Dhruv?'

'I think we can directly go into the talent round. But before I do that, I would humbly like to thank Aranya for organizing this Freshers' Day. She has worked really hard for it. Can we have a huge round of applause for her?' said Dhruv. The auditorium erupted. Aranya looked on, confused. 'I was hesitant of what I should do in the talent round and had it not been for Aranya I wouldn't have been able to pick my performance. We slaved for hours together to perfect my routine. Thank you, Aranya. If I'm good in my talent round, then the entire credit should go to ARANYA!' Dhruv shouted, blew a kiss towards her and smiled. A few boys in the crowd whistled, the professors nodded approvingly. But Aranya knew that smile. That fucking smile.

He motioned for the music to start. An orchestra with violins and pianos and cellos and saxophones started to blare out of the speakers. He threw the microphone on the side.

Dhruv took a deep breath and started to sway his hips to the music. The lights went out. A spotlight shone on Dhruv, it split into two, red and green and revolved around him, as Dhruv gyrated. Dhruv swayed his hips faster, his hands on his chest, slowly and seductively slipping down, and he tugged at his shirt and pulled it out. He came to the edge of the stage and winked at the crowd and slowly started to unbutton his shirt.

Now, he was looking at Aranya who stood frozen.

Three more buttons were unbuttoned and he ripped his shirt off. The music reached a crescendo. He was stripping. No doubt about it now. It was a goddamn striptease. People gasped. The professors were too stunned to react. Dhruv jumped into the crowd, shirtless, and started twerking and grinding like Beyonce on steroids. He grabbed his crotch and thrust his pelvis rhythmically towards the crowd.

'Do we grab him!?' the bouncer asked Aranya.

'. . .'

'Do we grab him, Aranya?' they asked again.

'. . .'

'Say SOMETHING!'

'. . .'

His jeans came off. Well, at least partly. Aranya felt bolted to the floor. She couldn't move, her head spun, and the voices of the screaming Prof. Mitra, the laughing guys, the gasping girls, were one homogeneous mix in her ears, and while she was falling to the ground she saw him shirtless and laughing in his red printed boxers, the three bouncers tackling him and punching him in his face. Her eyes shut, thinking of his murderous smile, his bare torso and Prof. Mitra's tragic face.

20

Dhruv was still shirtless in the guys' washroom having lost it in the scuffle with the bouncers. Sanchit had offered him a metaphorical blowjob whenever he was in need of one and a spare T-shirt.

'THAT. WAS. EPIC.' Sanchit gushed.

Dhruv inspected the bruises on his stomach. Any other day he would have taken them, but they came from behind, and he was distracted by the white-faced Aranya.

'I should have done abs this morning.'

'You're ripped, dude. I think I heard women come in the crowd.'

Dhruv played it cool like he didn't give a fuck. 'Whatever. Did you see that girl's face?' he asked.

'Which girl? Oh her! I think she passed out or something,' said Sanchit. 'Serves her right for whatever she was trying to do. It's karma and you were God-sent to kick her ass.'

'She passed out?' asked Dhruv, not sure whether to feel guilty or victorious so he did a mental toss and settled on victorious.

The thumps of bass from the speakers started to filter through to the washroom. The Freshers' party had started. 'Come. Get drunk today because tomorrow Mitra is going to screw your happiness,' said Sanchit.

They left the washroom and walked towards the amphitheatre where the DJ was playing pirated CDs of bygone hits. Most of the students were sitting on the topmost stairs of the amphitheatre. As Dhruv trained his eyes he saw a handful of students dancing out of tune.

'Dhruv, you will die a good, honest man for saving our college's heritage. And to celebrate it, we have to get drunk,' said Sanchit and dived into his little black polythene bag of clanging bottles.

They got drunk on a mix of Romanov, Royal Stag and Old Monk. Sanchit was a masterful bartender but a lousy drunk.

They walked back, their feet unsteady, Sanchit struggling to light his cigarette, the lights of the auditorium piercing their pupils.

'They look like they are being tortured,' Dhruv said, pointing towards the dance floor.

'I would give my critique having learnt all Indian dance forms including Kuchipudi and the extremely demanding Chhau,' said Sanchit, 'but I'm kind of fucked up right now and all I can see are colours. I need to sit.' He sat and got up immediately. 'My head's spinning. I need to walk. Hold my hand.'

'I'm not holding your hand,' snapped Dhruv.

'It will not be gay. It will be like Sylvester Stallone and Arnold after a long drunk night.'

'I'm sure they would chew on glass before they hold hands.'

'Hold me.'

'Fuck you,' said Dhruv and walked away before Sanchit could hold him. Dhruv walked towards the crowd, leaving behind Sanchit, who walked unsteadily, still trying to light his cigarette.

The girls, a few of them drunk, were dancing without caution now, their facial hair and unchecked sideburns glistening with sweat. The boys looked around themselves to copy steps from each other, big, wet patches on their shirt underarms making them extremely desirable.

Dhruv closed his eyes, forced himself to think that the music played by DJ Raju—a twenty-year-old boy with brown streaked hair and betel stains on his teeth—was still relevant and there was no harm in dancing to Katie Perry.

He started to dance alone with his eyes closed and his arms in the air; he was never a good dancer but who gave a damn.

21

'I understand. Now if you don't mind I have some work to do,' said Prof. Mitra who assured her he knew that she wasn't at fault.

'Goodnight, Sir.'

Despite the undiluted praise heaped on Aranya for conducting a perfect Freshers' Day with all but one unruly incident, Aranya sat there, on the stairs of the training and placement department, staring blankly at the boys and girls dancing, for whom the incident was just a blip, something they would forget, maybe joke about later, but she was crying.

'Care for a drink?' a voice said from behind.

'Go away,' she said without looking.

The man sat next to her. What he carried in his right hand was a curiously shaped bottle, Vodka she guessed, and two plastic glasses and orange juice in a tetrapack in the left. He looked straight ahead at the students dancing, the strobe lights, the eager young men and the shy young women, the madness.

He poured what looked like a lot of vodka in one and kept it aside. He filled the next with orange juice and offered it to Aranya who readily accepted it. Having now recognized the man, she was finding it tough to not fling herself in his direction.

'I got your mails and the notes you slipped into my room,' he said.

Aranya hyperventilated. 'I'm sorry, Professor Raghuvir.' Aranya wiped her face into her sleeve leaving her snot on it. She smiled like a silly schoolgirl. He was handsomer than the pictures in the newspapers. At once she was jealous of all the female reporters who got him to pose.

'There's no need to be sorry. It's always good to hear from serious students.' The professor smiled. There was something very Christian Grey about him. Like a young, toned–down, sane, cute, not a psychopath, Christian Grey.

'It must be tough to be perfect all the time, isn't it?' Prof. Raghuvir asked and whipped out a cigarette. Not like a boy, but a man, experience and habit reflecting in his jagged, swift moves. He could kill a puppy right now and still look gorgeous.

'. . .'

'You did a good job though,' he said. 'You shouldn't cry about it. Accidents happen. He was an asshole. Forget about it.'

'. . .'

Aranya didn't know what to say because saying anything would mean telling him about eight years of body image problems, the constant urge to cry, to shake every person who had ever seen her differently and ask them what her fault was: to tell them all the depressing details of how it was all brought on by Dhruv, the spite in her heart, the vengefulness, which resulted in her overtly competitive spirit, and the crushing inferiority complex carefully hidden by the veneer of superiority she had steadfastly maintained.

'Dr Raghuvir, professor of advanced physics.' He thrust out her hand. 'But you know that already.'

She grinned and shook it. Snippets of information about Dr Raghuvir bounced about in her frenzied brain.

13 years, made a high-powered telescope and found three asteroids. All named after him. 14 years, completed Bachelor's of Engineering from MIT. Filed eighteen patents. 17 years, completed Master's of Engineering in nuclear physics from MIT. Filed thirty-three patents. 19 years, was part of the team in France that successfully executed the first controlled fusion reaction. 20 years, he went missing.

And it had been nine years since then. His reputation in the scientific community had been of a self-aware prick. He knew he would change the world. If he thought he was right about something, he would obsessively bulldoze others with his theories, deride them, question them and make them believe in him. He was a temperamental, obsessive, control freak, manic genius—like all geniuses should be, the stuff legends are made of.

During the latter days of his illustrious career as a young path-breaking researcher it was speculated that he became a bit of a philanderer, stumbling from one relationship to another, ending up an emotional wreck. He had made a habit of dating and breaking up with beautiful women—young struggling models and actresses and students who found Raghuvir's limitless intelligence extremely attractive. When these relationships ended Raghuvir was often found blaming a lack of common ground for the failure. A less talented man would have made a fool of himself but not Raghuvir; he had the choicest quips for anyone who still doubted his abilities. Slowly, he had snuck out of limelight.

Who didn't know about him? He was a little celebrity in his time, a child prodigy, the nation's hope pinned on him, the hero, like Kalpana Chawla, like Vinod Dham, great minds, more successful in a country that wasn't theirs.

'I am a fan and I have fantasized about you. My room is on the first floor and you can come over. Though we can't switch on the lights because then you would know I'm ugly and you could have erectile issues. Shall we go?'

She could have said that but she chose, 'I love your work, Sir. I thought you don't come to college.'

'Why would you think that?'

'You were on the visiting faculty list so I thought you would be busy carving your name in the annals of history, being glorious and unforgettable,' said Aranya.

'The glory you're talking about is overrated,' said Raghuvir, pointing carelessly at the crowd, cigarette dangling from his fingers.'

'I see a bunch of drunken idiots.'

For twenty-nine, he was rather young. That day, he was in a plain black T-shirt which he didn't quite fill up, and beige coloured trousers with a pair of black worn-out loafers. He still looked like a PhD student who lives in the next building, a bit nerdy yet unobtrusively good-looking. His slightly longish hair flopped around his head and he sported a three-day-old stubble. He had these big black pools for eyes which no contact lenses could dull. To Aranya they were huge, like portals to another world of love, puppies and rainbows and supercomputers.

They both continued sitting there, separated by silence, with translucent plastic glasses in their hands, the darkness punctured by the revolving lights of the disco ball hanging from the DJ's console in the distance, and in that poignant moment she was slyly Googling Raghuvir to make intelligent conversation.

'Why did you give everything up for teaching? I'm sure there are laboratories out there which would kill to have you on their payrolls.'

Raghuvir didn't answer. From where she sat she saw his face bobbing, infinitesimally, to the beats in the distance, his eyes were closed and she envied the calm on his face, but more than that she admired the man's sharp jawline, the deep scar hidden beneath the stubble.

'Got lost for a while,' said Raghuvir.

Aranya frowned.

'But that's a discussion for some other time,' Raghuvir continued and turned towards her. He picked up the bottle of vodka from the floor. 'Enjoy the night. It won't come again.'

'. . .'

'Have a good night,' he said patting her back, and walked away, leaving her to think about this lost genius, his boy-next-door-like gorgeousness, and his stupid decision to give it all up to be a stupid professor in a stupid college with stupid students who were having a good time while she was sipping the stupid orange juice from a plastic glass.

22

'This is the last song for the night! Hope you had a good night. As per directions from the dean, girls are supposed to go back to their hostels and sign the register!' the DJ announced. Everyone swore and threw empty plastic cups at him.

The students had made the most of the time left—some danced, boys emboldened by alcohol asked for the numbers of the girls they'd liked and got turned down, still others looked for their lost cellphones and ID cards.

Dhruv's buzz had faded by now. He found Sanchit bent over a hedge at a distance, throwing up his intestines, rubbing his mouth clean and repeating.

'Are you okay?'

'Tell my parents I love them. I won't survive this,' said Sanchit and barfed again.

'You seem to be in control,' Dhruv said and walked away wanting none of the responsibility.

The music stopped, the lights went out, the party dispersed and students walked back to their hostels, their shirts and dresses drenched in sweat, smelling like horse pee. Facebook posts went up immediately, grammatically incorrect sentences suffixed with emoticons were tweeted, pictures were Instagrammed with sepia tones and hashtags: #collegedays #partaayyyy #bestdayofmylife #bitches #fuckyeah #drunk.

The roads of the college were deserted. The students were in their beds, sweating under creaky fans, checking the likes and hearts on their photos. Dhruv walked around, his hands deep in his pockets, kicking an empty Budweiser bottle.

He had just turned a corner when he heard someone vomiting behind a parked car.

'You're still here, Sanchit?' asked Dhruv.

On the other side of an old Honda City he saw a girl, dressed in a little yellow floral dress held in place by thin straps, her knees scraped and muddy, her hair in tangles and her make-up all smudged.

'Shouldn't you be in the hostel? It's late,' asked Dhruv.

'Huh?'

'I don't know why I just became the hostel warden.'

'Can you hold my hair? I need to throw up a little,' said the girl.

Dhruv did as asked and held her hair in a bunch while the girl grunted like a hyena while she tried to vomit. At one point Dhruv saw her thrusting a finger inside her food pipe and try again. Quite classy.

'Did you—?'

'Shut up and hold it well,' the girl said and regurgitated her brains out. 'I'm done.' The girl got up and dusted her knees. She was barely 5'4" but she had a flat stomach and very taut quads.

The girl fetched a little sealed bottle of water from her pretty-looking handbag and rinsed her mouth. She sanitized her hand.

'Are you alright?'

'Why?' asked the girl.

'You looked drunk.'

'I wasn't drunk,' said the girl.

'Pregnant, then?'

'Not yet. I just had a little too much to eat tonight. Had to flush that out of the system. Didn't want those extra calories. You know what I mean, right? But thank you and see you around.' She thrust out her hand to shake. Dhruv bowed and turned away from her.

'Hey?' the girl called out. Dhruv turned. 'I liked your performance today.'

23

Three hours later, he was on the ledge of the hostel roof, soaked in the emptiness of the hostel campus. Sanchit wasn't around and the alcohol hadn't completely worn off. Every time he closed his eyes, his world started to spin and it felt like he was falling.

At a distance, he could see the girl's hostel, and a little blinking light on its roof. He ran and got a pair of binoculars from his room. It was one of the many gifts his mother had sent him over the last eight years, one he had kept but never used. *How would she know what he wants?* She didn't. So she sent him a different gift every year. Once it was a paintbox, in case Dhruv had artistic pursuits, and the other time it was a mini tool box, if he was into boyish things.

He trained the binoculars in the direction of the girls' hostel, adjusted the knob for maximum magnification, and it worked like a dream even though he ritualistically cursed the binoculars and his mother.

He saw Aranya slumped over the laptop, crying.

Was it because of him? he wondered.

Minutes passed and he kept looking at her.

'DUDE!' a voice startled him and the binoculars dropped out of his hands. Fuck. He watched them fall to the ground below and shatter.

'Shit!'

Sanchit was standing behind him, leaning on a pillar for support.

'You are into voyeurism? You earn my respect today.' Sanchit saluted him. 'We should invest in a high-powered telescope. I know a guy in customs who can get us that. Cheap. It even records.'

'Get the fuck out of my face.' He pushed Sanchit away and ran down the flight of stairs to the ground floor where the broken binoculars lay.

As he picked them up, he surprised himself at how clearly he remembered the day they had arrived at his doorstep, wrapped in a red gift paper and an orange ribbon.

He had cried himself to sleep that day, imagining his mother with her new daughter, cradling her, loving her, his half-sister who had a full family while he rotted with his alcoholic father. Fuck you, Mom.

The binoculars were beyond repair. While he walked back to his room his phone rang; it was from an unknown number.

'Hey!'

'Who's this?'

'Ritika,' said the voice.

'Ritika?'

'The girl you helped a couple of hours back?'

'Where did you get my number from?'

'Is that important?' asked the girl.

'Only if you're a psycho stalker.'

'No, I'm not. Your voice sounds strange. Were you sleeping? Should I call later?'

'It's nothing,' said Dhruv, wiping the tears off with his sleeve. 'I was just trying to forget something.'

'Can I help?'

'Can you?'

'I can sure try. I owe it to you,' said the girl.

He walked to his room and found Sanchit slumped outside his door, passed out. He climbed over him and slammed the door. He spent the night talking to Ritika while he clicked through 489 pictures of her in twenty segregated albums on her Facebook account.

24

Two weeks had passed since her breakdown on Freshers' Day and that's about the time she used to take to bounce back into the scheme of things.

The Freshers' Day would still be treated as a success, a sign of things to come, and Dhruv would be branded an outcaste. She hadn't seen much of him in the last two weeks though it had become common knowledge that he had been dating Ritika, a girl who shared a paper-thin wall with Aranya in the hostel. Needless to say, Ritika was a run-of-the-mill pretty girl—curly hair with a hint of brown in them, average height, always knew what to wear, fair and decent features, and thin, too.

What did you expect out of someone like Dhruv? That vain bastard?

Ritika had already found herself a group of girls in the hostel with similar interests. They were nice girls but a little too silly and a little too obsessed with their own faces. It used to be somewhat odd for Aranya to be in conversations where only Facebook, Instagram, Snapchat and Whatsapp were discussed.

Her Facebook picture was a bird.

She found herself on the same bench as Ritika whose carefully curated style could be called *hastily put together* and *bohemian*. She almost never had any make-up on and relied on the natural blush of her skin and the good fortune of her genes.

Ritika was quite the blabbermouth. 'So yesterday, we went to Greater Kailash and this guy was staring at me like there's no tomorrow. You have no idea what Dhruv did. He just went and smashed the guy's head into a pole. Like literally. It was straight out of a movie.'

The girls gasped.

'And?'

'He held me and took me away from there. That guy had a few friends but they didn't dare to cross Dhruv's path. You should have seen his eyes.'

Aranya shook her head and concentrated on the assignment they had to submit the day after.

'Tell us more!' a girl asked.

'You're getting nothing out of me.' Ritika blushed, knowing fully well where this conversation was heading.

'Tell us!' prodded another girl.

'No!'

Aranya sighed and stared at Ritika with puppy eyes. 'We really want to know. I will not be able to concentrate on my assignment unless you tell me. Please, I beg of you. You will really make my day.'

'Okay, fine, though I did catch the sarcasm there,' said Ritika. She continued as if she was doing a favour, 'Dhruv is a little old school. He wants to take it slow.'

The girls were disappointed and impressed at the same time.

'You mean NOTHING happened?' asked a girl.

'Nothing. He held my hand though. He has strong arms,' remarked Ritika, a little lost. 'And he kept holding my hand all through after the little incident. He kept me from looking anywhere. He told me "You're too pretty not to attract attention. So don't look anywhere or it will get bloody again." I'm here, look at me.'

'Did you check for a beard, a turban and a suicide belt? Sounds an awful lot like Taliban.' said Aranya.

The girls groaned.

Aranya gathered her books, not wanting to get into a conversation about not letting a guy walk all over you but she had to complete the assignment. It's was Prof. Raghuvir's pre-class assignment and the assignment was her one-way ticket into his good books, his research team, and probably even his heart and pants. Who knows?

'It's good to be loved,' said Ritika.

Aranya pretended she didn't hear that. 'Hey, I need all of you to submit Prof. Raghuvir's assignment by tomorrow morning.'

'Have you completed yours?' asked Ritika's friend.

'I'm going to the library. Will Dhruv allow you that in a few days? Or is it too radical?' asked Aranya and winked at Ritika.

'I like how he is,' Ritika argued.

As she walked away cradling her books, the girls shouted, 'WE WILL COPY YOURS.'

'Of course you will,' muttered Aranya.

25

It took Aranya six hours, four missed classes, and six reference books to complete Raghuvir's assignment. Solving a Rubik's cube blindfolded using only toes would have been easier.

On and off, she had been unwittingly thinking about Ritika and Dhruv, imagining the details of their date, putting the pieces together. Ritika wasn't as dumb as she thought. She clearly lied about Dhruv being old school and wanting to take it *slow*. Of course, they did it. That bitch. It was too hot for that muffler that she wore to hide a possible love bite.

That night her assignment was passed from one group to another in the girl's hostel, and everyone stayed up copying every word. Some sparkling examples of the Indian education system ended up copying her name.

She was the first one in class that day, fresh and well rested. Some girls had missed breakfast and were still copying her assignment. She sat on the first bench with her carefully organized registers and books.

'Hey, I need a favour,' said Dhruv striding in. His knuckles were bandaged.

'Excuse me?'

'Ritika hasn't done the assignment yet. We were out all night and she didn't get the time. You need to ask for an extension of a couple of hours from Raghuvir sir,' demanded Dhruv.

'And why exactly would I do that?'

'Because I'm requesting you.'

'You're bending over my table and you're breathing into my face. This hardly looks like requesting,' snapped Aranya.

Dhruv stood straight and folded his hands. 'I request you. Give her time.'

'There's sarcasm in your voice.'

'Just like there was in yours,' said Dhruv and put his hands into his pocket.

'I'm not the one being a girlfriend's mouthpiece,' retorted Aranya.

'But you're being a scheming bitch, aren't you?'

'Excuse me?'

Dhruv whipped out a Xerox copy of Aranya's assignment from his back pocket and flipped it to its end. 'Here.' He pointed to the last step of the question. It was encircled with a blue pen and it was labelled as '*HAHAHAHAHA*'.

'So?' asked Aranya.

'So you want me to believe that someone who managed to crack this question faltered on the last step? A simple calculation error? Do you think I'm that naive?' asked Dhruv.

Aranya acted shocked. 'Shit. How did I get this wrong?' exclaimed Aranya.

'You're a shitty actress. You knew if you wrote it the class would copy it.'

'I would never do that! Why would I!'

'Raghuvir would know the entire class copied and you would be riding an easy wave into his projects or whatever he does.'

'Stop being an overthinking vamp.'

'Look who's talking.'

'So, even if I did. Who's going to believe you over me?' asked Aranya and smiled at him. She watched the smile drain away from Dhruv's face.

'You know what, FUCK YOU.'

Dhruv walked off. 'Go, run to your pretty girlfriend!' she called out.

Dhruv waved a middle finger while leaving the class.

Aranya won.

Yes, she was keeping score.

26

'I don't want to get a zero in the first assignment itself. We shouldn't have gone out. I could have copied the assignment in time,' complained a scared Ritika on the phone.

'Raghuvir is not a fool. He would have seen through it, that you had copied. Trust me. You will not get a zero.'

Dhruv had made Ritika submit pages with only her name neatly scribbled on the top. He had told her he would handle it. Ritika, Instagram-obsessed and a raging bulimic, had not really struck Dhruv as someone who would care about missed assignments.

'I love you,' said the girl.

'. . .'

'Why don't you say it back?' asked Ritika.

'You wouldn't want me to.'

'Why is that?'

'Because when I do, I tend to stick to it and it doesn't end well. For me as well as the girl I am in love with. I will be an asshole at the end of it all and you would be a crying mess,' answered Dhruv.

'You don't scare me,' said Ritika.

Dhruv imagined her rolling over her nice and clean bed, maybe in a tiny pair of shorts and stringy spaghetti.

'I need to go,' said Dhruv.

'What are you going to do?'

'Leave that to me.' Dhruv disconnected the call, put on a T-shirt and knocked on Sanchit's door which was shut but not locked. He found Sanchit supine on his tattered bean bag. The room reeked of alcohol and weed and unwashed boxers, and there were two women touching each other on his laptop screen. He was watching it with such piercing intensity one would think it was *The Shawshank Redemption* playing on his laptop.

'Hey.'

'Shut up, this is my best scene.'

Sanchit never took the pain of turning the volume down during his private porn screenings. The dirtiness is in their moans, he used to say.

'Are you high?' asked Dhruv.

'Will you try to charm my pants off if I am?'

'Maybe later, but for now, we have to break into Raghuvir's room.'

'The second-year guy? Sorry, can't do. It's beneath my dignity.' Sanchit frowned.

'The professor, Raghuvir.'

'When do we strike?' asked Sanchit.

'Now.'

He hit the pause button, put out the cigarette. 'We have to be discreet with this sort of a thing.' His tone suddenly changed to resemble someone from the Secret Services. 'One mistake and it's all done.'

'Stop being melodramatic.'

'I'm not in if we are not giving names to each other. I'm Black Hawk, you're Charlie.'

'I'm doing it alone. I promised Ritika and I wouldn't let her down,' said Dhruv and left the room. Sanchit followed closely.

'Why are we doing this for her? And what exactly are we doing?' whispered Sanchit as they scaled the locked gate of the faculty building.

'She's my responsibility. And I will tell you.'

'I didn't know Ritika was a toddler.'

'I don't want to be the guy who falters,' Dhruv argued.

'Dude, you have severe control issues.'

'You would have issues too if you found out about your father's weekly trysts with prostitutes far uglier than your mother while you wait for him to sober up and get your mother from another man,' said Dhruv.

'That's too much information to be shared amongst men. I think we should be married now.'

'. . .'

'But I'm sorry.'

Both of them walked across the lawn gingerly as if they were inmates running to hide from the prison light.

'You didn't strike me as rich,' said Sanchit.

'I'm not. What's that to do with anything?'

Sanchit spoke as they jumped over the last fence. 'It's just not a very middle-class story. If your father was a rich businessman with a few gold teeth, it's digestible. Or a kid of a wayward celebrity,' remarked Sanchit.

'But what if it is a very middle-class thing, and we only don't look out for it? What if? Think about it, Sanchit. The belief that the middle class can't put a foot wrong morally is so deep that you wouldn't even begin to think about those overtimes in the office, those short office tours to Jaipur or Agra or Bombay were not office trips but moments of weakness spent in the arms of the women they bought, little fragments of happiness in the lives of husbands and fathers battling with car and house loans. It sounds ridiculous if you imagine your father doing the same, but ask yourself, how difficult is it? Check his browser history. Check his phone. Check what he watches late at night on television. Is it always news? Why wouldn't you check? Because you believe in him. Just like I used to.'

'Frankly, I'm disappointed,' said Sanchit.

'Did you just hear what I said?'

'Stop being such an attention whore. Yes, you said something about happiness. But look, we are already here,' said Sanchit pointing to Raghuvir's nameplate on the door. 'This was too easy. There was no challenge.' The guards were sleeping, drunk, or busy masturbating to *Grihashobha*. An army tank could have rolled past them unnoticed.

'Here's the challenge.' Dhruv pointed to the lock.

'What are we trying to achieve here?'

Dhruv showed him a corrected copy of Aranya's assignment, and explained that they had to break in cleanly, copy it on Ritika's assignment and leave.

'I have seen that girl look at Raghuvir like he was red velvet cake.'

'How do we break in?'

'Why are you asking me?' asked Sanchit. The lock on Raghuvir's room was one of those six-lever ones.

'What? You look like the kind of person who could pick a lock,' said Dhruv, exasperated.

'And you deduced that because you're the last product of the Sherlock Holmes sperm strain? Talking of which, did you also know that my father works in the Public Works Department and my mother is a housewife? That my cumulative percentage from seven semesters is 83 and my department rank is 4 and that I'm placed with Microsoft which essentially makes me the King Nerd?'

'What?'

'What what? I can't pick locks.'

'This should be right up your alley, dude! Then what is the weed and the porn and the metaphors and the alcohol about if you can't pick a small lock?' Dhruv clenched his fists and punched in the air angrily.

'I don't see the connection!'

'You're such a fucking disappointment.'

'Now who's being melodramatic?' asked Sanchit. Dhruv threw a murderous look his way. 'Fine. I do know someone who can make a key for you. I have used the guy earlier. In first year I used to lose my key all the time, but now I have just chained my desktop to the window railing. Third–year bastards still steal my soap though.'

'I'm sure it hurts your government servant dad's FDs.'

'No need to get personal here.'

An hour later, they were driving back in Dhruv's spluttering motorcycle, a dummy key in his pocket.

'So do you like to pretend the motorcycle has broken down and be all rustic, grubby and manly while you repair it? This thing is a chick magnet, isn't it?' Sanchit teased.

Dhruv ignored him and revved the bike harder almost knocking Sanchit over who clung to him afterwards. 'If you wanted to feel my boobs you should have just told me.'

Dhruv drove on. 'The key better work.'

'I never liked Raghu. He's too brilliant, way too brilliant,' said Sanchit. 'I have known girls who want him to write equations on their cleavages.'

'Raghu? Is he a friend that you call him that?'

'I wish he was. He's GOD, dude. Women slit their wrists if he misses class.'

'Okay.'

'No, serious. Some write him letters in blood.'

'Gross.'

'I'm not joking.'

'You need to shut up.'

'But you got to admit, that guy brings everything to the table. Even your girl, Aranya, is like a deer caught in the headlights with him. I have been told she's smitten.'

Dhruv parked the motorcycle outside the college building. 'Ritika. That's my girl's name, the one I'm dating. And she doesn't give a shit about Raghuvir. And Aranya's the bitch.'

'But you seem to think an awful lot about her.'

'No, I don't.'

'But she's good. I read the assignment on the way. Nice touch to get it wrong on the last step. That's a mark of genius and a girl desperate to be in the good books of Raghuvir,' remarked Sanchit.

'You need to stop talking about her.'

'But weren't you in love with her in school? I have been told.'

'Who tells you all this crap? And no! I wasn't. Have you seen her? She looks like shit. I hated her then and I hate her now.'

'Hmm. But I should tell you that it's a lost cause.'

'. . .'

'Raghuvir isn't foolish to think your girl, *Ritika*, would solve the question correctly while *Aranya* couldn't. You can't fuck with Raghuvir. He's smarter than you.'

Dhruv jemmied the key into the lock and it didn't work.

'He's known to ask the students to solve it on the board and he grills them. It's not going to be easy.'

Dhruv dropped the key and kicked the door. The screws that held the latch came loose and it hung limply from the door frame; the door was now wide open. Dhruv walked in and started to look for the bundle of assignments.

'DUDE! What are you trying to do?' asked Sanchit.

'Accidents happen. Things get lost sometimes. If we can't get her marked in the assignment, we can at least make the assignment go away.' Dhruv stuffed the assignments of the entire class in a polythene bag.

'What now?'

'I have an idea,' said Dhruv and hurried out, Sanchit trailing him, jumped the fences, ran across the field, ran up the stairwell of his hostel and pointed at the girls' hostel roof where Aranya was working on her laptop.

'ARANYA. ARANYA,' he shouted.

Aranya put the laptop down and looked in their direction. She walked closer to the ledge and squinted her eyes.

Dhruv waved the bundle of the assignments in the air. 'FUCK YOUR ASSIGNMENT! FUCK YOUR ASSIGNMENT!' shouted Dhruv.

Dhruv kept the stack of assignments on the edge of the roof. He poured Vodka out of a bottle over it even as Sanchit kept saying, 'Enough, enough, don't waste it!' and lit it up.

Aranya screamed in disbelief.

'FUCK RAGHUVIR. GO FUCK HIM!' shouted Dhruv and started to walk away from the fire.

'That was a bit extreme even for me,' said Sanchit. 'Why did you do it?'

'Because I hate her.'

'Hate doesn't push you that far, only love does.'

'I'm sure you haven't heard of ISIS.'

'Oh. Political references. Respect! But your reference is incorrect because the ISIS guys love Islam.'

'Fuck off.'

'But tell me something, why didn't you do the assignment?'

'My mother's a bitch and my father's an alcoholic. Doing assignments is out of my domain,' Dhruv said and walked back to his room.

27

'But Sir, I saw it! I saw him burning the assignments,' complained Aranya, choking on her tears.

'That's the twenty-third time you're repeating the same thing, Aranya. And what if he did? Let it go,' said Raghuvir, leaning back in his chair.

He wore a spotless kurta today with the same pair of jeans she saw him in on Freshers' Day, and leather chappals. Dhruv was leaning against the door, yawning for dramatic effect. Despite the heat he wore a leather jacket, a white shirt, a frayed pair of jeans and black loafers. Careless hair carefully done.

Eight years separated Dhruv and Raghuvir but they looked the same age. Dhruv looked the vain, brash movie star, and Raghuvir, the sincere, piercing, intelligent technocrat with a dress sense borrowed from the founder of Facebook. In a parallel world or in a cheesy novel, they would be brothers who fall in love with the same woman.

Aranya should have been angry, and maybe she was, somewhere deep inside, but she was also a little dizzy, a little disoriented sneaking glances at Raghuvir's tired, painfully cute, beautiful face, which she was convinced was one of her horrcruxes. She had spent hours, wrong, days Googling about Raghuvir, downloading his images on her laptop, day-dreaming about being intelligent and funny and mysterious in his class and yes, also songs, they had danced on songs together.

Fuck you, Aranya. You're a grown, intelligent woman. Stop staring at him as if he's God.

But he is like chocolate. With cream and sprinkles.

Stop talking in Internet meme language. You're not retarded.

I'm sorry, but look at him.

Exactly. And look at you, you're ugly enough to be a different species.

Whatever.

I hate you.

I am you.

Raghuvir continued, his voice suddenly grave, 'And Dhruv, you need to keep your attitude in check. The anger is cute. But I'm not one of your girls. I'm your professor and I have seen dozens of you strut their fake machismo over the years and all of them amount to nothing. You're nothing special. So the next time you're standing in front of me, you stand like a f . . . student. Do I make myself clear?'

Aranya felt like giggling but she restrained herself.

'Sir, but what do we do to make sure it doesn't happen again?' asked Aranya.

'Dhruv, you can go. And stay out of trouble,' said Prof. Raghuvir, pointing his pencil at him. Dhruv walked out without a second look.

'And Aranya,' said Raghuvir. 'This isn't school so stop running around after silly assignments. You're meant for greater things.'

'But I don't think anyone will hire me based on the ashes of my assignments, Sir.'

'Answering back won't help either.'

'Sorry, Sir. I didn't mean to—'

'It's okay. It's better than being a sycophant.'

'I didn't get you, Sir.'

'I heard Professor Tripathi say a thousand good things about you. In a conversation between Tripathi and a wall, the wall would win. And if you're running around trying to impress that God-awful professor who can't tell a quark from a proton, you're wasting your time and mine.'

Despite being chastised, Aranya blushed, embarrassed as if she were naked and he were staring. 'I'm sorry,' said Aranya.

'You can go now,' said Raghuvir. 'And I had read your assignment when you had submitted it. Good work.'

'Thank you,' said Aranya, making the slightest of fist pumps.

Aranya left the room with a sense of victory but the feeling died instantly when she saw Dhruv waiting for her outside, arms folded across his chest, his nervy, overbuilt arms on blatant display, a far cry from Raghuvir's understated yet overpowering awesomeness.

'Aw! Look at that blush,' said Dhruv.

'You need to get out of my face,' said Aranya and walked away from Dhruv.

'I just wanted to congratulate you for your efforts inside that room.'

Aranya stopped, turned and walked up to him, and stood so close she felt she would choke on his cheap cologne. She said, 'The next time you do something like that, I will crush you. I'm not saying that in the figurative sense of the word but I will crush you. I will make your life a living hell, so dare you cross me again. I can throw anyone, especially a smug, vain bastard like you who thinks he's better than everyone, under the bus if push comes to shove and no one knows that better than you. I know you seek revenge for what I did to your poor little heart, but you're going to stop now. If you don't, it's going to rain misery on you and you're going to regret the day you dared to stand up against me. I have seen guys like you talk a big game and then crumble to dust. Go to your little, insignificant world of porn, protein supplements and little slutty girls, all of which will slowly disintegrate into a life of slaving for people like me, people with real talent and drive, who reign over minions like you. Go, live your days, slave, for the future will only bring wretchedness to you and it will make whatever happened to you in the past seem like good old times.'

Dhruv looked straight at her, held her stare, and then broke out in his ridiculous smile. 'That was almost poetic. Did you like read a book yesterday and mark out lines that you would say to me today?'

Aranya started to walk away from him when she heard Dhruv say, 'Crumble to dust I might, but what about you? And what about you and Raghuvir? Did he notice your sly smiles and your flushed cheeks and your little nervous knee shakes? Or were you just another of the nondescript girls who fawn over him? And yes, I might be insignificant in the future but who on earth has seen the future! RIGHT NOW, I'M THE FUCKING KING AND YOU'RE INVISIBLE. TO ME AND TO HIM! You're the ugly duckling, the spotted, ugly, loathsome toad, dude. You always were. Don't you look into the mirror? No matter what you try to do, you are never going to wash off that skin. You will always be repulsive,' Dhruv said and walked away.

28

Aranya felt nauseous about how he had used the word *dude*—wannabe and gender-inappropriate—and how honest Dhruv was in declaring her an ugly toad.

She missed her dinner that night and thought of going for a run but settled for quantum mechanics instead. She didn't want to be seen running. It was too embarrassing. Instead she would jog on the spot for thirty minutes in front of the mirror and slump on the ground, crying and exhausted and hungry.

She could feel a wave of depression washing over her. It happened every few months for a couple of weeks. She wouldn't eat, she wouldn't be able to concentrate on work and she would spend hours in front of the mirror wishing she looked better.

For the next few days, Dhruv was too involved in pandering to his *pretty* girlfriend's wants and kept out of her way. She had been avoiding Raghuvir too, wondering if he felt the same way about her as Dhruv did—an ugly, loathsome toad.

She went on another one of her depressing crash diets that made her weak, irritable and cranky, and crushed her feminist, beauty-is-skin-deep soul. Her class performance started to dip infinitesimally which no one but Raghuvir noted.

'What's up with you?' asked Raghuvir having called her to his staffroom.

'Nothing, Sir.'

'You're slowing down in class. What's the matter? Only weeks ago you were up in arms about a guy burning your assignments and now you're listless even when on the first bench?'

Raghuvir led her to a chair and his touch was strangely comforting. 'What's troubling you?'

For the next ten minutes, Aranya stayed mum and Raghuvir waited for an answer.

'You wouldn't get it, Sir.'

'Do I need to read out my CV again? People think of me as quite intelligent, you know.'

Aranya sighed. 'There's this girl, a cousin of mine. She just got married.'

'Okay. That seems plausible. What about it?'

'She's pretty. Her Facebook, Instagram and Twitter profiles have a cumulative strength of 764 pictures, with an average "Like" and "Comment" rate of 123 and 34 per picture respectively.'

'I still can't see where you're going with this.'

'She hasn't read a book in her life and thinks Africa is a country. Blue, red, pink, purple are the colours she got streaked in her hair in the past nineteen months, none of which looked ridiculous on her, in fact they looked very pretty. In the pictures she wears spectacles she's called a nerd, an intellectual even. She poses with books and coffee mugs. The only consolation is the grammatical mistakes in those comments.'

'So what's your point?' asked Raghuvir.

'Her fiancé is Harvard-educated, lives in Mumbai and is a hedge fund manager. He drives a loan-free Audi.'

'So?'

'Do you have any idea how much pressure that puts on me, Sir?'

'No. I'm not in marriage dealings or I would have known.'

Aranya took a deep breath and collected everything she had been thinking in the past few days into a cogent argument. 'I ignored her for the majority of my childhood and adolescence despite my parents' constant reminders. While she blossomed like those women in fairness ads, I bloated and battled with my disease, my weight problem and my facial hair. While she wore little black dresses to family functions, I wore sweaters and jeans and thanked God for not giving me polio instead. I was either invisible or someone to maintain one-arm distance from to my extended family and she was talked about in verses. I waited for my time to come—the tenth standard board exams. Something that separates the winners from the losers, and I knew it was my time to shine. I scored a 97.9 per cent and she came down with jaundice and passed with 43 per cent. *She* was the success story, the brave one who battled a life-threatening disease, not *I*, who would have preferred getting jaundice for a lifetime over what I have. Later she took humanities, because she claimed to be artistic. Imagine! Humanities! A subject where marks don't matter and people lose track of how to judge you. How would I ever outshine her? I knew that no matter how successful I am, I would never trump her. It's like comparing a liquor baron with a painter.'

'What does it have anything to do with her getting married?'

'I was getting to that. For all practical reasons, she's illiterate and I hoped karma would bite her in the ass, that some day she would have to get married to a rich, fat businessman with an intelligence of an ape. And that's when I would parade us, my future man and me, the power couple, the ones who can talk business, politics, art, philanthropy with equal panache. I intended to smash her ego, her pride, her superiority to smithereens. But guess what? Her fiancé has a blog where he writes about the political scene in the US and its ramifications on the Indian economy and is a part of an NGO that cares for cancer-stricken children. Imagine! CANCER CHILDREN! How am I supposed to compete with a man like that? How am I supposed to win? Why are men blind? How hard would it have been for God to give her a husband who believed in dowry and hated children?'

Raghuvir scowled. 'Is this where I tell you that you should be proud—'

Aranya snapped, 'I'm a fucking feminist, okay, a struggling one, but I am. I think men are disasters and we are better than them because, you know, periods and labour pains and higher emotional intelligence, but what the hell is wrong with you men? Like what? And it's not easy to look at yourself in the mirror and wonder if guys will ever like you! It's too much pressure. And the worst part is when you know you shouldn't think of it and yet you do! AND THAT SUCKS. Why can't I be ugly and fat and still be wanted? Why is the girl in biotechnology more talked about than me? She can't even tell an array apart from a pointer!' She felt exhausted and slumped in her chair, her body in severe deficit of carbohydrates she had ruthlessly cut out of her diet. Whoever said sharing makes you feel lighter must have written the quote on a shit pot while taking a dump, because right now all she felt was embarrassment, and the silence in the room was making it worse.

'I think you're pretty.'

'Stop making fun of me. I'm borderline suicidal.'

'No, you are. I would pick you over that cousin a zillion times. I have been in that guy's shoes more times than you can imagine. Going for a face that is said to be conventionally beautiful when beauty is all but a construct of the media, fed through movies and television and music and advertisements. I have been down that road and it blows. It's no fun dating a face. I have had my heart broken a million times—not by the women I chose to date but the mistake I did by choosing them. And that guy is making a mistake too and he will know that soon. Though I do agree with you that men are flawed and unfair. But that's why God made women like you to set things right. Law of averages. If I were you I wouldn't sulk in a room.'

'Then?'

'You should go to your sister's wedding and engage the guy in conversation about the situation in Darfur and talk about the fiscal deficit and then leave the conversation midway and walk away, giving him time to soak in your brilliance and realize his folly.'

Aranya smiled imagining the situation in her head. 'No, I can't do that. She's my sister after all. She's family, so can't hurt her.'

'Then stop feeling bad about yourself,' remarked Raghuvir. 'And where did it all start from?'

Aranya debated whether she should say it and she decided to anyway. Screw it, he already knew everything. 'Dhruv. We were in the same school and he has followed me here. He called me an ugly, loathsome toad.'

'What?'

'And he told me the rest of the world thinks the same of me. Which is sort of correct because my own parents and relatives think of me as a disaster.'

'But he's not your sister or your family. Feel free to exact your revenge,' said Raghuvir and smiled at her.

Aranya thanked him and left the room. She desperately wanted some cake.

And a little revenge.

29

The burden of genius isn't an easy one to carry.

Twenty-nine years of lugging it around had worn Raghuvir down. He had stopped treating it as anything other than a curse. It was fun in the beginning, he had to admit. The effortless exam scores, the feeling of superiority, the unabashed admiration, it was all quite heady to be honest. But slowly, the pressures that came with all this started to mount.

He was put into groups with other boys and girls with similar or greater intelligence, sent to competitions where he was reduced to a really slow computer.

And slowly, the headstart of having a greater IQ faded. Numbers stopped to matter and hours spent teaching himself courses way ahead of his time went up. The competition between geniuses is fierce and it stripped Raghuvir of everything else in life. He was the only twelve-year-old who refused to go on family vacations, or watch cartoons, make friends or even go outside and play. Instead, he would stay locked up in his room and attempt questions of advanced calculus. He had practically brought himself up. His parents, concerned at first, had resigned to their kid being abnormally precocious.

The only relationships he had had were with his teachers and professors. It wasn't until his late teens that he learned to hold down conversations. These were little sacrifices though. He wouldn't give up his position as a child prodigy, and later a promising young scientist, for anything in the world. He had got used to the attention, the promise of a legacy he would leave behind.

He spent a good eight years of his adolescent life locked up in labs, or in his room poring over books, research papers, publishing his own reports, criticizing the reports of others. The scientific community is a hostile, unforgiving place. New discoveries, inventions, technologies are frowned upon at first, looked at with suspicion and envy; most scientists are driven by the fear of being left behind.

But just like in every book, every movie, every play, he fell in love and everything changed.

The girl was a young and beautiful understudy, and Raghuvir was a young, good-looking professor. Their conversation started at the laboratory, and soon they were talking about their dreams and aspirations, things they loved, cuisines they liked and movies they hated. In a month's time Raghuvir knew she was the girl he wanted to spend the rest of his life with.

He had finally found love outside his research and his quest to leave a mark on the scientific community and the world.

It was the most beautiful thing he had ever experienced in his life, something science or logic could never explain. They were the best six months of his life. He got quite obsessive with the idea of love and how powerful it was.

Every turn in his story had been a cliché and so was what happened next—the girl left him.

She went to Germany on a research scholarship. Raghuvir was ready to go along but the girl insisted she would go on her own. Having just found the joy of having someone to love and be loved by, Raghuvir was miserable and lonely without her.

For the next few years, he was quite lost, but more than that he was just lonely. Love is quite an addiction. It trumps research, glory and all that bullshit by a mile.

He tried to write a book and failed. Like everyone who has lost in love, he tried writing a song for her but he couldn't rhyme it. He tried a host of other jobs but couldn't stick to any for too long. There were always a slew of job offers lined up for Raghuvir, now tagged as the irresponsible, reclusive genius, but Raghuvir knew it wasn't what he wanted.

What followed were whirlwind relationships with a bevy of beautiful women, none of which lasted. They were all faces he could fall in love with but never be in love with for a really long time. It's not to say that he didn't enjoy being with them at the beginning. He would never admit it but for the most part he would be with them for the sex and think that the love would come soon. How hard could it be to find love again? Especially when the women were beautiful and willing? Quite hard, he had come to realize.

Even though he flitted from one relationship to another, he couldn't quite find what he was looking for. In fact he got lonelier than ever. Slowly, his reputation as a philanderer caught on, his respect as a breakthrough researcher dwindled and he quietly stepped out of the limelight and people's minds.

Increasingly, he believed that love was good, but only as a concept. Only relationships existed and only those relationships endured where people were willing enough to compromise on love, careers and sexual freedom.

A year back, he got an offer from a leading engineering college in India. He wouldn't have taken the job had they expected him to be on his top game. But one meeting with the dean, Prof. Mitra, told him that he was just required to be a poster boy of their faculty, nothing more. It worked out well in the beginning, but slowly he was drawn back to the laboratories and the research. It was the only thing he was good at. And soon, he dived headlong into it for it was the only thing that could fill the void left behind by love.

And then walked in Aranya, the most vulnerable, insecure, adorable girl he had come across in years. She was a little, fat Raghuvir in a female body. That's what he remembered thinking the first time he met her. Strangely, he never noticed the discoloration on her face, her body. And even before Raghuvir had started taking classes for her batch, she had slipped in little notes of appreciation for Raghuvir's work, the list of numericals she hadn't been able to solve, and a comprehensive list of alternative solutions to the prescribed questions.

She was nothing like the girls Raghuvir had been with earlier. Maybe that was a sign?

Curious, he had first tracked her down to the library where she sat at the far corner, almost hidden behind the tower of books. It's strange to say this, but it was love at first sight. Unlike Raghuvir, or the girl he was in love with, Aranya was a hard worker. Her assignments reeked of years of back-breaking work she had put in to sharpen her mind. She wasn't gifted, but her attention to detail was exemplary.

By now he had heard stories about her Hitleresque leadership but there was something very honest about her behind the carefully constructed facade of being indestructible.

It was hard for Raghuvir to tell when he really started to feel something for the girl who walked the corridors of the college alone, always clutching an armful of books. At first he mistook it for pity. But time passed and he knew it wasn't so.

He wanted her to be around. She was nothing like the other girls who fawned over him. She was different and he began to think that maybe she was the answer. He was looking at all the wrong places. Maybe she was the normalcy he was looking for.

She reminded him of his old days when he used to isolate himself from the rest of the world as if meeting common people would erode his intelligence.

He was a lonely kid as well. He was just like her.

30

Dhruv's commitments were always severe. He took that shit seriously.

So while Ritika was getting her legs waxed, he sat patiently flitting through glossy magazines on a leather couch in the reception area which had outlived its intended use.

Unmindfully, he was running his fingers over the scar on his right palm he got as a kid.

'What's up?' a voice said, startling Dhruv.

Dhruv looked up to see Sanchit standing tall over his head. Sanchit had now started faintly reminding him of Betal from *Vikram and Betal*, the pale white ghost hanging from Vikram's shoulders. 'What are you doing here?' asked Dhruv.

'Dean wanted me to conduct a pep talk for the first-year students. Tell them about my glorious achievements and my struggles, you know. I would have found it hard not to talk about the dean's stupidity and his wife's massive breasts so I ran.'

Dhruv shrugged, trying not to think about the dean's wife and her massive breasts, but when you're trying not to think about something you only think about it more. He got back to the glossy.

'I'm just making sure you don't get bored. Hey, by the way, I never noticed that scar on your right hand. It looks pretty badass,' prodded Sanchit.

'It's a birthmark,' deflected Dhruv.

'Unless a baby actually came out of it, it is not a birthmark, dude. I'm departmental rank 4. I ask questions from the first bench till the professors break down and take to heroin.'

Dhruv sighed. 'Long story.'

'No offence, but your girlfriend's hairy as a yak. They are probably making wigs out of her armpit hair and that's going to take some time. Tell me your story.'

Dhruv wanted to kick his teeth in but Sanchit's skinny face only evoked pity, much like little National Geographic kids, only fairer.

'A door banged on it.'

'That's a short story, not the long one.'

'I banged the door on it,' said Dhruv.

'James Joyce's *Ulysses* was 265,000 words and that was a long story and you're shit but yours had just eleven words. I'm sure you can do better. Let me guess. Was it around the time your parents got separated?'

'A little before that.'

'You fit every cliché in the book, man. It's like watching a bad soap and you are the intense, brooding hero with a heavy backstory. You're an insult to every normal kid from a broken family.'

'Fuck off.'

'Fine, fine. Tell me. Stop being a girl!'

Dhruv waved his middle finger in Sanchit's face. He didn't say a word for the next ten minutes or so. Sanchit sat there calmly, staring at the wall in front of him, and Dhruv envied him for his stillness. Dhruv was always restless, bristling under his skin, always looking for confrontation, excitement, disappointment, he wanted life to fly at him, keep him occupied, unlike Sanchit who could sit and do nothing and be nothing.

'I had to miss a cricket match,' Dhruv finally started.

'I'm listening,' said Sanchit.

'I was seven. It was a Sunday morning. They had been fighting a lot. I knew they wouldn't talk about it if I stayed in the house, if I could just make them laugh or cry or be concerned or anything that would keep them together. I wanted to stay in the house.'

'What about the match?' Sanchit asked.

'My friends kept shouting from below, "Dhruv! Dhruv! We have a match, we have a match," and that I couldn't ditch them at the last moment. They were right. I had led them to the finals of the local tournament and deserting them would have meant sure loss. They were sulking outside. So I slammed the door on my wrist.'

'And?'

'The doctor said it was a hairline fracture. My parents sat there crying for me, together. Seeing my hand in the cast, the opponents agreed to postpone the finals till my wrist healed, and my team was ecstatic.'

'Not sure if you're a sorry bastard or an evil mastermind.'

'Let's go outside,' said Dhruv when a few more people walked into the waiting room. Sanchit lit a cigarette and offered Dhruv one. Dhruv took it.

Sanchit was now staring at the poster of a C-grade movie stuck on the wall in front of them. 'You could have said no to

Ritika today. Your raccoon girlfriend could have come with someone else.'

'I can't say no to her.'

'You can't keep everyone happy all the time, Dhruv. It's not your responsibility. Who the fuck cares if you lost that match? And if your parents eventually got divorced? Who eventually lost?'

The tone of the conversation had suddenly changed and it unnerved Dhruv and he wanted to run. 'It doesn't matter how it ended. But I can't be the one who fucks it up and neither will I allow the other person to fuck it up.'

'Did you win the match?' asked Sanchit.

'No.'

'Did you win the next year?'

'I don't know,' said Dhruv. 'I didn't play the next year.'

They smoked in silence. Little did Dhruv know this was the calm before the storm, that Aranya had been plotting her revenge while he waited for Ritika to get over with her business.

Dhruv, Sanchit and Ritika came back to college, riding triple on his motorcycle, and Sanchit stared at Ritika's legs throughout the ride.

31

Aranya had had her cake, red velvet no less, and she had been waiting for Dhruv in the canteen for the last three hours, plotting every second of her revenge.

People think of debaters as people with the gift of the gab and spontaneity and that might be true, but the pioneers are ones who plan every detail to the last second, who control the entire narrative and sit there smiling as it slowly unfolds. And with revenge, it just makes more sense to plan it out and understand the ramifications and how it will rupture the future, than just react in a knee jerk and not know how it will all turn out.

It was already seven-thirty and the canteen was deserted, the helps were cleaning the tables, stacking up chairs, and Aranya twiddled her thumbs nervously. Nervousness is always good, it keeps you aware, she had heard somewhere. She had done what she was about to do on Skype previously, on a call, on texts but never while looking into the eyes of a pervert.

It was seven forty-five when she saw Dhruv walk in with Ritika and Sanchit, his arm firmly around Ritika's shoulders. They sat on a table at the far corner of the canteen. She hated Ritika's hot pants, an anomaly in an engineering college like theirs, a blasphemy of sorts, and like 'how-could-she!'

She reminded herself of Dhruv's words and the missed meals and the little slips in class participations and gathered them all in a little snowball that she intended to transform into a fucking avalanche to drown him out.

And it was showtime. It was her stage and the audience was in ridiculous hot pants. She strode towards Dhruv as Dhruv looked at her walking towards him.

She cocked her head to one side and said, 'Hi, I want to talk to you.'

'I don't,' said Dhruv and waved her away.

'Are you sure?' asked Aranya and braced herself. She was mush inside. It reminded her of her first debate; she was a nervous wreck, close to a breakdown, but outside she appeared a rock. She reminded herself. Be a rock. She bent over and breathed her words into his ear. 'Are you sure you don't want to talk?' If there's one thing Aranya could do to seduce, it was to modulate her voice, and right now she could have been a voiceover artist to leading porn stars. 'Is that because I'm ugly? Or is it because you think my intelligence turns you on a little? Is that because you were in love with me once? Or are you still in love with me? The girl who destroyed you forever?' Her lips hovered dangerously close to his ear. 'Don't tell me you don't like a little challenge? A little intimidation? The feeling of your balls and your cock being in control of a girl. Aren't you one of those boys who like their hair to be pulled back and slapped a little?' So predictable, she thought. Dhruv reminded her of Sameer and his rodeo impression on Skype. Dhruv's breathing got heavier, just a little, but enough. Say the word *cock* to a guy and he's yours. She could see Dhruv freeze in his chair. She made her next move, a dangerous one, like throwing an unchecked statistic at the interjector hoping he or she wouldn't catch your bluff. She placed her hand on his thigh. 'Don't tell me you wouldn't like it if I maybe . . . tie you up? Hit you across your face? And you hit me right back? Don't tell me you haven't imagined that? You have, haven't you? You have touched yourself thinking of it.' She moved her hand towards his crotch and could disgustingly find Dhruv harden. 'Don't tell me you're not thinking about it right now? You are, aren't you?' Dhruv was looking at her, like a leashed puppy, helpless. And she grabbed his crotch and he was hard. 'You're thinking of me, aren't you? Tell me you are.' Dhruv nodded his head, just a trillionth of a fraction, even a slow motion camera wouldn't catch the movement, but in moments like these that's enough and Aranya pushed him away and took a step back and smiled derisively at him.

'SCREW YOU, DHRUV,' bellowed Aranya. 'FUCK YOU. Look down, you pathetic excuse for a guy. Look at that.

You're fucking hard, Dhruv. You're just a helpless boy, Dhruv, and you dared to cross my path. You call me hideous? You call me an ugly, loathsome toad? It took me just a few words to get you salivating. JUST LOOK AT YOU.' The blood had rushed to her face and she was aware that it was her war face, a face no one had fucked around with. She pointed a finger at his face which went pale. 'So the next time you dare to even think that I'm ugly, think of this moment when I made your world come crashing down on you, when you were powerless, the moment when you agreed to cheat on your pretty girlfriend. Remember this moment because this defines you.' Aranya wiped the frown on her face and smiled. She turned her gaze towards Ritika, smiled kindly and said, 'All yours. Nice legs, though.'

She strode off with a smile on her face, fully aware of the three pairs of eyes on her.

In her hostel room she washed her hands and sanitized them, and then ate three oily burgers to wipe out the memory of the battle and savoured the victory.

32

'It's not really her fault, dude,' said Sanchit.

As a part of Dhruv's mourning process, they were sharing a joint, and a Pepsi bottle topped with Old Monk on the roof of the hostel.

Ritika wasn't receiving his calls, wasn't attending classes and was crying her heart out, letting the entire world know what a nice fucking guy Dhruv was.

'Tell me something I don't know, asshole.'

Dhruv had spent the last five days in a drunken haze, dialling her number over and over again, waiting on the pavement facing her first floor hostel window, sending her long texts and numerous e-mails begging for another chance. He felt like shit for letting Ritika down. He even toyed with the idea of slitting his wrists to prove a point but the mess that would follow deterred him.

'*You have always* led her on, you didn't tell me you and she had a thing in school!' Ritika had complained.

But I called her ugly, how is that leading her on, Dhruv had argued.

She turned you on, how can I trust you any longer, Ritika had cried.

Sanchit unscrewed the cap of another bottle of Old Monk and poured it into the empty Pepsi bottle.

'I'm in love with Aranya. She's my dream woman,' said Sanchit.

'She fucked my happiness, dude. Ritika's never going to forgive me for this. How the fuck am I any different from my fuck-all father, fucking shit.'

'You're drunk.'

'I'm drunk? You are the fucking one who just said you fucking love that bitch!'

'Mind your language there, Dhruv. I'm married to her in my head,' quipped Sanchit.

'Is that why you're watching that?' asked Dhruv, pointing to *Bookworm Bitches—Megan Goes to School* video playing on his laptop.

'Fine. Let me prove it to you,' said Sanchit and clicked on the porn folder which was labelled as Important Documents and paraded his painstakingly procured collection, now categorized and cross-referenced.

He pressed the ALT key and his finger lingered over the DEL key. He asked, 'Should I?' And before Dhruv could answer, he pressed the key, a bar appeared and slowly, hundreds of pixelated naked bodies disappeared. 'See? Not even a second thought. Aranya is hot. All my fantasies are going to revolve around her now.'

Dhruv didn't see the point of arguing. They drank and smoked silently, Dhruv blissfully unaware of the approaching mid-semester examinations. It was the time when the hostels remained abuzz with activity till early mornings, study groups were formed and the dynamics of friendships changed.

They ran out of alcohol and lay on the rooftop, staring at the sky as if there were stars visible to appreciate. Dhruv's phone had run out of battery from the incessant calling.

'Should I get her name tattooed? Do you think that would work?' asked Dhruv, once he felt a little less hammered.

'Get it in Chinese so that you can fool your next girlfriend. Even the Chinese don't understand their script.'

'I'm not breaking up,' said Dhruv.

'Have you decided your kids' names yet?'

'When the right time comes, then why not,' answered Dhruv, the ridiculousness of the question and the answer ringing in his ears.

'You're stupid as hell, man. You have got to be kidding me if you think you and Ritika are meant for life. I don't think you're even sad. You're just acting sad!'

'Why would you say that?' asked Dhruv, curious.

'For one, you're twenty and there are ten more years for you to think from your dick. And secondly, how's it love? Love's not waiting for a couple of hours outside a parlour reading gossip magazines while she's getting rid of her fur. Love's when you can say fuck off, I'm not coming, and I don't care you're a hairy mess for I like your hairy mess.'

'That sounds like a fetish,' said Dhruv.

'I'm no Freud but you might be the first guy who suffers from the opposite of commitment phobia. Commitment philia?'

'This conversation is over.'

'Want to watch some porn together?'

'I hate porn.'

'Don't ever say that again or we might not be friends any more,' said Sanchit.

'Random girls fucking random boys for money? I'm not into that. It's just not my thing.'

'Aw! Don't tell me you think about their families and their boyfriends and their kids?'

'Why not?'

'This conversation is over, Dhruv. We are not friends.'

'We were never friends.'

'. . .'

'. . .'

Dhruv continued, 'Morever, two men watching porn together is gay.'

'What's wrong in being gay now?'

'Nothing.'

'Good.'

Dhruv sat up and drank the last sip from the bottle of Pepsi. 'Didn't you delete all your porn?'

'Which self-respecting guy doesn't keep a backup? But I did delete it without a second thought and you still don't have the tattoo on yourself,' said Sanchit and smiled. 'Aranya is hot.'

33

Aranya's life had crawled back to being awesome and unfit; samosas and cupcakes were being eaten without guilt, questions about thermodynamics were being answered in a flash, her dominance in class participation and internal class tests was on an all-time high, and most importantly, Raghuvir was happy about her comeback. He had even expressed interest in enrolling her as a student researcher in one of his projects, which was the kind of thing that turned Aranya on. It was a montage of life throwing good things at her.

She sat in her usual seat, the first bench, alone and sharpening her pencils, smiling. The first register of the semester was filled up and today she was breaking in a new register. The smell of new registers, and sharpened pencils always filled her with a sense of eagerness and anticipation. It was Raghuvir's class today and she hoped he would walk in wearing a niqab for her to concentrate on his words better.

More often than not Aranya was content placing herself at the centre of the universe and not caring about the insignificant people orbiting around her, but today was different. On the stairs outside the class, Ritika sat crying, bawling, snot running from her nose, looking like nothing anyone would love. In the past few days, she had become rather ghostly. She had lost weight and looked pale, one could find her standing unblinking on empty balconies and walking listlessly through empty corridors late at night, and since Aranya lived right next door, she heard howling from her room every night. Aranya told herself that it wasn't her fault but Ritika's and that the girl was cuckoo, and it would all be over and time would exorcize the ghost soon. But today she took it on herself to be the priest and show her the cross.

She walked out of the class, cursing her feminine instinct.

'Ritika?' said Aranya.

'Get lost!' snapped Ritika, her face streaked with tears.

If this wasn't an example of overreaction, she didn't know what was.

'I'm sorry it had to be like this between the two of you, but you have to know that there's nothing between the two of us,' said Aranya, trying hard to sound concerned but this entire situation was a little too stupid to be taken seriously.

'Nothing?'

'Well, if there's something between Dhruv and me its unbridled hatred, anger, and related synonyms. I would happily see his body in a blender.'

'But I just can't let go of whatever happened that day,' said Ritika and started to cry like a child again.

'Ritika. You need to get your shit together.'

'And you need to keep your hands off my boyfriend's crotch!' retorted Ritika.

'I would rather dip my hands in acid.'

'I don't want to talk to you.'

'What do you want to do then, Ritika? Quite frankly, I'm starting to feel guilty about what I did and I want to apologize and get it over with. And I need you to look at me and say that it's okay,' said Aranya.

And then, just like that, without warning, a hand came rushing to meet her face, and her fat cheeks reverberated with the impact and her teeth clattered. The slap reminded her of her father, who's favourite pastime was hitting her.

Aranya gathered herself, clenched her fingers into a fist to hit the bitch's face, but then thought she probably deserved the slap and took a deep breath and said, 'Okay, maybe I deserved that. But you need to move on from here now. Or I could slap you and it would go on and then I will win when I sit on your face.'

Ritika didn't reply. Aranya thought to sweeten the deal. 'Fine. This is the most I can do. You don't have to submit the next five assignments.' Yes, now the dumb bitch was listening. Ritika nodded and wiped her tears.

'I don't know if I can forgive him.'

'That's a call you have to take, but don't send me down another guilt trip.'

She ran an awkward hand over her head, looked at her like she gave a shit, and walked back to class. Ritika followed soon after and took a seat at the last bench of the class. Aranya could now go on with her life without a twinge of guilt or remorse.

A little later Raghuvir walked in in all his splendour, well not really, because he wore a tattered T-shirt from the technical fest last year, trackpants and slippers, but yeah, still too much gorgeousness. He had shaved so his smooth baby skin was glistening.

'Today we are going to study Heisenberg's uncertainty principle in detail. You might have studied it in school but we will go down the nitty-gritties of it today. So brace yourself because this is tough and boring and I will make sure I put in a few questions in the examination from this topic . . .'

Write down everything he says.

But look how gorgeous!

WRITE. STUFF. DOWN.

But?

What but?

I said butt. Look at his butt.

And look at yours, fatso Aranya.

What about it?

It's like a continent. And his is like a cute little island. There's no way the tectonic plates of yours and his are going to meet.

Fine.

Fine.

Raghuvir wielded the chalk like a samurai and no one saw how it happened but the board was filled with equations so dizzying it looked like they had spilled over to the walls, slowly creeping up to the windows, and would soon engulf the students in their wake. He made physics trippy.

Aranya's daydream of Raghuvir as a celestial DJ who spun out equations was rudely interrupted when the door was banged open and Dhruv crawled in, smelling like rug rat, face swollen, eyes bloodshot and his hand extended like sculpted warriors at traffic intersections. He was still in a pair of strategically torn jeans and white linen shirt with three buttons open, his muscular cleavage visible from afar.

'Excuse me?' asked Raghuvir.

With Dhruv's hand still pointing in Ritika's direction, he answered Raghuvir. 'I love her.' He looked at Ritika who was now crying. 'I love you. Don't try to run from me. I really do.'

Such a *fucking* drama queen, Aranya thought. This is a physics class, damn it.

Ritika stood up from her seat and said she loved him too, snot and tears obscuring her face. Beautiful, just beautiful. Aranya held her head, embarrassed. What was happening? How can this be a self-respecting college and why wasn't Raghuvir aiming the duster at Dhruv's head? Raghuvir stood there, amused, and Aranya felt like apologizing to him like it was her fault.

The bell rang and Raghuvir collected his books and walked out like it was business as usual.

Aranya watched him go, objectifying his butt and thinking what he must look like when he showered every morning and whether he and the PhD student, Smriti, were in a strictly physical relationship as the rumour went. Of course it had to be true. She was beautiful, just like the ones Raghuvir was often seen with in the past. She wished Smriti would die.

She heard people clap. She turned to see Dhruv and Ritika hugging each other, muttering apologies into each other's necks, and the girls in the class were clapping and crying at the reunion of a drunken bastard and a wailing drama queen. *When did people stop respecting sanity?*

Aranya walked to the teacher's table, banged it thrice with the duster, and announced. 'Mr Tripathi's assignment is due tomorrow. I need it in my mailbox by 11 p.m. tonight.'

She saw the happiness drain out from the faces and they were no longer clapping, instead they were discussing the assignment and from where they would copy it. Aranya had successfully ruined a beautiful moment, vile and disgusting to her.

34

Sanchit had never had a girlfriend, which gave him ample time to analyse girls and relationships deeply and intensely, be it through porn or books which he did out in the open, or through glossy magazines which he downloaded on his phone and read while on the shit pot every morning.

It was the tenth year since he hit puberty and he had researched enough to know that Ritika and Dhruv's relationship was a sham, there was no love, maybe a psychological warfare of a different kind but definitely not love. Dhruv wanted to possess her and then unwittingly suffocate her with his overbearing possessiveness and destroy her, and Ritika who was an intelligent girl had turned into a bumbling idiot in love. But then girls love to be destroyed by men who take them on a bad trip, make them feel loved and despised, keep them constantly on tenterhooks, and ruin them for everyone else. Dhruv was that mad love that forty-year-old women write about in their books while they are married to sedate office-goers with paunches and white patches on their wrists from wearing the same watch for decades.

But he loved Dhruv because Dhruv lived. He was always too angry, too happy, too agitated, too alive, too sad, like living four lives at once, like he was made of nerve endings. While the entire world was like a sleepy, herbivorous, gigantic argentinosaurus, ambling slowly, target in sight, the lush leaves on the top of a tree, Dhruv was an angry tryannosaurus rex, a complete fucking bastard with no sense of fear, absolutely aimless, ripping out trees and dinosaurs far bigger than his size and soaking in the glory of it all, remorseless.

For the past two weeks Dhruv had been chasing him and a near-impossible dream to top the mid-semester examination, an honour reserved for the nerds, the half-humans like Sanchit.

Dhruv had fumbled with the reason why he wanted to top the examination, concocting stories, but Sanchit wasn't Ritika and he didn't buy his shit. He would have pretended to be too drunk, too busy, too stoned to teach him but he had relented for Dhruv had some inherent niceness in him, you could sense it and you were sure it existed, but you couldn't get to it, and he respected that. It was also the reason why girls made him a project and fell in love with him.

Sanchit saw through the stories Dhruv tried to sell him but he knew all too well why Dhruv was poring over books, wasting precious paper and missing his morning cardio. He couldn't help but think that it had to do with Aranya's meteoric rise in the social fabric of DTU in the past two weeks, which had been nothing less than legendary. Sanchit, the reigning King Nerd of DTU, had been surprised when he attended one of the classes Aranya held to help out the weak students of the class (she had started with teaching one girl in her hostel and the crowd had swelled to thirty-three at last count). The girl was good, better than most professors even. And the college was rightfully talking about it. Sanchit knew this girl would go down in history. People would talk about her long after she was gone. The professors already were.

Sanchit remembered the last time it had happened, he was at the centre stage of it all. He was a young, untouched boy from a small town, hard-working as fuck and sharper than three grandmasters put together. In a college that prided itself on its research, a student like Sanchit was a virgin gold mine. No sooner had he topped the mid-semester examinations than he was drafted into the projects of three top-notch professors and he couldn't say 'no'. Three months of sleep deprivation and mind-numbing research pushed him to the brink, and in that brink lay the undiscovered world of alcohol, cigarettes and weed. It consumed Sanchit completely, robbed him of his desire to blow his professors' cocks to be in their good books, and he dropped out of the projects unceremoniously. The professors were pissed but alcohol and weed make you a hell of a good liar and when he told them, tears in his eyes, hands shaking, about his brother (non-existent) who had died in a gruesome road mishap, they decided he needed time to grieve. Since then, Sanchit had been grieving.

History was repeating itself and the girl was being courted by covetous professors who wanted mules to carry out their dirty, dreary, tiring research work, but Aranya had held her ground. She had become quite notorious for rejecting projects from the bigwigs in the college. He had heard Prof. Mitra, the dean, wasn't impressed by the rejection at all (no one had ever rejected the dean).

His dislike for Prof. Raghuvir, the genius, was never hidden. But Aranya had nothing to worry about, with Professor

X, Raghuvir, behind her there was nothing to worry. And of whatever little Sanchit knew, he guessed she was looking for Raghuvir to offer her a research scholar spot.

All this made Dhruv uncomfortable.

Sanchit guessed Dhruv was a big deal in his school, a brat, a hooligan even, the perfect anti-hero who walks into the class ten minutes late with an open wound on his forehead, blood dripping on to a crumpled white shirt now untucked courtesy the recent fight with a senior. In college though, no one gives a fuck. So while Dhruv with his little skirmishes in the hostel and the campus was fading into oblivion, the girl was searing her name into people's brains. The only reason people still talked about Dhruv in the college was because he was dating Ritika, who looked kind of okay and 'kind of okay' is a big deal in any engineering college.

Or maybe, just maybe, he was falling in love with Aranya again. Sanchit believed Dhruv wanted to take her head-on. He was attempting to keep hating her because loving Aranya would mean a lot of pain for him.

35

Ritika had dated before. Three boys to be precise, and with the last two she had gone all the way. With the first one because he was 'oh my god, so hot' and with the second because she thought she would end up with him. But she didn't enjoy it much and thought sex was overrated.

But she wouldn't dare discuss her previous sex life with Dhruv, who bristled at the mention of ex-boyfriends, forcing

Ritika to modify the stories to sound like they were innocent puppy crushes and might well have happened when she was six and the boys were still shitting in their half-pants and picking food stuck in their braces when they were dating. She had since then deleted, blocked, threatened her ex-boyfriends. It was for their good.

Dhruv was different. He wasn't kind or thoughtful or gentle or considerate, no Sir, instead he was ruthless. She used to imagine herself in a period drama where she's neglected yet aggressively loved, taken for granted yet always The One, bored but infinitely aroused and prickled, wife of a merciless dictator with the world in his hands. Ritika used to love to revel in the fear and unabashed domination Dhruv used to exude. No boy or man had the guts to look at her more than the accidental eye contact. She was *his* girl. And no one messed with Dhruv's girl.

In the past few weeks, she had broken up quite a few fights Dhruv had found himself in, always a few minutes too late though. It would start with a casual raise of an eyebrow from Dhruv to the target, warning him, and then he would clutch her hand tighter, look at her and tell her that he would be back, his face would be flushed, hair standing on his arms, and he would stride and without a second's hesitation throw a punch right between the ears of any guy who dared to hit on her. Ritika would stand there, shocked, but secretly admiring Dhruv's furious love for her, and then run to save the poor boy from Dhruv's unrelenting assault.

'I love you,' she would say.

'I love you, too,' Dhruv would answer back, still panting but calmed, and she would feel like she were dating the Hulk. *What more could she have asked for?*

But the last two weeks had been less than ideal. Dhruv had been studying uncharacteristically hard and often at the expense of the time they used to spend together and talk about Dhruv's unending hatred for his parents and for Aranya or Dhruv's time in school which Ritika noted was riddled with stories of disgruntled parents of other kids, three-day suspensions, rustications, and bloodied noses of his classmates. Dhruv had failed thrice and changed three schools but not before leaving an indelible mark on the schools/students, his rate of disfiguring faces of young men higher than celebrity plastic surgeons.

The sheer amount of time Dhruv spent with Sanchit, the creep, discomfited her. Sanchit's hatred for Ritika radiated from him even though they hadn't exchanged a harsh word. Not that she liked him but it would have been good to have the approval of Dhruv's only friend in college, no matter how dirty his bed sheets and his mind were.

Speaking of bed sheets and dirty minds, Ritika hadn't been able to keep her hands off Dhruv. She often felt he was turning her into a nymphomaniac but there was something in the way Dhruv made love to her that kept her thinking about it for days, reliving the moments repeatedly. Physiologically and mechanically, everything was still the same, in fact sometimes it was uncomfortable because of his muscular arms and rough hands, but there was something incredibly sexy in the way he kept saying that he loved her, that he would never let her go, and that he would kill anyone who would try to wrest her away from him. Quite frankly, the first time he said these things she thought of him as a clingy psychopath, which he was, but slowly she started warming up to his fiercely protective demeanour. And then got addicted to the angry, scorching sex they had.

She had started missing it now; Dhruv was studying too hard and their stolen sessions in empty classrooms, the corners of the library and the far end of the football field had come down to a trickle.

Two weeks before the exams had started Ritika dragged Dhruv to the cavernous hall in the basement of the electrical department which doubled up as the table tennis room to a host of shirtless boys in boxers playing matches for money. But that day it was empty, and their voices echoed and it was a bit sexy and thrilling and wrong. Sitting on a bench in the far corner of the hall where it was the darkest, her arms wrapped around Dhruv, she felt shamelessly aroused.

But no sooner had she started to nuzzle against his shirt and into his rock hard pectoral muscles, trying to be adorable, than a screeching sound pierced through the silence and a yellow neon light flickered to life at a distance. She crinkled her eyes, and saw Aranya drag and push one-half of a table tennis table against the wall. Aranya stretched—she could touch her toes, Ritika would have never guessed that—eyed the wall as an opponent, threw the ball up and swirled her TT bat like she owned it. The ball spun and hit the wall and she smashed it on its return and smashed the return too. Aranya moved nimbly on her toes and soon the hall echoed like someone was firing an AK-47. She didn't miss many shots, and on the rare occasion that she did, she cursed.

Ritika frowned when she saw Dhruv looking at Aranya shuffle like a pro, returning smashes to her own smashes, beating her own shots.

'Let's go,' said Ritika.

'But didn't you want to be here?' asked Dhruv, his eyes still on Aranya, who had broken into a sweat and whose deft feet reminded Ritika of a video she had seen of Muhammad Ali.

'Not any more. I didn't know the fatso would be here. Do you see what she's wearing? Bleh. She should keep those legs hidden.'

Dhruv had nothing to add. A pissed Ritika got up to leave. 'Are you coming or should I leave?'

Dhruv stood up and they walked across the hall; Aranya didn't notice them leave, her Zen-like concentration unbroken. Outside, Dhruv and Ritika walked in silence.

'What do you think of Aranya?' asked Ritika.

'I don't think of her.'

'You don't? She's the most popular girl in college right now. Everyone loves her.'

'I don't care.'

'She's holding classes for everyone, fights for extension of deadlines with professors and is the vice president of the debating team. She might make it to the Students' Council as a first-year representative. Everyone's talking about her and you want me to believe you don't think of her. The entire college knows you loved her back in school.'

'She made it up. She was just a friend. My parents were going through a divorce and she was around. That's that.'

'But didn't she get you kicked out of school?'

'Can we stop talking about it, please?'

'I'm just saying. Didn't Sanchit tell you? Guys from his batch have sent her letters and messages on Facebook and what not, proclaiming their love.'

'I'm sure it's Sanchit sending out all those messages,' snapped Dhruv. 'She's just a nerd with a strange face.'

Ritika rolled her eyes. 'Not really a nerd, is she? She's making it to the TT team at least.'

'It's table tennis. No one gives a shit about TT.' The way Dhruv said it, it felt like he did give a shit. 'And will you stop obsessing over her? She's nobody.'

'Really?'

'Yes, really,' growled Dhruv.

They didn't make out that day. Dhruv said he had to study and left Ritika thinking about Aranya, which she did with abandon in her free time. Since that day Ritika noticed the accidental but carefully orchestrated glances Dhruv threw at Aranya, who was being a curious mix of Mother Teresa and Cruella de Vil, strict and kind; friendly and professional. She had noticed the hatred in Dhruv's voice whenever they talked about Aranya, which they had started doing a lot these days, and it bothered her. Dhruv would keep talking about how fucking populist Aranya was, a total attention whore, an average-looking girl seeking validation by being extra sweet, extra hard-working, needlessly intelligent. His words were harsher when he put Raghuvir and Aranya in a sentence, and he would find reasons to bunk Raghuvir's classes.

'You're overthinking,' Dhruv would say when she mentioned his obsession and wrap his arms around Ritika.

But that didn't stop Dhruv from staring at her like she was a specimen, an alien, disgusting maybe, but also intriguing. She hated Aranya with a vengeance, and so did Dhruv, but the nature of their hatred was quite different.

36

The tables had turned since the Temple Run incident.

Aranya walked the corridors of DTU like she was the reigning queen, and the rest lowly courtiers. Dhruv could have learned to live with that. But he always felt everything Aranya did was to spite him, to tell him that she would always be the puppeteer, manipulating his life. Sometimes he felt like she laughed at how stupid he was to be in love and continue to be in love with her.

The little smirks she threw in Dhruv's direction were far too many to be coincidental. If only she was a boy, he would have him called out, lodged a right hook into his ribcage and then smashed his face with a quick elbow move.

But now Dhruv was prepared.

The countless nights spent with Sanchit were about to pay off when he would crush the mid-semester examinations and he would show Aranya that her presence meant shit to him. That he would happily crush her over and over again.

He was sitting on the last desk, smiling in Aranya's direction who, with her back towards him, was revising. Ritika shot him a look but he ignored it. Lately, she had started throwing a fit at the littlest of pretexts. Dhruv would try to explain to her what was really going on but Ritika wouldn't get it. He wasn't sure if even he got it.

The bell rang and the exam started. It was going to be a cakewalk. He marked out all the questions that were easy pickings and solved them within the first two hours of the exam. Then he sat back and sighed, flipping proudly through his answer sheet. He had managed a constant neat handwriting throughout the answer sheet.

'Sir! Extra sheet!' shouted Aranya.

Dhruv was still to use the last three pages of his answer booklet. He frowned.

'Me, too!' shouted Dhruv. Ritika who had finished whatever she knew within the first hour and now was dozing off looked in his direction, shocked. This happened three more times. Dhruv's answer booklet was glaringly empty now.

But Dhruv didn't know what to do with the answer sheet. The two questions he hadn't answered till now were from chapters he had chosen to leave out. He fished his cellphone out from his pocket and fired it up, taking care no one noticed. Over texts, Sanchit and he decided to meet in the boys' washroom.

Just before he could ask permission to go, Aranya asked if she could go and Dhruv slunk back into his seat. He waited fifteen minutes for the invigilator to busy himself and forget about the missing girl and then asked if he could go.

'Sure.'

Dhruv ran to the washroom to find Sanchit smoking, with none of the books he had asked him to bring.

'Dude! Where are the fucking books?'

'I am Miagi and you're my Karate Kid. You can't cheat! That's insulting my genius.'

'I will tell you what will insult your genius,' Dhruv grabbed his throat and pushed him till Sanchit's head hung over the ledge.

'I was just kidding,' said Sanchit. 'The books are in my pants. You think any guard would have allowed me inside with books in hand.'

'. . .'

Sanchit rolled his eyes. 'Such an amateur!' He plunged his hands into his underwear and grabbed around. Dhruv grimaced. He brought out a little booklet of the book photocopied at a size one-fourth of the original. He tossed it in Dhruv's direction who handled it like pissed-on banknotes.

'Chill. I wore two pairs of underwear.'

'I would have shat on your bed if you hadn't.'

'In fact I wore none,' said Sanchit, flashed his ass and ran.

Dhruv shook his head, hardly amused. He would get back at him later. For now Dhruv had to look for a safe, empty washroom. In the distance he saw Aranya looking over her shoulder before skulking inside a women's washroom. Dhruv followed.

A smile broke out on his face. Wouldn't he just love it to be busted together for cheating? Who cared if he did well or not? No one would give a shit if his paper got cancelled because he was found in a washroom with a bunch of notes down his boxers. In fact it would have been expected.

But what would happen if they found both Dhruv and Aranya in the washroom, cheating the system, a degenerate and a nice girl?

History repeats itself?

People love to revel in other people's misery and they would have loved to see Aranya go down.

It would destroy her if the image she had painstakingly created of being holier than thou exploded in a single moment of weakness. What would the professors say? Would they still want her in their projects? This was great! And what if he was the reason for all her misery? AWESOME. He would have his revenge.

He tried opening the door to the washroom but it was locked. He kicked in the door and found the faces of two terror-stricken girls looking at him.

'What are you doing here?' growled Aranya.

'I'm expected to be here. What are you doing here?'

'. . .'

'I think I should start drawing attention. Wouldn't it be heartbreaking for Raghuvir to see his pet student cheating?

'PLEASE DON'T DO THAT!' cried out the girl who was standing next to Aranya. The girl's face looked like she was constipated. Her body was convulsing and tears had started to flow abundantly which made Dhruv roll his eyes.

'And why shouldn't I?'

Aranya put her hand around the girl. 'Dhruv, stop fucking around with people. You're better than that, I hope.'

'I'm kind of not. And I'm deeply inclined to take down both of you with me right now.'

'You will not do that,' said Aranya with an authority that belied her position. 'This is between you and me.'

'I don't care. And I'm pretty sure I will.'

'Please DON'T!' the girl howled. 'I will fail the exam. Please don't.' And the girl rushed to Dhruv and stood a hair's breadth away from his face.

'Dhruv, the girl just recovered from jaundice. Give her a break! She deserves to pass!' yelled Aranya.

Dhruv felt like an asshole and suddenly couldn't bear to look at the girl. 'Fine. Fuck off,' said Dhruv.

'THANK YOU!' howled the girl, still crying. She was about to leave when Aranya called her back and gave her two answer sheets filled with numbers. 'Here,' whispered Aranya in her ear. 'I have solved the questions. Just append them to your sheets.' The girl nodded. 'It will be okay.' The girl literally ran past Dhruv and out of the washroom. Dhruv, from the corner of his eye, saw the papers in the girl's hand, the same supplementary sheets Aranya had asked for in the classroom.

Aranya jumped on to the ledge of the washbasin. 'So? Now you're going to call the security?'

'Wouldn't I just love to see you repeat the first year?' said Dhruv.

'I'm still the hero here, Dhruv. I was merely helping a girl out who couldn't study because she had jaundice. The girl will make sure the entire college knows that. You will still be the villain in all of this. What happened last time won't happen again. I will always be wanted here. And you will still look like you have always looked—a pathetic, spineless boy lost in love. You destroyed my life once but not again. You have already given me more pain than I hoped to endure in one lifetime. You made me feel hated for all my growing-up years but it stops now. You can't do anything worse to me now, Dhruv. So fuck off.'

Dhruv laughed. 'Let me try at least?'

'It's all for a cause, Dhruv,' said Aranya. 'I don't mind going down for it.'

'Of course you do, Aranya. The first blot on your perfect curriculum vitae. I wonder how your father would react!'

'Can you spell vitae?' Aranya chuckled.

And just for that brief moment, Dhruv thought he saw a stray tear in Aranya's eyes, who was being totally nonchalant about repeating a year and was being a total badass about it. Maybe it was the thing about her father . . .

'I'm still waiting for you to call the guards. Or are you scared?' said Aranya, her voice quivering a little. Dhruv didn't say anything, his eyes stuck on Aranya trying to gauge if she was just putting on a brave front, winning a psychological battle against him.

And just then, Dhruv heard footsteps approaching the washroom door. Multiple footsteps. The guards were talking to each other, wondering if they had heard students talking. Dhruv looked at Aranya whose face had drained of colour, her jaw was wide open, scared. She had frozen in her place.

'Fuck,' muttered Dhruv and strode in her direction. He pulled her off the ledge, picked her up and literally threw her in the bathroom stall. 'Stay. Don't fucking make a noise. And put your damn legs up.'

Aranya was in tears now, her brave front now in tatters in front of Dhruv. 'STOP FUCKING CRYING,' growled Dhruv and she did. Dhruv closed the door and jumped on the ledge. He started muttering the equations on the notes loudly as if he was mugging them up. The door flew open and two guards marched in.

'*OYE! Kya kar raha hai?*' shouted the guards. '*Saala. Cheating kar raha hai! Pakad saale ko.*' They grabbed hold of Dhruv and seized the notes.

'Sir, please, Sir, I will fail the exam, Sir,' pleaded Dhruv. He fell on the guard's feet who refused to listen.

'Check the other stalls,' one guard said to another.

'Sir, please, Sir. Sir, please,' said Dhruv and grabbed the guard. 'I had jaundice, Sir. I couldn't study. Sir, sorry, Sir. Sir, please.' The guard who was about to kick the bathroom stalls open stopped and told Dhruv that he should prepare for repeating a year. Dhruv broke down in fake tears. Dhruv's histrionics distracted the guard and he didn't bother to check the washroom stalls.

'*Lekar chal ise.*'

37

Dhruv was suspended from the examinations and he was to repeat the first semester.

Despite this Aranya saw Dhruv take all the examinations, often matching her supplementary sheet to supplementary sheet, and looked past her like she was made of plexiglas. She wasn't sure if she had to be apologetic or grateful so she chose to stay confused. In her head she tried to justify why Dhruv would take the blame on himself but always came up with naught.

Aranya had a hard time concentrating on the examinations; Dhruv had already won the examination, the Olympics and the Nobel Prize with his little gesture.

The exams ended without incident and Aranya calculated her expected score in each of the subjects. The cumulative total would beat the previous highest held by Sanchit when he was in his first year. She kept her fingers crossed.

'Thank you, Aranya,' the girl she had helped out said.

'Are you better now?'

'Yes, much better. I can't tell you how grateful I am.'

'Anyone would have done the same.'

'My friends and I are going to a club near the college tonight. It would be great if you can come. We have already talked to the warden. She's okay if we come back by two.'

'I'm sorry, I can't,' said Aranya, reflexively. Years of turning down plans that hampered intellectual progress had altered her DNA. She didn't even have to think before tanking plans. 'But thanks for asking.'

'Do let me know if you change your mind.' The girl hugged her and she left smiling.

While other students would celebrate the culmination of mid-semester examinations which counted for a measly 20 per cent of the final score, she would start out on the roadmap to tackle the remaining 80 per cent. She had already made a glossary of topics with decreasing order of importance and she had to strike off two of them from the list by the next morning. There was no time to waste.

The first hour passes by in a jiffy and adrenaline courses through her veins as she thinks of her thumping victory two months from now. But somehow, from some damned place inside her vast brain, a flash of Dhruv saving her from losing everything hits her. That tiny sliver of a microsecond where he had picked her in his arms with an urgency of a paramedic, that look in his eyes and the strength of his last utterly romantic words 'Stop fucking crying' resonated through her entire body and she slumped on the desk. All her wins, the little trophies, the medals, the certificates, everything that she would win from that moment on would now be stained with the memory of him saving her in that weak moment. Her crying and his concerned face flashed in front of her eyes, and she wanted to metaphorically slit her wrists. 'Why the fuck did it have to happen that day!' Because no matter how big a jerk Dhruv was, he did save her when she thought all was going to end. She would owe all of her wins to him.

She walked to the library, lugging all the books she needed, and settled at the far corner of the empty library. She hadn't realized but the mid-semester examinations and the extra classes had taken a toll on her. She had drifted off; head resting on a book she had drooled all over. She woke up with a start and felt someone's eyes on her. On the table, Raghuvir was sitting smoking a cigarette, reading a book.

Aranya wiped the drool off her face with the T-shirt sleeve. 'Ummm?' said Aranya to catch his attention.

'Oh, hi,' said Raghuvir and closed the book.

'That was very Edward Cullen of you.'

Raghuvir made himself comfortable on the chair next to Aranya's. Aranya smiled weakly. Raghuvir, the hot, brainy professor she dreamt of nine nights out of ten, was right in front of her. 'There's something I need to tell you. I have waited for really long to tell you this,' said Raghuvir.

Shit. His voice quivered just a little bit. He chose the right place to pause. It reminded Aranya of the 10 Best Wedding Proposal videos on YouTube. 'You know I have been noticing you since the day you first walked into my class. You have been better than the rest, impeccable and just perfect. You have stood out. No wonder after today, I

will be the envy of everyone around me.' Raghuvir's eyes
bore through Aranya, reducing her to a molten mess inside.

Aranya's dream was coming true. Her face flushed and her
body felt prickly and numb at the same time. Raghuvir continued
with a smile to die for on his face. 'I know we will make a great
team and I can trust you. I need to ask you something.' He
paused. This was big. This was going to change everything. Her
heart pounded like it would pop out of her mouth, or ear or
whatever.

'Will you be my research assistant, Aranya?' asked
Raghuvir and handed her a file of her latest research project
to go through.

Aranya could die happily now. This was the happiest
moment of her entire life! She, quite frankly, wanted to
cry and lunge at Raghuvir. She was just asked what every
girl dreams for. A research project for Professor Raghuvir!
Someone should have captured the video of this happening,
uploaded it and made it go viral.

'Yes,' said a trembling Aranya, wanting to burst out in a
puddle of tears like a beauty queen.

'Cool. We start work tomorrow,' said Raghuvir, shook
her hand, and left the room like he hadn't changed her
life forever.

Aranya sat there dazed for the first few minutes, and then
jumped around and pumped her fists and did a little jig to
celebrate it. She called her father to tell him about it.

'So?'

'He's a big professor, Dad. His recommendation means a
lot. I can apply to MIT after my graduation.'

'And scholarship? Where will we get the money from?
And how's college? I hope you're staying away from boys.
Don't embarrass us again,' grumbled her father, like it was

only yesterday they were called to school. He had never let Aranya forget it. And reminders often came in the form of slaps and punches thrown at her.

Her father just knew how to be a killjoy. She regretted calling him.

'I can try for a full scholarship, Dad,' said Aranya.

'Try? There's no trying. You have to get it, Aranya. You know how hard we have worked to get you where you are now. Your cousin, Madhuri? She's getting married in June next year. The boy's an engineer in Microsoft.'

'Okay.'

'Don't disappoint us further,' said her father as if it was her fault.

'I won't.'

'And don't make us come to your college again and make us feel like we made a mistake by trusting in you again.'

She cut the phone not wanting to hear anything further. Fuck it. What was she hoping for? A change of heart? Her family embracing her success?

She called up the Jaundice Girl and told her she would love to join them wherever they are going. And in a rare moment of courage she texted Raghuvir to ask if he wanted to join in as well. *Go on, I will come if I get free on time*, said the reply.

She took a long, hot shower, did her hair the best she could, and put on her little black dress, the only one she had. She twirled in it in front of the mirror.

Two hours later, thirty-three girls were packed in Liquid, a dump of a place, but what it lacked in ambience it covered up in the low prices. Didn't help Aranya though because she didn't drink and soon she was bored, sitting on a couch that stank, alone. Everyone else was drunk. This was such a mistake. How could she think loud music, drunken girls and boys falling over each other, shouting dumb jokes into each other's ears could mean a celebration for her? Raghuvir had texted her that he would come, but a little late, and that was the only consolation.

She started to read newspapers on her phone. From the corner of her eye she could see Ritika and Dhruv having a good time on the dance floor.

She couldn't help but wonder what would have happened had it not been for Dhruv. She would have had to call her parents again. They would have slapped her, berated her, called her names, and hated her existence.

Dhruv who had put her through it the first time had now repaid the debt.

It troubled her. She owed it to Dhruv and it was eating her up inside, infinitesimally, making her feel hollow.

And that bastard was dancing without a care in the world.

38

Dhruv couldn't wait for the night to be over. Ritika was too drunk and there were moments when he wanted to smack her face, leave her and the club. There she was flailing her arms around, trying to kiss Dhruv all time, and being a fucking nuisance.

'She's going to puke, man,' said Sanchit.

Dhruv helped Ritika to the washroom. The girls judged Ritika, and Dhruv swore at them. 'Should I stare at your stubble?' snapped Dhruv at one of them. The girls looked away.

The line outside the men's was shorter.

'SHE'S GOING TO PUKE,' shouted Dhruv and the boys parted and made way for Ritika and Dhruv.

'I'm not going to puke.' Ritika smiled at the boys who were sniggering.

'Shut the fuck up,' said Dhruv and took her inside the boys' washroom where he threatened everyone to leave within the next thirty seconds or he would smash their heads on the mirrors. The three boys who were fixing their hair slunked out.

'I'm fin—'

And Ritika puked all over the floor, falling to her knees. Half-digested food, bile and alcohol spilled out on to the floor and a murderous stink rose from it.

Dhruv held her hair while she retched and emptied her bowels on the floor. Doctors should have been on standby to collect a spare kidney lying on the floor. 'This is the last fucking time you're drinking.'

She kept on retching and muttering apologies in broken words and grunts, feigning innocence and blaming the strong, cheap vodka.

Dhruv called Sanchit to ask him to get lemonade but the call went unanswered. Meanwhile Ritika had nothing left to vomit but hot air. She was smiling like a guilty puppy that had soiled the carpet. 'I feel much better.' Dhruv wanted to smack her square on her face.

'Are you sure?' asked Dhruv. She nodded. Dhruv picked her up and made her sit on the slab around the washbasins where she crawled to the tap and washed her face. He took the mop and cleared the muck as much as he could. Little sacrifices you have to make when you date someone who fucking doesn't know when to stop drinking. Dhruv was trying not to explode, but Ritika, having flushed the alcohol out of her system, was sprightly and ready for another round.

He helped her down and they left the washroom. The boys waiting outside cursed them and crinkled their noses when the ungodly smell of Ritika's insides wafted in the air. Dhruv made her sit down and suck on a slice of lemon. He looked around for Sanchit and found him sitting with Aranya in one corner, laughing, God knows discussing what. He saw Sanchit put on his best smile and nudge Aranya into drinking, which she reluctantly did and they both laughed and drank.

Sanchit had never hidden his admiration for Aranya, calling her hot, intelligent, Geek Queen, whenever he got the chance. It made Dhruv squirm. He told himself it was because he was possessive about Sanchit and didn't want him to cross enemy lines.

For the next half-hour, he kept a count of how many drinks Aranya had. Their laughter kept on getting louder, their high-fives more intense, the jokes more intimate. Dhruv imagined walking up to them and socking Sanchit's face. He kept sending Sanchit texts asking him where he was but Sanchit, who seemed mesmerized by his company, didn't check his phone.

Dhruv got his chance when Sanchit excused himself and walked towards the men's.

'Will you be okay?' asked Dhruv. Ritika mumbled.

Dhruv followed Sanchit into the washroom, bent over to check the stall and spotted Sanchit's jeans crumpled against his army slippers. Dhruv entered the washroom stall next to his and banged on the common wall.

'It's me, you bastard,' said Dhruv. 'What the fuck do you think you're doing with her?'

Sanchit grunted. 'We are just talking. I think I'm in love with her.'

Dhruv banged on the door.

'What's wrong with you!' exclaimed Sanchit. 'I'm trying to concentrate on potty here.'

'You fucking can't be in love with her.'

'It's not really in my hands, dude. What is in my hands is this faucet, though, and if you bang on the wall again I'm going to rain water on you.'

'She's the enemy, Sanchit.'

'She knows the Schrodinger equation by heart.'

Dhruv banged the door again. Sanchit aimed the faucet at Dhruv who returned it with a toilet paper roll.

'Stop that, you juvenile asshole. And once you get out of this washroom, you have a choice to make. Either you talk to her or you talk to me.'

'Stop being a melodramatic bitch, Dhruv. I got to go to her. Not because I'm in love with her, which I am, truly and deeply, but because she's drunk now. I can't leave her alone. Also, we are discussing horror movies, Mithun Chakroborty's *Gunda* and Indian politics, man.'

'Why the hell would you get her drunk?' grumbled Dhruv.

'What the fuck is your problem?'

'I just don't want you around her, okay,' warned Dhruv and stormed out of his stall.

Ritika was sleeping, stretched out on the couch. Dhruv ordered a drink to take the edge off. He watched Aranya sway to the music in the distance, clearly drunk, a happy smile on her face and shouting out an occasional 'Woohoooo' like any other normal girl would. He couldn't take his eyes off her. Sanchit walked towards the bar to get another drink.

This was Dhruv's chance to talk to Aranya. About what, he didn't know.

But before he could start walking in Aranya's direction, Raghuvir walked in, dressed up in a nice shirt for a change. Dhruv felt a gut-clenching ache. Aranya almost threw herself on Raghuvir and they started to talk animatedly. 'He is a fucking professor for God's sake!' muttered Dhruv angrily. She should have shown some respect, not shoved her breasts on to him.

'What are you looking it?' asked Sanchit, now sitting next to Dhruv.

'I don't even know who you are,' said Dhruv.

'We have shared holy faucet water. We are brothers.'

'We aren't even friends,' snapped Dhruv. 'Go, fucking laugh with her. Why are you fucking sitting here?'

'You have a very limited vocabulary, both of you. She kept saying fucking, fucking, fucking. She's damn hot, dude,' Sanchit said, his tone not sleazy but serious. 'Look at her. Shit.'

Aranya snapped her fingers and ordered another drink but Raghuvir, the protective bastard, waved the waiter off. A few students looked at Raghuvir and Aranya and whispered to each other.

Dhruv saw Raghuvir call for the cheque and a little later, they left the club.

'I will be back. Take care of Ritika,' said Dhruv and left before Sanchit could form a coherent sentence.

Outside, he saw Raghuvir bundle Aranya into the front seat of his car, a well-maintained Honda Prius. He wanted to slam the car's door on Raghuvir's hand, drive the car away, dragging his body hanging from the door. He had heard of Raghuvir being quite the womanizer. A man in his position always had women fawning over him and he couldn't be blamed if he slipped once or twice. Moreover, no one had heard any of the women he slept with complain about him. Most of them didn't even admit to having had an affair with him. It was all quite strange. Dhruv was convinced that Raghuvir was a good manipulator no matter how many people talked about him being the nicest fucking person on earth. He found Raghuvir's niceness rather creepy.

He had heard stories of his torrid fling with Smriti, the PhD student (who by the way had a boyfriend waiting for her back in her home town—Kanpur), amongst many others. He tried not to draw parallels between the charming principal of his school who wrecked his life and Raghuvir who had just driven off with a drunken Aranya in his car.

He waited for them to leave, then kick-started his motorcycle and followed them.

For a good part of the drive, Aranya had her face stuck out like a dog, laughing and shouting and making fun of people they'd left behind. The car missed the final turn to the college and swerved left and finally stopped in an empty parking lot. Dhruv turned off the headlights and killed the engine.

Raghuvir helped Aranya out of the car and they sat on the bonnet. Dhruv couldn't quite make out what they were talking about, the sound of chirping crickets was louder than the degenerates out in the open. Sanchit kept calling him and he kept disconnecting the calls.

Irritated at not being able to listen to their conversation, Dhruv lobbed a stone in their direction and it crashed against the boot of the car. They ignored it. The next one cracked the rear windshield, making an intricate web. Raghuvir inspected the damage, shouted '*Kaun hai*' into the dark, his voice deeper and angrier than Dhruv had expected, and then instructed Aranya to get into the car. They were going back to college.

Satisfied, Dhruv hopped on to his bike and drove off. He stopped at the police picket and pointed at the car Raghuvir and Aranya were in and said, '*Bhai sahab. Gaadi andhere mein parked thi.* (Sir, the car was parked in darkness). God knows what the couple was doing.' And he drove off. In the rear-view mirror he saw the police guy stop Raghuvir's car and ask for his licence.

Dhruv rode back to the college, and almost forgot about Ritika back in the club. He called Sanchit to check on her, who told him that he had dropped her to the hostel, and Dhruv wondered how little, if at all, he loved Ritika. Later that night, he bought the Security Room guards with a bottle of Red Label and they handed over the security tapes of that night to him. Dhruv had never been of much use with computers but he spent that night carefully editing a video of Raghuvir and a visibly drunk Aranya entering the college, and Raghuvir helping her to the girls' hostel.

It wasn't incriminating. But people have fertile imaginations.

39

Ritika woke up with a bitch of a headache. This was the closest she had felt to death. She spent the morning vomiting, grunting and moaning, dehydrated like a century–old mummy.

She was rolling on the floor, the cold mosaic calming her down when the Jaundice Girl walked in. She made Aranya sit on the bed, marshalled her girl troops, none of whom seemed hung over, and they nursed her back to normalcy.

'Are you coming for the class?' asked the Jaundice Girl.

'I will decide,' said Aranya. Lazily, she looked over the timetable. It was Raghuvir's class. She dragged herself out of the bed and washed her face. She owed Raghuvir an apology for last night. She had been a pain in the ass, she remembered, begging him not to drop her to college, to go on a long drive. She faintly remembered Raghuvir talking to a policeman, playing his professor card and wriggling out of the situation.

She was fifteen minutes late for the class and Raghuvir still wasn't there. The moment she walked in and took her seat, she sensed the class shift in their places, their voices lowering to a murmur. She could feel the stare of her classmates, and heard stray sentences with her name and Raghuvir's. And that's when she knew what it was all about. She remembered those moments faintly when she had walked through the college gate with Raghuvir the night before, leaning on him because her steps were unsteady and she was seeing things in triplicate. She had thought the college was deserted and was sure no one saw them. But she also knew it took only one person to concoct a rumour and make is spread like wildfire.

'Did you see this?' the Jaundice Girl came up and fired up a video on her cellphone. It was Aranya and Raghuvir stumbling through the corridors.

'People are saying you seduced him to get a spot in his research team.'

'Are they blind? Raghuvir would get seduced by me? Fucking retards.'

Despite knowing the truth, her eyes welled up. Everything intensified in her head. Despite her talent, the years of hard work, she would never be able to live this down.

Her options were clear—to wait for things to settle down or clear it out. The first was a defensive move and Aranya didn't play defensive. She reminded herself of the twenty-three trophies she had won in debates in the last decade, shredding her opposition to pieces, making them crawl on to her side, and she felt the anger rise and gust through her veins. She saw Dhruv sitting on the last bench, feet propped up, without a care in the world.

The tears were gone. Aranya's split personality took over. Like a manic werewolf she tore through her sobs and bared her canines. She walked to the teacher's table and wrote in bold letters on the blackboard and underlined it—PROF. RAGHUVIR IS HOT.

She sat on the teacher's table. She often leaned over the podium to show how relaxed she was. She had ten simple rules. She pointed at what was written on the board.

Debating Rule No. 1: Start with a fact and hook your audience with a question.

'Let's not pretend otherwise, right? He's hot. And let's start the conversation with a fact. Nothing happened between Raghuvir and me, and I regret it. Let me tell you why.'

She had the attention of the class now.

Debating Rule No. 2: Flood the opposition with facts that may or may not matter. Make them feel underprepared and like a congress of baboons.

'At thirteen years of age, Rahguvir made a high-powered telescope and found three asteroids, all named after him. At fourteen, he completed his Bachelor's of Engineering from MIT and filed eighteen patents and sold thirteen of them. At seventeen, he completed his Master's of Engineering in nuclear physics from MIT and filed thirty-three patents. At nineteen, he was part of the team in France that successfully executed the first controlled fusion reaction.'

Debating Rule No. 3: Act like a judge, not a participant. Make the audience feel like dirt.

'At nineteen, you're still sleeping on month-old bed sheets and masturbating to Sunny Leone and asking your parents to pay for your cigarettes. You dress like you're homeless and you dare to talk about a girl who has beaten you in mid-semesters by a mile. You are students who shake in fear when he walks inside the class knowing that he was better than you can ever be when he was younger than you. And look at you!'

Debating Rule No. 4: Your body language should be such as to show that you have already won.

She laughed for dramatic effect and whipped open the class register.

Debating Rule No. 5: Attack the opposition. One on one. RIP. THEM. APART.

'Amit Singhal. I know you were talking about me back there. Yes, you. The guy who I just heard saying, "Obviously, they slept together. How else would she make it to the research team." There you are in your oiled hair, rubber chappals and the fake Diesel shirt. Look at you. So virginal. What are you sniggering about, Sameer Garg? It's not that you have ever talked to a girl. You know how easy it is for me to check what you searched for in your browser? You look flushed? What did you search for?'

Debating Rule No. 6: Threaten. Scare. Create fake panic.

'I don't think you took me seriously. Let me just tell you the IP addresses of your laptops. Let's check your mails. The desperate mails you would have sent to your ex-boyfriends, ex-girlfriends? No?' She fished her cellphone out. She played Temple Run on it.

Debating Rule No. 7: Douse the panic.

'Maybe I shouldn't be that cruel now, should I? Why share your misery with the rest of the class? So let's come back to the topic of you gossiping about Raghuvir and me. I feel blessed that you, who are as intelligent as a pack of chimps for Raghuvir, have decided to gossip about Raghuvir and me.'

Debating Rule No. 8: Address everyone. Divide the crowd. See them turn on each other.

'And don't kid yourselves, girls. You know you would rather be linked to Raghuvir than to any of these boys here. I don't mind if you keep talking about Raghuvir and me because I know, I understand, it comes from the deep-rooted feeling of wanting to be where I am today. We have all been jealous of the girl who has it all, haven't we? I have been in your place. And who wouldn't want to be linked with Raghuvir after all? I understand your envy. Last night, I saw many of you dancing with boys who don't deserve you and you knew that, but you rationalized in your head that it's the best you can get in our college. I don't feel bad when you talk about me and him. I understand.'

Debating Rule No. 9: The final blow. Leave them thinking that they were wrong from the word go.

Her voice was now soft. She made it sound like she was almost mourning for the class, like someone had died. 'I would like to thank you all for linking me to him. It's good for my self-esteem. I really needed that. In fact, I want you to keep talking about it. But I hope every time you boys talk about Raghuvir, it would NOT remind you of your own failures and inadequacies. And when the girls of my esteemed class talk about me, I request you to please NOT think of the last boy who had shown a smattering of interest in you and feel any less beautiful or accomplished than I am. I know it's painful to see someone have it all in life while you're stuck in a less-than-equal relationship. Everyone lied. God didn't make us equals.'

Debating Rule No. 10: Whatever be the result, celebrate your victory.

'Class of 2014, I wish the best of luck to you.' She beamed, bowed in front of the class, sure that it would be the last she heard of the gossip, and walked out.

40

Raghuvir put on a white shirt, tucked it into his freshly pressed beige chinos and prepared himself for a meeting he knew would end in an ugly way. Still, he didn't want to feel that he didn't put his best foot forward. Raghuvir knew what soiled reputations could do to someone's career. He had been way too careless in the past to not know that. An irresponsible philanderer, that's what people thought about him now, and for good reason. He had been doing things he shouldn't have for the last few years. Sleeping around with PhD students wasn't warranted, it was even illegal, but he had made sure none of the students opened their mouths. He was charming enough to keep them from saying anything.

But he had rotted long enough. It was time for him to change. He had found himself changing the day he saw Aranya. It subtly reminded him of a younger him, lonely, yes, but also ambitious. He was drawn to her. He felt something for the girl. You could call her his muse even. Even while he slept with Smriti (and others), he caught himself thinking about the girl and her unwavering drive. It rekindled something inside him, and that's why he wanted her to be his mentee. To kick-start a few projects he had been planning.

He wanted to get into the middle of things again.

While he waited outside for the meeting to start, knowing fully that he would have to leave the college, he knew he didn't want the girl to suffer. He wanted to make sure the girl went through nothing because of the video that surfaced that day.

Mitra made him wait for half an hour outside his office before he was called in. Childish, but nothing he hadn't expected from Mitra. Mitra sat behind his dark mahogany desk, the one he had bought recently and through suspicious means. He had also bought a new car. It was safe to say that the centrifugal machine he had just bought for the college wasn't as expensive as he made it out to be.

Raghuvir took his seat and waited for Mitra to broach the topic which he did almost immediately, mincing no words.

'The choice in front of the administration is quite simple, Raghuvir. Either you have to go or she will have to. If the transgression of the decorum of the college is from both sides, it will look bad on the college and we can't afford that.'

'With all due respect to you, let me get this clear. If I tell you I'm the person at fault, you will make me put in my papers and leave. And if the girl's at fault, she will have to leave the college.'

'Precisely.'

'It's clear in your proposition that you want me to leave the college, don't you? What I fail to understand is, why are you taking the step that you are?' asked Raghuvir, his eyes narrowing. Leaving Aranya behind, unguarded, was terrifying but necessary. So was letting Mitra know that others aren't fools.

'People talk.'

'That's very reassuring coming from the dean of an esteemed institution. People talk? That's your argument?' grumbled Raghuvir, barely managing not to get swept away by anger.

'Don't teach me my job, Mr Raghuvir. I have been running this college since you were a child,' said Mitra like every old person when they run out of defences.

'Then pray tell me, if that student were a boy would you have taken the same step?' asked Raghuvir.

The dean looked uneasy. He looked at his watch, at his cup of tea, his tongue floundered. 'You don't get to ask questions.'

'What do I get to do then?'

'All you need to do is to choose between you and her. I have other matters to attend to, Mr Raghuvir.'

Raghuvir leaned back in his chair and brought forth the crumpled resignation letter he had typed out that morning. Mitra read it with suspicion and kept it under the paperweight when satisfied.

'Your accounts will be cleared within a month.'

'That won't be necessary. But I do expect you to be nice to the girl.' he said before leaving.

Back in his room, Raghuvir dumped his sparse belongings into a big leather suitcase. He felt hollow. He had never liked being here in DTU; it was always supposed to be a stop-gap arrangement, something that would serve its purpose, some place he could move on from without attaching any nostalgia to it. But now that he was leaving . . . A few more days couldn't have hurt.

He would miss Aranya and the joy of having found someone he could relate to. All that radio talk about opposites being perfect for each other is nonsense. You always find someone who's exactly similar to you. With whom you can stick so close that only a vacuum can exist between the two of you.

He zipped the suitcase shut. He would miss Aranya. What was it in her? He certainly wasn't in love with her. And what was love anyway? He had been with way too many women to know it didn't exist. Maybe love was nothing more than finding someone who loved the exact things that you did. Love was *not* about loving everything about the other person, or being intimate, or being loyal, or being happy with sleeping with one person for the rest of your life; love was about finding yourself again. So he loved Aranya in that sense even though he really didn't! Love was not really a fairy tale. It was a practical relationship from which both the partners gained something. And he knew that though Aranya fawned over him, she was into Dhruv. Only a fool wouldn't understand that those two were supposed to end up together. So for now, there was no place for Raghuvir in the equation. Dhruv and Aranya were young and foolish and they didn't know the world like Raghuvir did. He had been like them once and had got burned. They would too.

A part of him hoped Aranya would bump into him and he would explain to her what love really was and maybe they would have a chance then. If not, he had the best in his heart for her.

Having resigned, he spent the next day locked up naked in the room with Smriti and left the college without a word.

41

Dhruv rejoiced at Raghuvir's disappearance from the campus.

No longer would he have to imagine Raghuvir and Aranya in the mechanics of a solids laboratory, working on lowering the friction coefficient long after stipulated college hours.

That day, every word of Aranya's speech in class had stoked his fear of having fallen in love with her. He had wanted to throw something at her to make her stop harking about Raghuvir but the ferocity and control of Aranya's words stunned him. Good riddance, Dhruv had thought.

Although he had noticed the funereal expression on Aranya's face, he was sure she would get over Raghuvir. It wasn't as if she was in love with him or anything. A few more weeks passed and Aranya was still behaving like someone had died. She would constantly be distracted in class, doodling away in her notebook, lost in her daydreams, hardly caring about who submitted the assignment and which professor threw her out of the class.

Sometimes, Dhruv would spot her hanging outside Raghuvir's cabin. She would do her assignments sitting outside his door, papers strewn around her, books stacked in a corner as if Raghuvir was just late for a scheduled meeting. Often he would find her with her eyes shut, as if praying for his return. More than a few times, he had seen her text him on his now-defunct number.

Irritated at the cuckoo behaviour and the insane devotion, Dhruv confronted Aranya one day while she sat outside Raghuvir's room.

'What are you doing here?' asked Dhruv.

'Assignments. And if you don't mind I am in no mood to have a conversation right now.'

'I just wanted to point out that in the last three assignments I managed a better grade than you.' Dhruv laughed and winked, hoping to anger Aranya.

Aranya scribbled away in her notebook, not once looking at Dhruv.

'I beat you. Are you not seeing that?' asked Dhruv.

'Good for you.'

Dhruv tried not to say anything more but couldn't help it. 'That man left. Get over it. Show that Raghuvir's leaving the college doesn't matter to you, that you're a heartless bitch because that's how I know you as! Because that's what you were. You fucking lied and ruined my life years ago when I loved you. And here you're waiting for a man to turn up? What did I do that you didn't stand up for me and fucking lied but you can sit here all day and rue about Raghuvir's absence? Did you regret my absence as well? Did you sit like this in the last bench where we used to sit? Did you miss me as well? Or were you busy protecting your stupid scholarship? Why him and not me?'

'You are getting nothing from me,' Aranya said calmly. Dhruv threw his hands in the air, exasperated and walked back to his room. The girl's unflinching devotion towards Raghuvir was excruciating for Dhruv. He would have preferred getting skinned alive.

A month after Raghuvir's resignation, Aranya had accepted offers from two more professors, Dr Sharma and Dr Mitra, to be their research assistant. Prof. Mitra, who had been waiting for his revenge on Aranya who had turned him down earlier, was exceptionally hard on her, making her work nights and days in succession, counting on her to either succumb or make a mistake, whichever came earlier.

It was the latter.

A couple of weeks after she had started working with Prof. Mitra, he came marching and shouting into the class with an army of teachers behind him. Apparently an expensive machine had shorted in the laboratory and there was a small fire.

'WHERE IS ARANYA?' shouted Prof. Mitra. Aranya who looked like she was expecting it stood up. 'Do you even know how much that machine costs, Aranya? ANSWER ME! DO YOU KNOW? How could you not keep the mains off? Don't stand there like a fool—answer me! What's the reason behind such carelessness? Will your parents pay for the damage? Tell me? Who will pay for it?' Prof. Mitra's face was flushed red, his voice shook with anger, his body convulsed like he was having a stroke. He addressed Prof. Tripathi, 'Mr Tripathi, now you tell me what I should do? On your recommendation I chose this girl and now she has ruined the incubator I had ordered from Germany. Thirty lakh rupees! It's all ruined. It's all wasted! What do I tell the trustees now?'

Aranya shivered, little drops of tears dropped on to her notebook.

'DARE YOU EVER COME NEAR MY LAB! And tell me what to do with that junk machine now? Should I just throw it? TELL ME.'

'It happened by mistake,' mumbled Aranya.

'MISTAKE? YOU CALL IT A MISTAKE, MISS ARANYA! Tell me, tell me, what do I do with it?'

Dhruv had had enough. He interrupted Prof. Mitra. 'Sell it for scrap. Do you want me to break it for you? Isn't the machine's delivery in college and your new car a delicious coincidence?'

'These students, I tell you. Disgrace. I will not take this. I will call your parents. And Dhruv, you should keep your tongue in check or I will have you expelled,' said Prof. Mitra and strode out.

Dhruv left the class. These old failed men needed to be taught a lesson. Even if Prof. Mitra whored out his whole family, sold kidney, spleen and heart, he couldn't have afforded a Mercedes CLA45 AMG. He strode to the sports room and issued a slightly old but sturdy Slazenger bat. Prof. Mitra's lab was on the third floor. He ran up the flight of stairs, heaving and panting, and found the laboratory locked. He held the bat upside down and slammed the handle into the lock which didn't budge even slightly.

'I thought you would need this,' said Sanchit who was walking towards the laboratory, a key dangling from his fingers.

'How did you know I would be here?'

'That's not too hard to guess now, is it? Prof. Mitra berates her in front of an entire class. So the boy who's irrevocably in love with her has to step in, right?'

Sanchit opened the door and pointed to the machine that lay in the distance, gleaming in places, charred in others.

'I am not in love with her,' said Dhruv and smashed the bat on the incubator. 'I got her into this mess. It's my responsibility.'

'Didn't you want to destroy her?'

'They are calling her parents.'

'You should be happy about that, right? You can repeat history here, can't you? What better opportunity than this?'

'I don't want to.'

'Because you're in love, Dhruv!'

'If you don't stop speaking I'm going to swing this in your face.'

'Speaking of swinging, wait for me,' said Sanchit and grabbed a long spanner himself.

And together, they smashed the machine to pieces.

42

A few days later, Aranya's father received a letter from Prof. Mitra about Aranya's behaviour in college. Prof. Mitra used the choicest of words to pull down Aranya and to highlight her waywardness in college. If his words were not enough, he had slyly attached with the letter the sign-in sheet of the hostel of the day Aranya had returned late in the night.

Her father called Aranya when he was done reading.

The letter lay in tatters on their dining table. Aranya's mother was in tears. The brother had shrugged and only said that they could not expect anything better from a girl like Aranya.

'Where were you that night?' Aranya's father asked in a menacing tone.

'T . . . the mid-semesters had e . . . ended. The entire college was out,' she mumbled.

'Did I ask you about the rest of the college? I asked about you, Aranya! You're not like them. Don't you know that? And what is this letter? What on earth are you doing in the college? Did we send you for this? Night outs? And breaking college property? Summons to come meet the dean? Why? Explain it to me. *Bol, Aranya.* Answer me.'

'. . .'

'What happened that night? I want to know why weren't you studying!' her father barked.

'All of us were there . . . us friends.'

'Friends? *Waah! Tere friends bhi hain? Tujh jaisi ki friends?* Who would be friends with the likes of you,' her father shouted. 'I hope you remember what you did the last time you had a friend. What did I tell you before going? You're not supposed to talk to anyone. And what are you doing? You're partying! You're staying out nights with your friends. You're destroying college property! Waah. I'm so proud of you, beta. Why don't you just kill us? Huh? We are tired of you. We do everything to hide you from the outside world and you leave no stone unturned to embarrass us. Why? What wrong had we done that you were born to us? Why would you do this to us?'

In the background she heard her mother sobbing loudly, cursing her wretched luck. 'God knows what I had done to deserve such a daughter. I wish she were dead.'

Aranya sat in a corner, hands wrapped around her knees, the phone stuck to her ear, crying, wondering what she had done to her family, as if her disease was by her own volition.

'*Aa raha hoon kal main. Theeka karta tujhe mai.* (I am coming tomorrow to set you straight),' said the father and cut the call. Aranya spent the night curled in a little ball on the floor shaking with fear.

The next morning, her father landed in the college, veins bursting out of his temple, fists clenched. He marched right to her hostel mess and slapped Aranya in front of the hostel staff. Luckily, it was a Sunday and most hostellers were sleeping.

Aranya was paraded for the next two hours, taken from one professor to another. Her father had begged and pleaded in front of the professors, apologizing for Aranya's shortcomings, her professors had nodded, appraising Aranya in the newfound knowledge.

'I'm extremely sorry for her behaviour, Sir. She will never do it again. She got into some wrong company I'm sure. She's usually not like that,' her father begged, hands folded.

'I understand.' Prof. Tripathi shook his head. 'I will make sure I am stricter with her. Also, Prof. Mitra would want to see you as well.'

'Thank you so much, Sir. And Aranya, say sorry to Prof. Tripathi again.'

They met all her professors. Numbers were exchanged between her professors and her father and promises were made to keep Aranya in check. Like she was a teenager gone astray with tattoos on her shoulders, a dildo in her bag and cocaine her in her bloodstream. However, despite her father's pleas, none of the professors took Aranya in their projects.

'Who would want a research assistant like you?' bellowed her father. They were made to wait for three hours for Prof. Mitra to get free from his meetings. He finally called for them. Her father shook Prof. Mitra's hand and immediately started to apologize for his daughter's digressions.

'Sir, I apologize for my daughter's behaviour. Her mother is still in shock. She has always been a perfect student, Sir. God knows what got inside her head. She must have fallen into bad company. I have talked to her. She won't create any trouble.'

'I would like to believe you, Mr Gupta. We all thought Aranya was a sincere student. Her indiscipline has shocked us too. The economic loss, the hit to the research, the spoilt machine notwithstanding it's saddening for a professor to see a good student waste his or her life by mixing with the wrong people. I believe she has been spending a lot of time with that professor—'

'Which professor?'

'Prof. Raghuvir. The professor was expelled after a disciplinary meeting. But also ask her to not associate with that boy from her class. He was caught cheating in the mid-semester examinations. And yet—'

'Boy?' Her father looked at Aranya.

'Who was that boy who got suspended from the mid-semester examinations?' Prof. Mitra asked the peon. 'Oh yes, Dhruv, that's the boy's name.'

The father's eyes were still on Aranya. 'Sir, I assure you she will stop talking to him right away.'

'Mr Gupta, since you are here and you seem like a nice man, I should also mention that the day your daughter returned to the college late, she was drunk. It was captured on the CCTV cameras. We have strict rules against that kind of behaviour in this college. We have been very lenient with her till now, Mr Gupta. We never expected this out of her.'

Aranya hands reflexively went up to save her face as her father swung wildly and smacked her face. She cut her lip on her teeth and tasted iron.

'*Tune daaru peena shuru kar diya?* YOU WERE DRUNK, ARANYA? *Kya bol rahe hain tere professor?*' The father stood up and asked Aranya to remove her hands from her face and slapped her again.

'Listen, Mr Gupta. Take it easy. I'm sure it was a mistake and she will not do it again. Take it easy.'

The father slapped Aranya two more times. She was crying now. Aranya's father held his head and slumped in his chair. He stared Aranya down and raised his hand again. Aranya cowered.

'Sir, I'm very sorry on her behalf. I will make sure she never gives you a chance to complain again,' said the father.

'Thank you, Mr Gupta. You can go now,' said Prof. Mitra.

'Sir, I have one more request if you allow me. I know my daughter has disgraced your institution but if you can give her some projects to do it will be great. We come from a humble background and she needs to keep her marks up.'

'I will see what I can do. Now I have a few meetings to attend. Thank you for coming, Mr Gupta. The peon will show you out.'

Aranya and her father left Prof. Mitra's cabin. Aranya's upper lip was bleeding.

'Call your mother and tell her what you did,' her father said. He dialled the number and gave the phone to Aranya. 'TELL HER EVERYTHING, *bhenchod*!' She held the phone and broke down. Her father snatched the phone from her and narrated to her mother the details of what the professors had said about Aranya, embellishing it with more imagined details.

Aranya sat with her head hung low, her lips bleeding.
'Take me to the boy,' her father told Aranya.
'Dad, I'm sorry. Nothing will ever happen again.'
'TAKE ME TO THE BOY.'

43

Aranya and her father waited in the canteen for Dhruv to turn up. The onslaught of slaps had ended for the time being but Aranya waited for it to resume. Her father had a striking memory when it came to her misdemeanours and it wouldn't take him long to recognize Dhruv as the boy from school.

By now, news had spread throughout the campus about Aranya's sweet and docile father.

The canteen had started filling up and they were all talking in whispers about Aranya and her father. She was eleven years old all over again, surrounded by kids who laughed at private jokes about her, and jibed her needlessly. It was as if she had walked into a time machine. Another four years in the labyrinth of soul-sucking sadness, of judging students, of her maligned self. Her life was in a fucking loop.

What did she expect? It was her fault entirely.

She had come to this college to study, maximize her scores, get her projects done on time, get a high-paying job and spend the rest of her life being a lonely overachiever. Why did she make the mistake of thinking that someone else would take care of her problems? Why did she have any hopes with Raghuvir? What was she thinking? That a

professor in shining armour and floppy hair would waltz into
her life, they would solve complex equations together, be the
greatest friends anyone had ever seen, maybe even fall in love,
and everything would be hunky-dory for the rest of her life.
All those fucking Disney films! Why didn't she notice that
only pretty damsels deserved to be rescued? What would have
happened to Cinderella if she were ugly? She would have
been rotting at her stepmother's still.

What happened to all the lessons she taught herself about
being alone in every battle of hers? How did she allow herself to
be distracted from the goal just because Raghuvir left the college?
Why did she let Raghuvir play such a pivotal part in her life?

So what if she thought for the first time somebody had truly
appreciated her and looked beyond her patchy skin, her less-
than-average face and her oddly overweight body? So what if she
felt loved for the first time, even acknowledged? So what if for
the first time she thought there was someone encouraging her on
in her life? So what if she felt loved? Cared for? Or even human
for that matter? She wasn't supposed to feel any of these things.

And Raghuvir? Did she really expect him to stand up for
her? Why would he stand up for a girl like her? Why would
anyone stand up for her? Didn't she learn that from school? Of
course he ran away leaving her to rot here. Of course he didn't
even call to see what became of her. Of course he switched
off his cellphone.

She deserved this. She had had one chance to fix
everything. One chance and she blew it. Her only job in the
world was to stay hidden and not embarrass her family even
further. Being born to them was enough.

Dhruv walked in. He looked different in his buttoned-
down shirt, a regular fit pair of jeans and clean sneakers.

'Hello Uncle, Dhruv,' he said and shook her father's hand.

'Sit,' her father said, still no recollection of where he had seen the boy before. But Aranya's life was one travesty after another and her good fortune didn't last beyond the first thirty seconds.

'You are Dhruv Roy? Janakpuri? Is he the same Dhruv? You're the same boy? *Bhenchod, tu wahi hai?*' asked her father, startled.

Dhruv nodded. Her father stood up stumbling, still a little stunned.

'YOU! You stay away from my daughter. Do you hear me? Or I will call your mother. Give me her number, give me her number right now. Did you not hear me? *Number de unka warna maar doonga.*' Dhruv stood up, too. Her father continued, 'GIVE ME THE NUMBER.'

'My parents are divorced, Sir. I don't think it will help to call my mother. I can give you my father's number,' Dhruv said giving out the number

Aranya's father dialled the number and it was unreachable. 'You stay right here,' he said and tried again. It was still unreachable. '*Saale, dekhta hoon tujhe abhi!* I will call your father and tell him what you're up to! I WILL TELL HIM EVERYTHING. You're behind everything. *Ruk bhenchod, tu.*'

'Yes.'

The call didn't connect. He turned to Dhruv. 'How would you understand, you bastard? You're a divorcee's son. What would you understand about family?' He looked at Aranya instead. 'Stay away from him.

'Sir—' Dhruv interrupted.

'SHUT UP! If I find you near my daughter again, I'm going to file a police complaint.'

And this time it was Dhruv's turn to bear the brunt of Aranya's father's heavy hand. It hit him square on his face.

Dhruv staggered backwards and leant on the table to steady himself. Her father continued to humiliate Dhruv, exhausting his entire vocabulary of expletives. Aranya closed her eyes in anticipation of what would follow.

Dhruv would stand up and laugh. He would clench his fist and throw her father to the ground with one blow. He would shout, you fucker, and would continually punch her father in the face till a few teeth came loose and he spat blood. He would spit on her father but that wouldn't still cut it. He would jab her father's ribcage with his foot and swing his foot on his face. FUCK YOU, he would shout. He would walk away from the scene with a smile on his face.

But nothing happened. Dhruv did nothing.

'Sorry, Sir,' he said and stared at his shoes.

'Listen to me.' Her father grabbed his collar. 'This is your last chance or I will kill you. Do you hear me? I WILL KILL YOU. Now get lost!' He let Dhruv go, who left without a single word.

He did nothing, absolutely nothing.

Aranya's father left soon after, promising Aranya that he would need a daily progress report, that he would regularly call all of her professors to keep track of her.

Aranya couldn't understand though how Dhruv let her father leave the college without a broken jaw and a fractured skull.

44

It was one in the night and Ritika was still on the other side of the phone, now talking about some girl in her school who was dating someone important, someone who drove a big car and was friends with quite a few club owners.

'She was such a slut in school. Always at the far end of the football ground with her skirt in a bunch around her waist,' Ritika grumbled.

The first hour wasn't a problem. It's the boyfriend's duty to keep his girlfriend entertained, to listen to mind-numbing stories about people he didn't know and didn't care about. He spent the second hour watching an episode of *Breaking Bad*, the phone on loudspeaker and earphone plugged in one of his ears.

'Are you even listening to what I am saying? Hello? Hello, Dhruv?'

'. . .'

'Hello?'

'Yes, yes, I'm there. I'm just a little tired,' said Dhruv. Ritika didn't get the hint and went on and on about another story about another girl in her neighbourhood who had been caught making out on her parents' bed and it became a big deal.

Dhruv was now sitting on the ledge of the roof. He didn't love her, he was sure of it now. At a distance he could see the flickering light from Aranya's laptop.

'I think I should sleep now,' said Ritika.

'Are you sure? I really wanted to talk to you through the night,' Dhruv said. Aranya wouldn't have missed the sarcasm.

'Aww, that's sweet. Tomorrow, baby. For sure. We will talk the entire night. Muah! Goodnight,' she said.

He sat there staring at the tiny light of the laptop on the next roof. Aranya never slept before four in the morning, Dhruv knew that by now. He had spent the last few weeks being awake with her, darkness and a few hundred feet separating them. She was making amends, trying to get her life back on track. Back on the projects for Prof. Mitra and Prof. Tripathi, she spent every waking minute trying to crawl back into their good books. The path was as hard and futile as Frodo's.

'Day twenty-three,' said Sanchit as he placed a small bottle of Vodka and two plastic glasses between him and Dhruv. 'You should go talk to her.'

'Why should I do that?' Dhruv asked.

'It's better than counting days here.'

Silence engulfed them and soon they were drinking directly from the bottle.

Sanchit said, 'This wouldn't have happened if Raghuvir hadn't left. He had quite a shouting match with the dean before he left. But you shouldn't be concerned. You have Ritika, don't you? The girl you're never planning to leave? The girl whose face you will wake up to every morning? The girl you will have kids with? It's Ritika, isn't it? The ONE?'

Dhruv nodded.

'Fuck off, Dhruv. You're in love with her. That flickering light in the distance—not that girl with an eating disorder.'

'I'm not in love with her,' mumbled Dhruv. 'And as you said, she's into Raghuvir. Look at her. Just look at her mourning the absence of Raghuvir. How fucking stupid is she? Why doesn't she just get over it?' If Raghuvir is who she wants, Raghuvir is who she will get.

45

That night, like many before, she sat on the roof preparing for the end-semester examinations like her life depended on it. Her blood was practically liquid caffeine. Between Mitra's project, Tripathi's stupidities and the end-semester examinations, she wasn't sleeping for more than a couple of hours every night. Her concentration was scant. Often she found herself looking towards the other roof, where she could see a silhouette, sometimes two.

Though Dhruv had kept out of her way since that incident in the canteen, she couldn't help but think about him, about how Dhruv stood up for her in the class when Dr Mitra censured her. How he even let her father slap him when he could have easily sent him back with a broken face.

'Hey,' a voice said from behind, startling Aranya.

'. . .'

'. . .'

'What are you doing here? How did you come here?' asked Aranya.

'I got something for you,' replied Dhruv and dangled a piece of paper in front of her. 'That's the address and the home number of Raghuvir. I have called on the number but the line is disconnected.'

'I have nothing to do with him,' said Aranya.

'Of course you do. None of this would have happened if he had stuck around.'

'But he didn't. He left me here to face the music.'

'Well, that's true. But that shouldn't stop you from bringing him back. Here's what I think would have happened. Mitra would have accused you and him for being drunken teenagers, upsetting the decorum of the college, probably doing something juvenile in a closed, dark classroom—'

'Dhruv!'

'I'm just saying! And Raghuvir would have stood up for you. Mitra must have thrown at him a choice between you and him, and he would have chosen to walk out of the college sacrificing himself, the gentleman that he was. Because, if I were a stuck-up dean, I would have thrown you out.'

'What makes you so certain?'

'Sanchit says I watch a lot of television drama.'

'Why are you so concerned?'

Dhruv didn't say anything. He sat next to her, his arm inches away from her. Aranya could see Dhruv squirm even as he said this. 'I'm doing this because I might have sourced the CCTV video that night. The rumour too was started by Sanchit and me.'

Aranya's throat went dry. 'YOU?'

Aranya had lived the past twenty-four days in a flash, not knowing where things had gone wrong. None of this would have happened had Dhruv had the decency to not try and destroy her life.

'Yes, it was me. And with the reputation that Raghuvir had, it wasn't hard for people to believe it. Now don't throw a fit and cry and curse me because we have been through it before. Can we just skip to the part where you think I'm doing this to wash away my black soul?'

'And why would I help you do that? I have been to hell and back, Dhruv. And you think this is a damn game, don't you? My father slapped me!'

'He slapped me too. Which part of "let's skip that" did you not get?'

'The part where I kill you!' growled Aranya and lunged at Dhruv. She grabbed his collar.

'You're crazy! Let me go.'

'Am I crazy? What did you get out of it? Were you totally out of your mind?' she screamed.

Dhruv drew himself up and pushed her away and she staggered backwards. 'Enough. We can still get Raghuvir back and you can still have your happy ending, walking hand in hand with him into the sunset, or in your case, the lab.'

'I can't leave the college. And who knows where he is. He could be anywhere by now,' Aranya said, weighing her options. 'And, moreover, my father would come to know. The professors talk to him every day.'

'Who says you have to miss classes? Go now.' Dhruv unclasped her palm and put the paper in it. 'You will be back by morning. I will take you.'

'I'm not going,' said Aranya.

'Why not?'

'Why should I? Why should I free you of your guilt? And where did this come from, this feeling of remorse?'

'I feel no remorse.'

'I do.'

'Excuse me?' asked Dhruv.

'I won't go until you tell me you're going to get your father to talk to Prof. Tripathi.'

'My father?'

'I talked to Prof. Tripathi after you were barred from the examinations. He said if your father talks to him, he will let you go. I found your father's number from the college database to call him here but seems like he hasn't paid his bills.'

'What? You called him? You're fucking psychotic, Aranya.'

'Look who's talking. You're not repeating the year because of your kindness and your sacrifice!'

'Blah. Blah. Blah,' grumbled Dhruv, inches away from Aranya's face.

'I will cut you a deal. I will come with you but I don't want to see you in college for the next three years, looking at every milestone I cross and telling me that I wouldn't be there if it weren't for you sacrificing your first year for me. I won't take that. Talk to your father. Ask him to meet the dean, apologize for what you did that day, and the dean will let you take the exam. I don't want to owe anything to anyone. Least of all you!'

'What would you do if I don't? I like the idea of torturing you, and not letting you enjoy any of your spoils.'

'Don't kid yourself, Dhruv. You wouldn't have got me here if you weren't sufficiently guilty of what you did. And what you did was shitty.'

'It's a deal.'

Dhruv walked to the ledge of the roof and stood there for a brief second, surveying the perimeter like he was Bruce Wayne.

'Come,' he said and gave his hand to her.

Aranya's heart leaped at the sense of adventure her decision would take her on. It took them fifteen minutes to jump the parapets and reach the parking lot, and she felt her heart would give way any time. By the time she felt solid ground crunch under her feet it felt like she had been through fifteen straight episodes of *Man vs Wild*.

'You look like you died.'

'I did. Thrice.'

'Take this,' said Dhruv and handed the only helmet to her.

'What about you?'

'I would die to live in the blazing glory of having saved someone.'

Aranya rolled her eyes, knowing all too well that Dhruv was in love with her again. The ball was in Aranya's court now.

46

Dhruv intended to bring Raghuvir back to college. But as they drove out of the college, with Aranya clinging on to him for dear life, his resolve started to melt away.

'You better not brake and try something stupid. I have seen it in the movies.'

'I wish I could have. I feel like I'm driving with a blue whale clinging to my back. It's a surprise the front tyre is still on the ground.'

'With your bike, it's a surprise it's still running,' snapped Aranya.

'We could go on and you would lose.'

'Try me.'

Dhruv liked that in her, that fight to have the last word. She could lose some weight though. One month of HIIT would take off the cellulite from her jiggly vibrating arms. Post that an intensive three-month weight training schedule could make sure her stomach was taut and hard and indestructible.

'Why are you smiling?'

'I imagined you running.'

'It's like imagining you studying.'

'I actually did study. You can check my answer sheets,' said Dhruv.

'. . .'

'. . .'

The ease of conversation, the possibility of rekindling an old relationship, the prospect of him straying, made him queasy, a bit disgusted, and he revved the old engine to its limit. The engine groaned and in the noise, Dhruv came to analyse what he felt.

The mere thought of Raghuvir and Aranya in the same room gave him nausea. Then why the fuck was he taking her there? Why the hell would he want them to be close again? She was sad and she would get over it.

Reasons and feelings and the beating of his heart muddled up his head and he concentrated on the road instead. At this time of the night, highways were dangerous. Also terribly romantic, with the long stretches of darkness punctuated with light from distant houses, little stars if you could find some, and silence. But he reminded himself that he was with her, Aranya, not with the girl he had promised to love and be committed to. How would he be any different from his mother?

For a moment the name escaped his mind. Ritika, he remembered. The names got blurred as he drove on.

Ritika. Before her it was Satvika. Another girl he had committed to love for life before it broke down and came to nothing.

'Can you stop? I need to pee. Right now,' shouted Aranya in Dhruv's ear.

'There's a petrol pump after a few kilometres.'

'NOW.'

'You can't pee here,' shouted Dhruv and went faster weaving between trucks and buses.

'That's only going to make it worse!'

'Where will you pee?'

'ANY DAMN WHERE.'

Dhruv stopped the motorcycle at a sufficiently deserted stretch of road and gave her an earful, deriding all womankind and their weak bladders.

Aranya got off the bike, stepped closer to him and dug her index finger in his chest. 'And listen closely. If you or anyone comes even close to me when I'm doing my business I will reach for your intestines through your mouth, pull them out, rip them apart and hang them around your neck. So don't even dare to move an inch from here.'

She walked away till she was just a shadow. Dhruv heard the crunching of leaves and then nothing. He didn't move an inch. Aranya came back after five minutes; a smile had replaced the murderous look. He drove without a word, though all he wanted to do was to keep looking at her and talk.

'That was pretty intense back there, the intestines around my neck thing,' said Dhruv after a while.

'I don't like people around when I'm not dressed. How is that hard to understand?'

'But even when you're not, you will always have those layers of fat covering you!' Dhruv laughed and waited for a piercing retort. He had hit a raw nerve. He drove a few kilometres without a word. 'I'm sorry.'

'It's okay.'

'You're not really fat, just a little healthy maybe.' Dhruv added after a pause. 'By my standards.'

'. . .'

'How your body should look is no one else's business really,' said Dhruv.

'. . .'

'It's all media fed. Who cares if you're fat or you have abs?'

'. . .'

'As long as you're not dying, it's fine.'

'. . .'

'And you're not dying.'

'Dhruv?' said Aranya.

'Huh?'

'You need to shut up.'

For the rest of the drive, he forced himself to think of Ritika and how much he was missing her, which he wasn't at all.

That's the cliché about love. You don't choose it. It chooses you.

47

When they had started out from college, their reasons to be together were rather clear. Dhruv didn't want to feel guilty any more and Aranya wanted her success to be free of Dhruv's benevolence. As the night progressed, their reasons became increasingly ambiguous.

Dhruv, the guy who appraised people in body fat percentages, had just talked like a feminist. And sometimes when he drove too fast, Aranya held him tight without feeling the need to wash her arms with acid.

To cut the awkwardness of the conversation, Dhruv asked. 'So why is Raghuvir that important?'

'What do you mean?' asked Aranya.

'You clearly lost your shit once he left.'

Aranya didn't answer. It wasn't as if Aranya hadn't thought of what was there between Raghuvir and her. But the thought was so flawed that she didn't dwell on it. Raghuvir had dated models. And she was . . .

Raghuvir had never acknowledged Aranya as anything more than an infatuated student. Which he had proved by running away.

They reached Noida at three in the night. They spent the next hour trying to find their way to Raghuvir's house.

Dhruv parked his motorcycle fifty yards away from the steel gate of Raghuvir's modest one-storey house and said, 'I will wait here.'

Aranya had been thinking of what she could say to Raghuvir and she had zilch right now. She rang the bell thrice before there was any movement inside the house. A couple of minutes later, Raghuvir emerged in his A&F trackpants and an ill-fitting T-shirt.

Pleasantries were exchanged after Raghuvir expressed suitable shock. He invited her inside, still trying to get over her uninvited, creepy presence.

'How did you get here?'

Raghuvir closed the door behind her. Through the steel gauze of the gate, Aranya could see Dhruv bent over his motorcycle, frowning.

'Sit,' said Raghuvir, collecting the stray papers on the couch into a bundle. Raghuvir switched on all the lights but they weren't enough for the large living room. The house was dying. The walls were lined with bookshelves bent with the weight of the textbooks. Big books with cracked spines and incomprehensible symbols lay upturned everywhere. Minus the seepage on the walls, the ruddy smell, it was exactly like Aranya had imagined. She had imagined Raghuvir and her working together one day, half-filled blackboards and half-empty coffee mugs surrounding them. Raghuvir clearly wasn't slacking. In fact he was on top of his game.

'Why did you leave, Sir?' asked Aranya.

'I had to,' Raghuvir answered.

'Why?'

'Mitra had wanted my head on a platter for a really long time. I gave him the opportunity and he struck. We had a slight disagreement and I had to leave.'

'What disagreement?'

'He wanted to throw you out. So instead, I volunteered. And I had a few offers lined up for me and I thought it's best for me to take them up. I have been down for far too long. It's time to get on the horse again,' said Raghuvir with a smile.

'So you can come back if you want to?'

'Technically I can, but I have things to do now. I have already accepted a job offer in Bangalore. They are funding all my research. It's a new start for me,' answered Raghuvir.

'You will never come back then?' asked Aranya, her voice desperate.

'No. Plus, I can't assure them what happened that day won't happen again. This student–professor thing really brings you down in the research community,' said Raghuvir, peering into some notes now and scribbling in the margins with a pencil.

'What?'

'Four years is a long time to just like you and do nothing about it,' said Raghuvir.

The words hit Aranya like a bus. Raghuvir looked at her, nonchalant. Aranya had tears in her eyes, God knew why, and she said, 'That's not funny. I didn't come here to be made fun of. That happens enough already.' She got up to leave.

'Sit down.'

Aranya listened.

'It wasn't supposed to be funny.' Raghuvir flipped through his notes like they weren't having a conversation where he had admitted to liking her, which at best was an insensitive, cruel joke. 'I just told you the reason, Aranya. I might just think you're an interesting person right now, but I'm afraid it will grow stronger.'

'What are you saying exactly?'

'That there might come a day I might want to be with you a lot more often. Because I like you, Aranya,' he said it like he had solved an equation, a predetermined sequence of symbols and numbers which would yield the same results without any deviation.

'You're joking. What is there to like in me?'

'You're smart, you're driven, and you're intelligent. There's not one thing I would change about you. Not a single thing. If I were to stay in the college, it would be for you. And so I can't,' said Raghuvir.

'. . .'

'Don't act so shocked.'

'This is ridiculous, Sir. Please don't joke around like this.'

How was all this not a joke? Or a dream she would wake up soon from? This was a fucking nightmare. He was making fun of her. Raghuvir? Liking her? The man who only dated goddamn goddesses? That was what it exactly was. She was a joke for everyone.

'This isn't a joke, Aranya.'

'I think it is and it's not funny. If what you're saying is true, why didn't I see this tone in your voice in college? You have always been just a professor to me,' growled Aranya. She felt her ears burn and she was moments away from crying. 'Why this sudden change? What is it if not making fun of me? And of what I feel for you? You know that, right? Sir? You are saying all this because you have seen how I look at you? Is this what this is all about?'

'You didn't see it because I was trying to be a professor in college. I'm no longer one. If I think you're an intelligent and interesting girl and I like you, I don't think that's hard to believe at all.'

'If all that you're saying is true, which it's not, then why would you run? If you feel what you do, why not stay?' Her voice barely audible, like someone had jammed a pen in her larynx.

Raghuvir took her hands in his. Aranya's body shuddered. No man had held her hand with such warmth and acceptance; she even felt beautiful. 'Let's face it, Aranya. We both have things to do and places to go to. We can't be stopping each other. There will be a time I will be a dead weight to you, a professor you were probably infatuated with, someone you thought you loved, someone who could fill up something in your life at that point in time. Or it could be the other way around. I have seen how attachments can lead you astray and I don't want that to happen with you. Or with me. It happened to me once and look how it ended for me. You need to make your own mistakes and I will not be one of the mistakes you make, Aranya. You shouldn't go down the path I have gone. If you're with me, you will give the relationship everything that you've got and leave your ambition behind, something that I did too and I don't want you to do that. There will be a time you will realize that love's tiring and worthless. Relationships need to be worked at. They are hard work and there are a lot of compromises to be made. And I don't want you to do it and I don't want to do it either. When it comes to relationships, pragmatism trumps love. You are too young to understand that.'

'You could have asked once what I wanted?! You never asked. You never asked!' Aranya hyperventilated. She stood up and walked around the room holding her head mumbling to herself. 'You will be a dead weight some day? I will leave you? What's all this? Why? How would I leave you? What? You're my professor? Am I in this room? You wanted to be with me? What? This is a nightmare. This is a very bad joke. This is a very bad joke. Why are you saying all this? Why are you saying this? Don't say this. Just shut up! Why!' She was crying into her palms now. Her shoulders heaved with every snort.

'I'm not joking. And I didn't need to ask you. I know how much you look up to me. I have been in your place. I have looked up to my professors, even loved them. But that's all they were. And you know what people say about me, right? Of course you know about Smriti and the other PhD students? What's to say I wouldn't do that again, huh? I can't promise that to you. What will happen if I stray? Love's too risky, too complicated, Aranya, and maybe it's not love at all.'

'We could give it a shot? Make rules and stick by them? Be pragmatic as you said? Couldn't we? And you said love and relationships are a compromise, didn't you? You could choose to not have any more Smritis and I could choose to still pursue my ambitions and so could you and we could be together! Unless you're joking. If you are, then I didn't say what I just did.'

Raghuvir took a long pause as if thinking about it. They had laid out their cards on the table. 'That night when you were drunk, you talked about Dhruv.'

'I hate him,' said Aranya, almost as a reflex.

'Isn't he outside? Leaning against his motorcycle? Not wanting to let you out of his sight? Hatred is a strong emotion, Aranya, and you don't feel it for someone worthless. And if he's worth something, he might be worth loving at some point. I don't want to risk anything. If you get into a relationship with me, it will end whatever chance you have with Dhruv once and for all. I'm not saying you should be with him—because quite frankly, the guy is a prick—but the question is, would you be able to live with that choice? There are way too many questions for you to answer, Aranya. I don't think you're ready. Neither am I. I'm just starting to get my bearings back.'

'So you gave up on me?' asked Aranya, wanting to fall in love with Raghuvir, however make-believe it might be, making all the compromises he was talking about, aching to hold his hand again.

'I didn't give up on you, Aranya.' He sat next to her and put his arm around her. She, despite her size, fit perfectly in his embrace. He sighed and said, 'Dhruv doesn't scare me. It's not the person I'm afraid of; it's the idea of perfect love that I'm scared of. I'm just afraid it doesn't exist and I don't want to give you an illusion that it does. I don't want your world to revolve around me or mine around you. We will both end up dissatisfied with it.'

'What if I told you that love is a concept alien to me as well and I'm ready to make every compromise to just stick with you?' Aranya spit out her words, still wary that he would laugh out and say 'gotcha'!

'It doesn't work that way, Aranya.'

And then they didn't talk.

Aranya sat there reflecting on what she had just said. She saw Raghuvir get back to his work, scribbling equations.

What had happened right now? Would she snap her fingers and find herself in her hostel bed? Snap. No. Why would he say all these things?

He disappeared into the kitchen and came back with a flask of coffee for the journey. Of course, she could love him. She was halfway there already. And they would make a ridiculously talented team. That's all that mattered.

'So you will not come back?' asked Aranya.

'No.'

'Just so you know, if you come back, I will be there for you. I haven't experienced love, imperfect or perfect, and I don't know how you can hurt me but I know this that if you ever think about us, I will be with you. Just know that I would be okay with making all the compromises that are to be made in a relationship. No matter how desperate that sounds!'

'That doesn't sound desperate at all.'

Aranya started giggling at the ridiculousness of it all, a pathetic, self-loathing, self-hating giggle. She plonked down on the couch, shook her head, trying to absorb everything. Something changed in her; she could feel it. Like gears set in motion, changing their orientation, slowly transforming her into another person, a better person. A few minutes later, she spoke. 'You know what, Sir?'

'What?'

'When I was little, I always craved for attention from the boys in my class. But I also knew I was unattractive. Even as a child, I would look at other girls around me and wish I could be like them. I would check my desk every day for letters from boys who like me. There were none for me even as others got dozens.'

'Why are you telling me this?'

'Because it matters.'

Raghuvir poured a cup of coffee for her from the flask and gave her the rest to carry back.

Aranya continued, 'So I started writing letters to myself and would keep them where people could find them and give them to me. The teachers finally caught on to it. I had to change my section because I was teased and chased down hallways. My mother thought I had lost it. My father stopped talking to me for an entire year. And so I started to teach myself to hate boys. Slowly, I became good at it, so good that I hated almost everybody. I still wanted attention though,' said Aranya, almost wanting to share the details of her Skype sessions. 'You don't want to know what I did for it.'

'You're lovely, Aranya. That's all I've got to say.'

Aranya should have been happy right now. This should have been her moment when she could look back at the world and shout, 'Fuck you, fuck you, world. Look at me now. Raghuvir is in love with me. RAGHUVIR. Fuck you for my body fat percentage, fuck you for the bad skin you gave me, fuck you for my complexion, fuck you for my shitty body. Fuck you naturally fair and beautiful girls with high metabolic rates. I have Raghuvir. What have you got?'

This was her revenge. This was where her movie should have ended. With a thumping victory. But it didn't feel like she was standing on the corpse of the world that had been unfair to her.

She just felt light. Like none of it mattered. She had never been spiritual but it must feel like this—liberating. She felt she could have a billion cupcakes right now without guilt wearing her down. She was free. She was now smiling and then started laughing and crying—all at the same time. Something definitely changed inside her. The hatred she had harboured and nurtured for herself, she felt that melt away.

'Are you okay?'

Aranya wiped her tears off. 'I have never been better.'

Aranya hugged Raghuvir. She told him that she would wait for him to come back to college and wished him luck if they never saw each other again.

'Thank you,' said Aranya and walked to the door.

Raghuvir held the door open for her. She hugged Raghuvir again. 'What did you thank me for?'

'Coffee. And if you ever change your mind . . . because I'm crazy good at making compromises. Been doing that all my life,' said Aranya and winked at him.

Raghuvir smiled weakly. She strode out of the door, smiling. She got on the motorcycle and asked Dhruv to drive.

'What happened?'

'He isn't coming back but it's okay. My work is done,' Aranya said.

She saw her reflection in the rear-view mirror of Dhruv's motorcycle and for the first time in years, she didn't frown at what she saw. It felt like love. She stared at her face and saw how beautiful she was; her eyes like little black pearls, her ruddy cheeks which would still be young at forty, and a sharp nose to kill for.

She was fucking stunning.

Raghuvir's words didn't make her fall in love with him, but with herself. She opened her hair, stretched her arms and felt gorgeous. She was in love. Right now, she could have sex with herself.

48

'Your blood isn't on my hands now, all right?' asked Dhruv. Aranya nodded, smiling widely. 'What happened inside?' Dhruv asked irritably, not wanting to let his imagination run wild.

Aranya didn't answer; the happiness in her smile was unmistakable and it bothered Dhruv. He drove dangerously, swerving and weaving between trucks driving with the high beam on to distract himself from thinking about the two of them. They were still a couple of hours from Dhruv's. Somewhere in the last fifty kilometres, Aranya had drifted off, clutching Dhruv.

'Huh?' Aranya woke up with a start and retracted her arms immediately. 'Sorry, I didn't know—'

'It's okay.'

Dhruv drove on, and Aranya, now wide awake, kept smiling foolishly, much to his chagrin.

'Why the fuck are you smiling?' asked an irritated Dhruv.

'Huh? I'm not smiling,' answered Aranya, crunching up her face in surprise.

'Of course you are. Tell me what happened in there. I didn't drive all the way from DTU to this professor's house to be played games with. I need to know what happened in there,' said Dhruv.

'The deal wasn't to tell everything!' argued Aranya, the smile still pasted on her face. 'Stop acting like my boyfriend.'

'Listen. If I were your boyfriend I wouldn't let you in sight of that man. I would have just ripped him apart. I have seen how he looks at you. Just tell me what happened inside.'

'Whoa. Calm your tits down, Dhruv,' said Aranya.

'It's not madness, it's love, and you do these things when you're in love. You keep nothing back and you give it your all. That's what love is about. Losing yourself in it,' said Dhruv, backing off.

'I have never been in love. Oh wait! I have been in love. You were asking why I was smiling, right? That's because I think I just fell in love.'

Dhruv wanted to drive back, drag Prof. Raghuvir out from his house and smash his head into his motorcycle's headlight. He tried hard to keep his words inside him but they bubbled to the surface and spilled out of his mouth. 'You're so fucking weak, Aranya, so fucking WEAK. You kissed him, didn't you? What did you do? That's why you're smiling, aren't you? You moron. He told you he loves you, didn't he? And you would have said you loved him back? What else can one expect from a girl like you.' Dhruv pointed a finger right at her face in the rear-view mirror. 'The moment a decent guy approaches, you give in! That's not fucking love. That's called being an attention whore and you're exactly that! It comes from a deep-rooted insecurity about being fat and whatever the hell you look like. Yes, I said it again. You're fat. You jiggle when you walk. The vibrations from your belly make the buildings tremble. Didn't anyone fucking tell you that?' And abruptly, Dhruv stopped talking. Aranya wasn't offended the least bit—she was grinning. In the absence of a rebuttal to his words they sounded juvenile and empty.

'I didn't kiss him. Yes, he told me he loves me. Something like that. Also, I WAS an attention whore. Yes, I'm fat. I can't say I'm particularly proud of it but I think I'm worth falling in love with. And today, I fell in love with myself. That's something worth smiling about, isn't it, Dhruv? Do you love yourself? Have you ever asked yourself that?'

'Whatever.'

Of course he loved himself. He was shredded after all, wasn't he? He put it back on.

Aranya asked after a little while, 'Your father must be sleeping right now, wouldn't he?'

'More like passed out. You remember how he was, don't you?' said Dhruv.

'You can choose not to go.'

'I don't go back on my word,' snapped Dhruv.

'Is that like your thing? You don't go back on your word?' Aranya chuckled. Dhruv didn't find it funny. 'Okay, fine, don't frown, Dhruv. But why don't you go back on your word?'

'Because our words define us, otherwise what stops the world from descending into chaos?'

Aranya frowned. 'So, you think if you don't go and talk to your father the world will descend into chaos? Mountains would implode, whirlpools would swallow civilizations? That's an exaggeration, don't you think?'

'It's called the butterfly effect. Today, I go back on my word and I don't go to my father. Anything can happen tomorrow. Tomorrow, I won't be in Ritika's class. She misses me and dumps me eventually. Angry, I take back my word and blame you for everything. Right when you're about to enter your all-important interview, I shit all over your mood and you don't get the job. Your parents, who had planned a party, start to hate you for it. I destroy Ritika's new boyfriend who happens to be your friend. You hit back wanting to destroy me, but obviously, I'm stronger and more ruthless, and knock down everyone around you. Vengeful, you get Sanchit arrested for possession of weed. His father commits suicide. His sister comes after you with a knife and kills Raghuvir instead.' Dhruv paused.

'This would make such a good B-grade movie.'

'There are consequences, Aranya. Everything we do has consequences,' said Dhruv.

'Why do you care?'

'I'm a consequence.'

'Dangling a line like that doesn't make you mysterious; it makes you boring and laborious.'

Dhruv wanted to smack her beautiful face. He drove, wanting the roads to stretch out interminably.

49

They hadn't talked for the last hour. Aranya pretended to be asleep. She saw Dhruv wipe his tears more than a few times.

She couldn't tear her eyes away from the rear-view mirror, from Dhruv's stoic face as he concentrated on the road. She wanted to comfort him but how do you comfort someone like Dhruv? Dhruv entered his neighbourhood.

The watchmen saluted him, so did the kids out for early morning football matches.

'This is where I live,' said Dhruv, pointing towards a balcony on the third floor in an old, yellow building with flaking paint. 'I will be back. You wait here,' Dhruv said and walked towards the building. His strides got shorter as he got closer to the building and then he stopped altogether, and stared at his shoes.

'What happened?' asked Aranya, walking up to him.

'Do you mind?'

'. . .'

'Do you mind coming with me?' asked Dhruv, almost ashamed.

Aranya nodded and held his arm. They walked up the dilapidated stairwell. The granite beneath their feet was cracked in places, and the corners of walls had spider webs, it looked like it had not been cleaned in ages. Dhruv rang the bell twice. Aranya noticed Dhruv alternate between abject helplessness and anger.

'Dhruv?' His father—bloodshot eyes, matted hair, every bit what Aranya had imagined drunkards to be—seemed surprised. 'Come, come.' Dhruv walked in and his father almost stumbled on the shoes lined at the entrance. He was wearing a pair of trousers without a belt and a vest riddled with holes. Dhruv helped him just in time. The house stank of fermented beer and rotting food.

He asked them to sit on a lumpy, creaky sofa and went to the kitchen. Dhruv sat there rubbing his hands, sweating, as if it wasn't his house.

'Here,' Dhruv's father gave them two bottles. Soda bottles filled with water. He sat in front of them, grinning widely. His hair was sparse and his skin was marred with little marks.

'You need to talk to my professor. I cheated in my exam and got caught. I might have to repeat a year if you don't,' said Dhruv, looking up, meeting his father's eyes.

'Actually, it was me who cheated,' butted in Aranya. 'He got caught saving me.'

Aranya saw Dhruv's hand creep up to the almost empty bottle of Vodka on the side table. He unscrewed the cap and touched it to his lips.

'DHRUV!'

Dhruv shrugged. 'What? Like father like son. Did you expect anything better?'

'You will NOT drink!' His father stood up and snatched the bottle from him. The drunken demeanour had been replaced by a murderous frown; his feet were no longer unsteady.

'You're a fucking hypocrite, Dad.'

'I will smash your head if you swear in this house,' thundered his father.

Dhruv turned away from him. He started to walk away. 'It was a mistake coming here. I should have just left you to your misery.'

'What else would you do?' shouted his father to his back. 'Go, leave me! GO! DO JUST WHAT YOUR MOTHER DID. GO.'

Dhruv looked back and stared him in the eye. 'And what did you do? WHAT DID YOU DO, HUH? DID YOU

FIGHT? NO! So fuck off and drink yourself to death.' Dhruv waved the middle finger at his father.

'Ha! My son! Full of innocent pride, aren't you? Showing off in front of your female friend how great and sensible a man you are?'

'I'm a better man than you were any day, Dad. You are nothing but a chronic disappointment.'

'Then pray tell me something, son, when you left this house a couple of months ago with similar bravado, waving your finger at me, calling me an incompetent father, a drunkard, a pervert, you said you wouldn't ask for a single rupee and yet I see you relentlessly swiping the debit card I gave you. What's with that? Where does the Dhruv who doesn't go back on his word disappear then?'

Dhruv clenched his fist; Aranya could sense a fight brewing. 'That's me giving you a chance to redeem yourself, Dad.'

His father laughed it off. 'So benevolent of you, isn't it?'

Dhruv's jaw tightened, he took a few steps towards his father, then backed off and walked out of the room without a word. Aranya kept sitting there, awkward, scared.

She wondered if she would one day be able to stand up to her father and assert herself like Dhruv had just done. But he wasn't an alcoholic and neither did he consort with prostitutes. A part of her wished he did. She got up to leave as well.

'Here's the professor's number,' Aranya said and handed over a piece of paper to Dhruv's father. 'Don't disappoint him please.'

She left and quietly boarded the motorcycle. Dhruv handed over the helmet to her. In the rear-view mirror, she could see his face muddled up in tears, and it made her cry, and she hugged him tighter from behind for she didn't know what else to do.

They stopped at the next petrol pump where Dhruv got his motorcycle refuelled. Dhruv's phone started to ring; Ritika's name flashed and Dhruv cut the call. 'She will ask too many questions. I don't think I can answer them right now,' he said as if explaining.

'You can just lie. I won't tell her we were together. You know, whatever.'

'I can't lie to her.'

'She won't rest in peace if you don't call her back,' said Aranya. Not that she knew Ritika very well, but if someone had to be in love and in a relationship with Dhruv, anything less than total madness was cheating.

'I will call her in some time to explain everything. I will have to tell her from scratch.'

'Ummm . . . she doesn't know about your parents?' asked Aranya.

'No.'

'Why?'

'I wasn't ready for that kind of intimacy,' said Dhruv.

Aranya didn't quite understand what Dhruv meant but she nodded. They got on the motorcycle and drove back to the college. Aranya thought of what Dhruv had just said and what intimacy meant for her. She kept going back to the time she had almost thought of stripping in front of that boy on Skype. The thought of being naked in front of the boy had scared her shit. The fear of the boy knowing everything there was to know about her had gripped her and she hadn't taken anything off. But Dhruv, driving heroically, stoically, felt naked to her, and so did she to him, for they had no secrets to hide any more and if that was not intimate then nothing was.

But of course, she couldn't fall in love with him again.

50

It was seven by the time Dhruv drove into the campus.

The students hadn't woken up yet, having slept only a couple of hours earlier.

He turned towards the girls' hostel to drop Aranya first. She hopped off the motorcycle, a little distance away from the prying eyes of her warden. A blip in his heart told Dhruv that he didn't want her to leave.

'Good morning,' said Dhruv to prolong conversation; leaving her meant going back to his room, being alone with the thought of having met his father.

'Will you be okay?' asked Aranya.

Dhruv nodded. Aranya turned to leave when Dhruv stopped her.

'I'm sorry.'

'For what, Dhruv?'

'For everything. For having called you ugly and repulsive and what not. I don't think you're any of that.'

'It's okay, Dhruv. I'm used to it now. Everyone calls me that.'

Dhruv smiled weakly and held her hand and said, 'The next time someone calls you that, you need to come to me.'

'And what will you do about it?'

'I'll make sure it's the last time that person gets to speak. I have a great right uppercut. You can ask all the boys who have tried hitting on my girlfriends,' said Dhruv and they both laughed.

And just then they heard a hyena cry out in the distance. It startled both of them.

He saw Ritika, still in her pyjamas, charge towards him, her arms flapping by her side. Her hair in disarray and her eyes sunken, quite clearly she had been up all night thinking about worst-case scenarios.

'WHERE WERE YOU? AND WHAT ARE YOU DOING WITH HER? I called Sanchit! He told me you were not in the campus. WHERE WERE YOU?'

Dhruv looked in Aranya's direction like he wasn't being verbally assaulted and said, 'Bye, Aranya.' Aranya, not wanting to be a part of their domestic squabble, quietly and quickly walked away.

'ANSWER ME!' shouted Ritika.

'Sit,' Dhruv said and cocked his head, motioning Ritika to sit on the motorcycle.

'I'm not going anywhere with you. Answer me, first.'

'SIT,' Dhruv said.

Ritika, her chest still heaving in anger, climbed up and he drove to the far corner of the college and parked his motorcycle. Ritika screamed her questions in his ear. Dhruv sat on the pavement, lit a cigarette and started to fiddle with his phone. Ritika snatched it and flung it in the bushes. Dhruv would have slapped her but he was reminded of three of Ritika's cellphones he had unapologetically smashed for talking to boys he had strictly warned her against. So he stayed put.

'Why didn't you pick up my calls? Were you out for the entire night? What the hell were you doing with her, Dhruv? I thought you hated her! And you were cutting my calls? Why? Dhruv!' Ritika took the cigarette from his mouth and threw it away. 'LOOK AT ME AND ANSWER ME, Dhruv. You can't just keep treating me like shit.'

'When did I treat you like shit?' asked Dhruv. 'And sit here.'

'Shut up, Dhruv. I'm tired of listening to you. Don't do this, don't go there, and don't talk to that guy. ENOUGH. I stay locked up in my room, and what the hell did you do?

You were out with a girl! What happened last night, Dhruv? Dhruv, look at me and tell me what happened. If you had to break up with me, you could have had the damn decency to look at me and tell me that!'

'I'm not breaking up with you, Ritika.'

'Neither am I, Dhruv. After ruining my life and shooing away all my friends, I'm not letting go of you that easily. Now will you just tell me what on earth happened yesterday? Did you touch her?'

'You need to stay calm, Ritika. Nothing happened.'

'Then why were you with her? All my friends told me that you were with her! Aashima even saw you guys leave, but I didn't believe her. GOD! I'm such a fool. Do you know how stupid I would look?' Ritika slumped on the pavement next to him, and cried into her palms.

'You're overreacting, Ritika. She just needed to talk to Raghuvir and I needed to talk to my father. That's all that happened.'

'You have destroyed me, Dhruv.'

'Shut up, Ritika.'

'I spend entire days trying to live like you want me to live. I don't have a single friend I can call my own. All I think about is you and you. You just come and go as you like. Why? Look at me and respond to what I ask, Dhruv. What have you asked for and I haven't given you, Dhruv? What else can I do to be a better girlfriend? For you to be like everyone else, like a normal boyfriend? Why do I have to settle for love in your hate? Why don't you make me feel loved?'

'I do everything a boyfriend does,' Dhruv said irritably.

'No, you don't, Dhruv. Just because you beat up anyone who comes near me and make me feel protected doesn't mean you love me. When was that one time you held my hand

and told me I meant something to you? Dhruv, despite your damned bravado, you're a scared little piece of shit inside. You don't have the balls to accept your love for anyone. You're just scared you will be the same wrecked shit everyone else is.'

'Ritika, you need to calm the fuck down and shut up.'

'What shut up. Say if it isn't true.' Ritika thrust a finger in his face. 'You're just crazy, Dhruv. You just pretend to be in love. And I'm tired of this. I'm tired of looking for signs to feel loved. Oh. Look at that. Dhruv just berated that girl, he must be in love with me. Oh. He just hit that boy black and blue, he must be in love with me. I'm tired, Dhruv. I'm just tired. I need normalcy. I don't give a shit if you cheat on me, if you're not committed, if you're still in love with your ex-girlfriend. All I want is for you to be in LOVE with me when you're with me. I can protect myself, Dhruv. I don't need you for that. I want love from you and you clearly aren't ready for it. And the FUCKING problem is that I can wait. I can wait for you to turn a full circle and come back to me.' Ritika got up. 'If you ever feel you're ready to be in a relationship, I will be waiting. But before that, please don't call me. We've broken up for now.'

Ritika walked away from him, crying. A tired Dhruv walked to his room and crawled to his bed. Sanchit walked in and closed the door behind him.

'Ritika called last night,' said Sanchit, his voice solemnly serious. 'I told her you were out. But I guess a friend told her you were out with Aranya.' Dhruv was too drained to talk about it. He stared at Sanchit like a corpse. 'When will you tell Aranya?'

'What?'

'That you love her, fucker.'

'I love Ritika. I need to get her back.'

'Why the fuck would you do that?'

'Because I'm not my father, dammit. I can hold down a relationship and not destroy people. I will get Ritika back and be the best fucking boyfriend the world has ever seen.'

'The world called. It said fuck you,' Sanchit said. 'And also, your father called. You need to call him back. He's in the hospital.' Sanchit left the room.

After much reluctance, Dhruv dialled his father's number after a few hours.

'Is that Dhruv?' an unfamiliar voice said from the other side.

'Yes. Who's this?' asked Dhruv.

'It's me, your father.'

'You sound strange,' Dhruv said irritably and was about to disconnect the call when his father told him he was dying.

He was at the hospital and wanted to see Dhruv before he died.

51

Aranya see-sawed between feeling slightly guilty and strangely glad.

She wondered if Dhruv and Ritika had patched up. Her heart leaped with joy at the possibility of them failing to understand each other. But Ritika knew Dhruv could have fended off the accusations with no more than a groan. Ritika, the airhead, would have forgiven him. Her shoulders drooped and she frowned at this imagined amicable reunion of sorts.

She had just settled down to get some shut-eye when she heard the familiar screeching voice from the other room.

'Hey?' Aranya knocked on the common wall. 'Are you okay, Ritika?'

'GO AWAY!' howled Ritika. Ritika threw things at the wall and Aranya smiled heartily. They were breaking up!

'We can talk,' offered Aranya.

She heard Ritika break down in uncontrollable sobs and felt like a heartless bitch when her lips curved into a celebratory smile.

After an hour of sobbing and cursing, Ritika invited Aranya over. Previously perilously pink and orange and delightfully decorated, the room lay in ruins and so did Ritika, legs splayed at odd angles and her hair a crow's nest. Aranya tried to feel as bad for Ritika as she did for the room.

'What happened?' asked Aranya.

'I fell in love with the *worst boyfriend ever.*'

'Listen, Ritika, I would have been really sorry for last night had something happened, but nothing happened between us. I mean I can't even think of it. I just had to talk to Raghuvir and he helped me with it.'

Ritika wiped her tears and drank greedily from the bottle of water Aranya had thrust in her face.

'I know you think I'm like a dumb blonde, don't you?'

'Me? Huh? Not at all,' lied Aranya.

'You're not that good at lying, are you, Aranya? And stop flattering yourself. It's not you why I have had enough of him,' Ritika said, steeling herself. 'I have saved my boyfriends from the likes of you a billion times before.'

'Likes of me?' asked Aranya, trying hard not to get offended.

'The pretentious, intelligent ones? The ones who think everyone around them is a goddamn fool. You think I slept my way into college? I scored 43 marks less than you in the entrance examination. And that's after I did everything fun and crazy one could do in twelfth grade.'

Aranya's chest heaved in anger but her debating instincts kicked in and she kept Ritika from digressing. 'It's not about you and me, Ritika. It's about you and him, isn't it? Do you want to talk about that?'

She felt important, suddenly, like a psychiatrist; she crossed her legs and rested her chin on her knuckles waiting for Ritika to pour her heart out.

Ritika chuckled and shook her head. 'I knew this was going to happen. He was always going to ruin me.'

Ritika started to talk endlessly about Dhruv's capability to make you feel immensely loved, even if it was for a fleeting moment. Ritika told her that no matter how hard she tried to hate him she couldn't. 'Because deep inside, he's a child, a boy, a rebel you want to protect and save but don't know how. Like all the other women in his life, I tried to change him. It was a selfish pursuit, I know that.' Ritika looked Aranya's way. 'I thought to myself, what if I can exaggerate how he loves me, and tone down how much he protects me and our relationship, I will have a perfect guy. I was so close, so close.'

'No offence, but aren't you too young for, like, a perfect guy?' asked Aranya.

'So my love doesn't count because I'm young?' Ritika stared at Aranya as if she was a repulsive, pea-brained lizard.

What Aranya really wanted to tell her was to stay the hell away from Dhruv! Why? She wasn't totally sure about the reason. Was she in love again? No! Was it pity for Dhruv? No, who would pity him? Then what was it? Aranya decided it wasn't the perfect time for monologues.

'I didn't say that.'

'Yes, you did, Aranya. You're one of those, aren't you? Love's for later? When your heart breaks, it feels just the same. It hurts more when you're young and you don't know the in and out of love, when you think it's ideal and incorruptible. For grown-ups, what's love if not a transaction? '

'I'm not one of those,' protested Aranya, suddenly feeling a thousand years old. She added after a pause, something she had heard in every break-up ever filmed, 'You deserve better.'

Ritika laughed and laughed and cried and laughed. 'Do you even know what you're talking about?'

'Didn't you just say he was the worst boyfriend in the world? So obviously you deserve better!'

'But it's still hard not to love him like life itself. I'm sure it's hard for you to understand that. You have never been in love, have you?'

'Why are you making it sound like it's a crime?'

Ritika shrugged. 'Of course it's not.'

Ritika's smiles were now irritating her and Aranya wanted to leave. 'Look, Ritika. All I'm saying is you deserve someone better. Why do you want to change someone you fell in love with in the first place? Which just means you fell in love with the idea of falling in love with him. You fell in love with what you thought you would eventually change him into. Of the little time I have spent with Dhruv, he's the meanest fucking bastard and he's never going to change. If you keep expecting him to change and be in this relationship and toe your line, it's not going to happen. And if you don't know that you can't claim to be in love with him. Stick by your decision of having broken up with him.'

'I don't think I'm that strong.'

'Of course, you aren't. Because it's Dhruv and he can make you feel immensely loved, even if it's for a fleeting moment,' said Aranya and stormed off. She had meant to be sarcastic in that last sentence but she wasn't so, not in the least bit, not at all.

The conversation with Ritika filled her with rage. Ritika didn't know the first thing about Dhruv. What she really wanted to say was 'He doesn't deserve you.' But she had yet to find out what Dhruv deserved and why he deserved anyone at all.

She had just managed to knock her conflicting feelings for that bastard Dhruv out of her head when Ritika came into her room and said, 'You're right. I need to stick by my decision. Dhruv and I aren't meant to be.'

Aranya found herself smiling after she left.

52

Aranya had slept peacefully that night. Little did she know what awaited her the next morning.

She had even smiled in her sleep thinking of the brief conversation she had had with Dhruv.

Aranya had lived the conversation in her head for five hours when she had been rudely awakened by her father banging on the door. 'I HAD WARNED YOU! I HAD WARNED YOU, ARANYA! *Bola tha nazar rahegi tujh par!*' Aranya's father had shouted that morning when he barged into Aranya's room, unannounced.

Aranya sat there wordlessly, rubbing her sweaty palms together, staring at the strewn books and registers her father had brutally torn apart. Her room lay in dismal disarray.

She wanted to cry but the tears didn't come, as if the boiling rage inside had consumed the tears as well. Her face still singed from where Dad had hit her. Her back hurt from when Dad pushed her against the chair demanding why she was still talking to Dhruv.

It wasn't Dad's fault, it was hers. She should have known better. Did she really think her little night out with Dhruv would go unnoticed? Nothing in her wretched life ever went unnoticed, no matter how hard she tried to be invisible!

Aranya had tried to tell Dad about Dhruv, about her hatred or indifference or whatever she felt for him but he had already called her a disgrace. If he weren't her father, he would have called Aranya a whore, a word she had heard her father use for other girls who had boyfriends. She was sure he was thinking the same about her.

So she had let her father hit her. Fighting back would be foolish, she thought.

'Do you think we don't know what you're doing in college? We know everything!' Dad had shouted. 'The warden told us. You were out of the hostel for an entire night, weren't you? WEREN'T YOU?' Aranya could hear girls of her hostel murmuring outside. Dad continued, 'When will you straighten your ways, Aranya, when? *Ya tu hume maar hi daalegi?*' He looked at Mom who had followed him in and stood crying the entire time. Dad had trained his eyes back at Aranya, his finger pointed at her. 'Listen, Aranya, it's not as if you're doing well in your studies. This is your last chance. Do you hear me? If I don't see your name on the merit list, I will cancel your admission and you will be a fucking receptionist somewhere. Bloody disgrace. Are you listening to me? ARE YOU?'

Aranya had nodded. Yet Dad's swinging arm caught her on the left side of her face sending her body careening into the cupboard. Her body slumped like a ragdoll. Her mother screamed and ran to get to her but Dad stopped her and shouted, 'LET HER BE.'

Next, Dad wrested her phone away. Before he left, he repeated the ultimatum, 'If I don't see you at the top of the merit list, don't even think of coming back home.'

Her parents left Aranya sprawled on the floor, staring at herself in the mirror.

You deserve it, Aranya.

No, I don't! What did I do? I did nothing wrong. I went to meet my professor. What's wrong in that?

You also fell in love, Aranya.

I didn't.

Yes, you did. Don't kid yourself. You're in love with Dhruv. That's why you left that night.

I would never love that asshole.

But you do! You so do! And you shouldn't. It isn't allowed. How can you waver from your goal?

What goal are you talking about?

Being like a robot. A very successful robot.

But why should I be that? What would I get out of that?

Because your family wants that, that's why!

Why should I do what my family wants! They don't even love me. I don't want to do what they want. Enough. I don't want to see them again.

Haha. That's bold. But what are you going to do?

I'm never going to see them again!

Haha! How are you going to do that? How are you going to run? Who is going to pay your fees? Three more years, Aranya, three more years.

I'm smart. I will find a way.

That's too optimistic. You can't leave your family, you know that. Even if they hate you, they at least love you more than anyone ever would.

I will find someone to love me and keep me forever. Like Raghuvir. Like Dhruv. They love me.

Till the time they find someone else, yes, they do. But are you willing to take that chance?

Maybe I am. For now I just need to get away from my father.

You wish.

Fuck you.

I'm you.

Mindlessly, she fired up her laptop to complete the assignment that was due the next day. PING. Her mailbox icon vibrated with one new mail.

From: T&P trainingandplacement@dtu.edu.in
To: aranyagupta@gmail.com
Subject: Summer Internship
Dear students,
This is to inform you that AMTECH, Bangalore, will be holding interviews for interns on 31 May 2014. Interested applicants may apply at the following link. http://on.fb.me/1sNmEgX.
The company would hire 1 student only from the first year.
Please attach a scanned copy of your passport with the application.
Regards
Arjun Johar
Training and Placement Department
DTU

She had three months to be battle-ready.

53

'Fuck him, fuck him, fuck him,' shouted Dhruv. He paced around the room, kicked things, threw things, broke stuff and punched walls. 'He's just being fucking melodramatic. I'm sure nothing is going to happen to him.'

'I called the hospital, dude,' said Sanchit. 'He's under treatment.'

'So?'

'He's not going to live for more than a couple of years.'

'A couple of years is a long time,' said Dhruv, pointing a finger right at Sanchit, as if convincing himself and not Sanchit. 'And that bastard said he was dying. He wasn't dying, he might die in a couple of years. There's a big fucking difference between the two. Why all the drama now? Couldn't he just have called me in two years when he was *actually* dying!' Dhruv picked an old beer bottle lolling on the table and smashed it against the wall. 'What, what would have happened? Suddenly it has dawned on him the wrongs he has done and he wants to make up for it! Well, screw him. I'm not going to go to him, sit by his side, listen to his side of the story, cry, forgive his imperfections and hold his hand in his dying days. It fucking won't happen. This isn't a damn movie!'

'Well, not yet.'

'What not yet?'

'It's not a movie yet but it could be if I decide to write about it. It could be a big hit, you know?' remarked Sanchit.

Dhruv smacked Sanchit's head. 'What are you talking about? My father is dying and you think it's a joke?'

'Me? No. You think it's a joke,' said Sanchit, turning serious. 'So what if he slept with hookers? So what if he didn't fight for your mother? So what if you always hated your father? Why shouldn't he get a last shot at loving you? You can spend the rest of your life hating him. He's not going to stop you from doing that, will he? So just go. I'm sure he needs you right now, Dhruv. Stop thinking about yourself for once.'

'. . .'

'I'm trying to make you feel guilty if you haven't noticed.'

'. . .'

'Well, it's already working, Dhruv. No matter how badass you are, right now, you're thinking what if he doesn't see you for the next two years and dies taking your name over and over again. What if he spends every waking second of whatever is left of his life staring at the door, waiting for you? What if he spends every shred of his life crying? And when all he needed was one chance to apologize.'

Dhruv breathed deeply. 'You're manipulating me. I can't fucking believe you.'

'Neither can I. Your father is dying and you're here talking to me.'

Dhruv slumped on the bed, face down, wanting to cry but the tears had dried out years before and said, 'I'm not going.'

Yet six hours later, he was running through the corridors of Eight Hills Hospital looking for room no. 324. When he reached the door, he calmed himself down, pushed the door open and entered the room. His father lay on an uncomfortable bed reading a magazine. There lay a set of machines by his side, not yet plugged in.

'Dad,' Dhruv said. He sat on the seat meant for distraught relatives—crying brothers and wailing sons, daughters and wives. Dad looked just fine. 'You don't look sick.'

'It's something with my liver. Too much drinking, they said. And I told them if it had been too much drinking I wouldn't be here.' Dad laughed and Dhruv failed to see the joke in it.

The words dried up and quite some time passed by before Dad said, 'I'm sorry.' Dhruv had already started to regret his decision to be there. He felt angry if anything at all.

'You kind of should be. For all the shit that you have done and made all of us go through. I just came here because my friends told me I should give you a chance to apologize. And quite frankly, it doesn't feel any different. Seeing you trapped in this bed doesn't make me cry. If anything it makes me fucking happy.'

'Don't swear, Dhruv.'

'You don't have any power over me.'

'I'm your father.'

'Yeah, you fucking were!'

'Don't do that.'

'I'm leaving. This was a mistake,' snapped Dhruv, jumped out of his chair and left the room, still not sure why he even visited him in the first place. Outside, he sat on one of the benches, desperately trying to feel sad about his father's imminent demise but all he could think of was the years of torment he had gone through. Was he being selfish?

He began to think how people cry even when their dogs die and Dhruv was failing to feel that emotion for his own father. How pathetic was that? Why? Why didn't he feel anything? Had even sorrow left him?

He was sitting there, nodding, trying to feel alright about himself when the first tears started to flow. And as if his mind had taken offence, the times he had spent with his father, however little and fleeting, came flooding to his mind in a sepia-tinged montage and he cried and cried and cried.

54

Dhruv had waited for night to come. All that crying outside on the bench turned his heart to mush and he wanted to see his father. Maybe even apologize. But he didn't have it in him to just walk in, sit by his side, and have a heart-to-heart conversation.

Instead, he had decided he would go in late at night when his father would be fast asleep, he would say what he needed to, complain, bicker, curse, abuse and drown him in his frustration.

It was two in the night. The deserted corridors looked straight out of a horror movie. Gingerly, he opened the door again; it creaked like in a cheap Ramsay movie. His father was sleeping.

He sat on the same chair he had sat in in the morning, feeling nothing, absolutely nothing at all but now, a few hours later, he felt like the ten-year-old Dhruv who would cry himself to sleep in his arms. He started to talk.

'Dad. You ruined my childhood. You ruined everything for me. I don't even know if I love you any more,' Dhruv whispered into the night. 'I hate you. That I'm sure of. But thinking of you makes me cry and I don't know how to label that. I have spent days thinking why you would do what you did and I still do hope it would all make some sense some day but it doesn't now. Why didn't you fight for Mom? If not for yourself, then at least for me? I still can't wrap my head around why you slept around after she left. Did you not think about what you were doing to me, Dad? I was little! I was *so* young! Why? Why did you do it? I know you wouldn't have an answer and that's okay. I have learned to live with it. At least you taught me not to trivialize relationships and to take responsibility for my actions by fucking my childhood over.'

He held his head and cried for a few minutes. 'Anyway, Dad, I need to go now. I have college to attend. Oh, by the way, thank you for calling my professor. Thanks.'

Dhruv stood up and turned away when he heard his father voice. 'Stay.'

'. . .'

His father looked at him, not groggy and definitely awake. That sly bastard had listened to the entire thing. He called Dhruv over to sit by his side. His eyes were unnaturally kind. For the first time in years, Dhruv had seen his father sober.

'There's something I need to tell you,' his father said. He held Dhruv's arm, firmly. 'Sit,' he said.

Dhruv sat down.

'I really loved your mother.'

'You sure did. It showed.' Dhruv felt the fury find its roots again.

'I did. I was in love with your mother from the first day I saw her,' Dad said, his eyes liquid. 'But she was never in love with me.'

'That's so typical of you. Still shirking responsibility! Blaming her! That's a cheap shot, Dad. Even for you.'

'Listen to me.'

'Fine,' said Dhruv, leaning far back into the chair, and looking outside the window. The room depressed him.

'We were really young. Our marriage was arranged by your grandparents and we were supposed to fall in love. And I did.' Dad sighed. 'But your mom didn't. Not when we got married and not in the countless days we spent together. But she never complained about it. She was always the good wife. At first, I really tried hard to make her love me as much as I loved her but realized it doesn't work that way. You can't force someone to be in love with you.'

'So you gave up?' asked Dhruv, exasperated, throwing his hands in the air.

'Yes, I did. It was hard not to. Years went by and it started making both of us unhappy, her more than me. I thought things would change when we had you.'

'Did they?' asked Dhruv, leaning forward, obviously interested how his conception was just a ruse to make his parents happier.

'Your mother and I loved you more than life. You brought joy and love into our lives. You were this little cute ball of happiness.' Dad's eyes lit up. 'Those years were the happiest for us, your mother and I. But slowly the sadness, the lack of love crept in again. It took me eight years to realize your mother would never love me. I realized I had to let her go, sooner or later.' He shook his head, a sad smile on his regretful face. 'Can you pass the water?'

Dhruv poured out a glass and gave it to him. 'What are you talking about? You were married. How does anything else matter? You can't just . . . '

Dad started to smile. 'You have to, Dhruv. You have to learn to let people go for their happiness and for your own.'

'So? What did you do?'

'I drove her away, Dhruv. I made sure she would never look back.'

' . . . '

'I slept with women, I started getting drunk more often, I shouted, I screamed and I fought with her. I made her hate me. I made myself loathsome.'

Dhruv listened to it, dumbfounded, trying to make sense of it all.

'She put up with it for a couple of years. But then she found love.'

'That's why you didn't fight for her? Because you actually tried to push her away?'

His father nodded. 'I couldn't see her unhappy any more.' His father laughed sadly at his devious, destructive, stupid, brilliant plan. Dhruv tried to piece together the memories of his childhood.

'Does she know you did this for her happiness?'

'Look at me. Do I look like a man who's strong enough?'

Dhruv couldn't think straight. 'I don't know.'

'Obviously, I told her! I, like a complete fool, told her how much I had sacrificed for her. I went to her place and said this in front of her husband.'

'Why did you do that?' asked Dhruv, looking at his father, the flawed hero.

'I was drunk. And maybe I thought she would fall in love with me seeing me being selfless! Maybe it was all a selfish pursuit.'

'Huh.'

'Men are petty, Dhruv. We need recognition for the sacrifices we make for our women. Your mother never complained about the ten years she had spent with me without a shred of happiness. But I complained every day.' Dad started laughing, slightly at first and then loudly, and Dhruv joined in and they both laughed and laughed and laughed.

55

Aranya had never felt so distracted. It was like her brain was in a blender. There were days she felt helpless and under a lot of pressure. She would see her father's face right in front of her, cursing and tormenting her for the entire two months she would have to spend at home if she didn't get this internship.

She would end up texting Raghuvir and they would stay up all night writing to each other. Not that it meant anything, but it kept her a little sane. She might have slipped a few times though, when she was at her weakest, asking him if *they* were a possibility. Sometimes Raghuvir would say *'Yes'*. But at such times she thought it was out of pity more than anything else . . .

But then one day, things changed.

ARANYA

I miss you in college sometimes.

RAGHUVIR

My sentiments exactly.

ARANYA

Which company have you joined?

RAGHUVIR

You will know soon.

ARANYA

Why such a secret?

RAGHUVIR

Just like that, don't want to jinx it. How's your prep going?

ARANYA

Good. But scared. What if . . .

RAGHUVIR

You won't have to go home. You're good.

ARANYA

*Found a replacement for Smriti yet? *wink**

RAGHUVIR

Haha. No. Not looking for one. Trying to turn over a new leaf.

ARANYA

millions of hearts break Why is the only Casanova from our domain hanging up his boots? Making a compromise for someone?

RAGHUVIR

You're too smart for your own good, Aranya.

ARANYA

TELL ME! Who's it for?

Though Aranya felt infinitely jealous thinking there might be someone else in Raghuvir's life, someone who had convinced him that their relationship could work, she told herself not to feel bad about it. Of course Raghuvir had found someone else.

RAGHUVIR

Shouldn't you be studying?

ARANYA

Fine, if you don't want to tell.

RAGHUVIR

Will tell you if I can keep up with it.

ARANYA

Name, please? Don't keep me hanging!

RAGHUVIR

Don't do this.

ARANYA

Don't want to jinx it?

RAGHUVIR

Exactly.

ARANYA

I would jinx it? Just to let you know that in Tanzania people like me are considered lucky.

RAGHUVIR

☺

ARANYA

Smilies mean you don't want to talk any more, so goodnight.

RAGHUVIR
Goodnight.
ARANYA
#foreveralone
RAGHUVIR
You're funny.

Aranya switched off her phone and got back to her preparations. She told herself not to text Raghuvir ever again, leaving him to his turning over a new leaf by not fucking around with pretty PhD students any more and having found someone who would have a perfect, logical relationship with him. Whatever happened to him thinking of Aranya as an interesting girl? He didn't take long to move on! Men are uniformly disappointing, she thought.

56

The day of the interview for the internship at AMTECH was nearing and she was yet to finish a considerable part of the course. AMTECH traditionally hired unconventional people with varied skill sets. Aranya had won thirty-four debates, not counting the ones she had come second in, and she was a zonal-level TT player. She was sure she would get through.

But despite her apparent nervous excitement, something was amiss. The smart girl she was, it didn't take her long to pin-point it—it was Dhruv's prolonged absence.

Ritika, who looked like shit now and had slowly been recovering from the break-up, told Aranya about Dhruv's father's situation. She had broken down in Aranya's arms, as if she herself were the root cause. 'I wish I was with him right now. I wonder how he's taking it. I haven't been good to him.'

'He will be okay. I'm sure he will call you if he needs you,' said Aranya and quietened her, stroking her like a stray dog, compassionate but still wary of catching rabies.

The thought of Ritika cradling a crying Dhruv was discomforting. Every night she would find a pretext to sneak out and see if Ritika was still in her room. In college, her eyes would follow Ritika to see if Dhruv was back, and if he had found a shoulder to cry on in her. Luckily nothing of that sort happened. She would rather have Dhruv's father die a long, prolonged death, than have him in the college, in Ritika's arms mourning his father's illness/demise.

When Dhruv missed three consecutive assignments, something she had been waiting and planning for, Aranya got the opportunity to talk to Sanchit about Dhruv's prolonged absence.

'I need to talk to him. He has not been submitting assignments. The professors keep asking me and I don't know what to tell them,' lied Aranya.

Sanchit laughed. 'It's not about the assignments. You're just missing him, aren't you? Aww. That's so cute, Aranya. Finally you found your heart beneath your umm . . . err . . . how do I put it without sounding gross or offensive . . . womanly chest?'

Aranya rolled her eyes. 'It's about the assignments. And they are called breasts.'

'Can you say that again for me?'

'Breasts. You're such a child.'

'That sounded so good! And if assignments are all you want, I will do them for him and give them to you by today evening but I know that's not all. There's no harm in saying you miss him. Hell, I miss him, too. He's the only friend I have. And that's when we are not even friends.'

Aranya shrugged like she didn't care. How blatantly Sanchit could proclaim his love for Dhruv, a flawed asshole at best? 'It's about the assignments, Sanchit.'

'I'm your senior, Aranya.' Sanchit lit a cigarette. 'And I was as loved by the professors as you were. I have their numbers on speed dial. Not only do I know that Dhruv's assignments are completed and submitted, but his attendance too is cent per cent. Now I wonder who made that possible.'

Aranya went red in the face; she felt dizzy and embarrassed as hell. 'I . . . I . . . was just helping out.'

'If you have already taken care of them, why are you standing here asking me about Dhruv's attendance and his assignments? Do you think I'm a six-year-old?'

Aranya didn't think there was any merit in continuing the conversation. So she just started to walk away. Sanchit followed her and said, 'He asked about you. Quite a few times.'

'What?'

'Yes, but in the same way you did. He had an even sillier pretext but let's not get into that.'

'What did you tell him?'

'I told him you were distracted and you keep asking about him. I told him I was sure you miss him.'

'Are you crazy? I don't miss him at all,' said Ananya showing fake anger; secretly she was happy about Dhruv missing her.

Sanchit smiled. 'Chill. He didn't ask anything about you and I didn't tell.'

Her heart sank. 'Good,' said Aranya and hurried into the library.

She heard Sanchit chuckle in the background and shout, 'Let me know if you need help doing his assignments. And can you say *breasts* again?'

57

Dhruv's father didn't last two years.

Hell, he didn't last two months. It was all so sudden. One night he was there and the next all that was left of him was white dust. Dhruv lost track of time and often he found it hard to believe that all of it actually happened. Relatives had flown down and suddenly there were so many tears that there were none left for Dhruv.

His mother had cried and so had others. He had not known what to say to his mother when he had met her. They counted days and performed rituals together, both stealing glances at each other, grappling for words they might use. The silence was deafening.

After the fourteenth day, his mother went back to her family. 'Will you be okay?' she had asked Dhruv while leaving and Dhruv had put up a brave front. Dhruv had lived most of his life hating his parents, crucifying them. But the twelve weeks he had spent with his dying father watching movies and reading to him had left Dhruv lurching with an identity crisis. His father took away all the bad memories with him, leaving behind a lump of good ones, reducing him to tears every time he thought about him.

He truly was an orphan now.

'Why don't you call your mother?' Sanchit had asked a number of times.

'What would I say to her, Sanchit? That I have suddenly forgiven her? That I'm sorry I hated her for twelve years but it was my fault? What should I talk to her about? She doesn't know me any more,' Dhruv would say, trying hard not to reduce to a puddle of desperate tears.

Dhruv was most scared of the days to come, the loneliness that would soon follow when the semester ended, when everyone would go back to their happy families and spend two happy summer months. Where would Dhruv go? To that empty house? To his mother's? What would happen to him? Why did he always fucking end up alone?

Dhruv didn't miss a single class. He spent days locked inside his room, studying. Time was slipping by like sand from a closed fist. The semester exams were near. The hostels would be empty after the exams, leaving him alone, he knew that. The loneliness would eat at him. He couldn't go back to an empty house. His mother had offered to host him with her family for the two-month break but it wasn't even an option. *Her family*—the words pierced through his heart every time he even thought of it. He would have to remind himself not to hate his mother now. Suddenly, his chaotic life of hatred had an unsettling stillness to it. Death left behind a stench.

'You don't have to stay in the hostel. You can come back with me,' Sanchit had offered even though Dhruv hadn't shared his fear of being alone in the hostel with him. 'My mom makes the best *bharta*.'

'Get some when you're back,' Dhruv had said. 'Thanks for the offer though.'

'But where are you going to go?'

'I still don't have an answer for that.'

The news of Dhruv's father's death had spread. His classmates didn't know how to respond to it so they changed ways to avoid bumping into him. What do you really say? I'm sorry? How would that change anything?

Ritika had tried talking to Dhruv a few times but Sanchit had asked her to stay away from him. Dhruv had enough on his plate already. Aranya, too, after a few failed attempts to bump into him consciously kept herself away from him. Dhruv didn't want pity; he wasn't even sure what he wanted anyway. Moreover, she would be busy with the exams, Dhruv figured. But he really did fucking want her. Maybe.

The fourth-year students, except Sanchit, were the first ones to leave; the third floor was empty. The day crept close when the first-year students would leave, too. He would be alone once again.

That day Dhruv was in his room revising induction motors when he heard what he thought was a girl shriek from the other room. On further inspection it turned out to be Amit, third-year mechanical, departmental rank three. It was him crying for he had lost his passport and he had until the evening to find it. Dhruv's nonchalance met with a caustic response. The boy shouted. 'What the hell do you mean it doesn't matter? How will I go for the internship? How will I apply? They WANT THE PASSPORT NOW!' He had started crying again and Dhruv thought it was best to leave.

Back in his room, Sanchit was waiting and before he could ask, Dhruv explained his absence. 'The guy in the next room was crying. He has misplaced his passport, so he can't apply for some internship.'

'Oh yeah, that internship has everyone's panties in a bunch. They are asking for passports so it's pretty sure they are looking for a long-term investment, someone they can hire for their headquarters in San Fransisco later on. But what the fuckers don't realize is that they would be ground to death, every rupee strained out of them. But then again, an American sweatshop is better than an Indian one.'

It hit Dhruv like a subway train. Dhruv bundled Sanchit out of the room and opened his college e-mail. The internship was for the exact two months he had been obsessing about. It was in the AMTECH headquarters, a software start-up, in Bangalore, far away from his empty house, from those memories, from the biting loneliness. They had one spot for the first-year students. Today was the last day to apply.

This was exactly what he wanted.

58

Sanchit didn't know whether to be impressed or terrified at Dhruv's ambition to crack the AMTECH interviews. Sanchit hadn't seen him sleep a wink in that month, and every time Dhruv tried to sleep, Sanchit feared he would pass away; cause of death—exhaustion and with traces of depression in the bones.

'Am I ready?' asked Dhruv the day before the interview.

'I taught you but today even I wouldn't go against you.'

'Do you think I can beat Aranya?' asked Dhruv.

'You can beat anyone,' said Sanchit. 'You should sleep now. Tomorrow is your big day, dude.'

Dhruv nodded and went to bed to spend a night of tossing and turning, sweating, the bed sheet sticking to his back, tears flowing freely. He told himself he didn't miss a mother who would calm him down before a big exam the following day;

he didn't need the encouraging words of his father. Sleep evaded him.

Sanchit found himself on the roof that night drinking alone when he spotted Dhruv's arch nemesis, his eternal love, Aranya ambling below with a book in hand. Sanchit followed her.

'Hey?' said Sanchit.

'What are you doing here?' asked Aranya.

'Checking out competition, what else? Dhruv is going against you tomorrow and you should be wary of him.'

'How's he doing now? Haven't seen much of him in college, is he alright?'

'Shouldn't you be more concerned about me threatening you?'

'I don't get threatened, Sanchit.'

'You turn me on,' said Sanchit.

'You're gross.'

'Keep saying that and I will cut out my heart for you.'

'What do you want from me?' asked Aranya.

'I love you, Aranya. The only problem is you're out of my league, and I'm a good friend to Dhruv. So it's my great sacrifice. Forgoing my love so that a great love story can take root.'

'I don't know what you're talking about.'

'Fine. Let's play a little game here, Aranya.' Sanchit faked diabolic laughter and raised an eyebrow for effect. 'You don't love him, do you? So under no circumstances would you let go of the internship for him.'

'No.'

'Because you have a Hitler-like father and you would do anything to run away from him, wouldn't you?'

'How do you know that?' asked Aranya.

'I am God. You will realize that later. But back to the point, what was I saying? Oh yes, the internship. Dhruv needs it or he will have to spend two months in the hostel alone. ALONE. His father just died and he doesn't have a family to go back to. Pretty tough life that kid has. I asked him to come with me but he refused. He's going to be depressed as shit here. He looks suicidal to me.'

'I don't care. I would see him go under a bus.'

'We will know about that tomorrow, won't we?' asked Sanchit.

'Sure, now if you don't mind I have to revise the course for the third time in two days to bolster my already lopsided chance of running your friend into the ground.'

'Damn. You're cruel! Did I mention that his estranged father just died and he has been drowning in depression? Or did you just miss that part?'

Aranya shrugged. 'Just so I know, did you give him the same choice? What did he pick?'

'Maybe I did. Wouldn't you really like it if I told you that?' asked Sanchit and walked away calmly, knowing full well he had destroyed Aranya's night. She would spend the hours battling whether to save Dhruv or save herself.

Love's cruel, thought Sanchit, and it won't be any fun if it's not so. Easy love is no love. Love's not love unless you're laid waste by it, unless you're destroyed by it, ripped apart and scarred for life by it. Puppy love is bullshit, it's for kids, hook-ups and sex. Real love is to see your girl humiliate you by getting into bed with your best friend and enjoying it, and still being with her, knowing it will destroy you and that you will destroy her. Love is a conscious decision to be destroyed. Love is being in a roller coaster without the seat belt, there will be highs and lows, you may be thrown out, trampled beneath the wheels, or thrown up to the heavens.

If you can do that, you can be in love. Otherwise, try again, maybe?

59

Aranya tried out three hairstyles; it was the longest time she had ever given to her hair. She looked good now, she thought, at least presentable. She thought of applying make-up but got into an internal debate—whether she was doing it for herself or the people around her. A quick Google search and YouTube video of John Green told her she was doing it for herself and she found the courage to apply a faint lipstick. Goddamn it. Her lips were chapped. Why did she even try?

She locked the room behind her and joined the minions whom she would mercilessly crush today in the training and placement room. Two sprightly young men walked into the room dressed in polo-neck T-shirts and distressed denims, quite a contrast to the applicants, all of whom were in crisp, suffocating white and black suits.

The two men, Indians but with accents, showed them slides of the offices they were supposed to work in, the cafeteria, the women, the men, and left everyone salivating in the room.

Aranya saw Dhruv walk in and sit in the last row. He was gorgeous in his suit that strained against his arms and chest, yet he looked like shit. While the others in the room were like lambs to slaughter for her, and she would do that with the stoic face of a butcher, she felt sorry for Dhruv.

She would be sad when she defeated him.

She wanted to cuddle him, tell him it was going to be okay, cradle his head in her arms, tell him she loved him, and then bring the knife to his throat and slice it open and cry when he bled dry. She was sure she loved him, for now he didn't look like Superman's Luther, or Batman's Joker, and even with a mean suit on, he was more like a furball, a little pug, harmless and lovable.

The two men left the room and the question papers were distributed. Nervously, she looked around to see if the questions befuddled the applicants, and on seeing people struggle a smile broke across her face and she bulldozed through the question paper. While leaving the room she saw Dhruv vigorously chewing the back of his pencil, sweating, but unlike others, not looking for help from the adjacent table.

The crowd filtered out and the question papers were collected for evaluation. Students milled about near the foyer, nervously and passionately discussing how their qualifying round went. Some of them had given up, others were preparing for the interview. Aranya fed on their nervousness and unpreparedness and hovered around like a dementor, sucking the happiness off people's face by confidently smiling at them.

At a distance sat Dhruv, his knees shaking. He was biting the skin off his nail. Just then one of the seniors put up the list of ten students from the first year who would be interviewed. While others rushed towards it, Aranya saw Dhruv say a little prayer, which wasn't like supposed to happen before Armageddon.

Aranya was through. And so was Dhruv.

The ten students waited in a line outside the room for the interviews to start. A little later, a third man joined the ranks to take the interviews. The students gasped as he shook hands with the other interviewers.

It was Raghuvir.

While passing the students, Aranya saw Raghuvir smile at her from the corner of her eye. Before she could ask what was going on, Raghuvir had already disappeared inside the room.

This was almost unfair. No one else even stood a chance now. Aranya was sure she'd get through and she wasn't as happy as she thought she would be. Raghuvir wasn't supposed to be here. He had said he was leaving soon. What was this then?

Names were called out at random and they were hammered and spit out from the interview room. It was hard to fathom that those innocuous-looking men could inflict so much damage.

They took a break for lunch. Dhruv, Aranya and a classmate battling nervous breakdown were ushered into a room and asked to wait. It took all the might in the world and more for Aranya to not start a conversation with Dhruv but she failed in the end and said, 'It's going to be okay.' She didn't know why she said that. She actually wanted to say, drop out and it will all be okay.

'Easy for you to say, Aranya. You're smart and you're charming. There's no way I'm getting through this. Plus, there's Raghuvir.'

The normalcy of the conversation threw Aranya a little off balance.

'You really want to get this, don't you?' asked Aranya.

'Yes, I do. And so do you,' answered Dhruv.

'I'm going to get it, Dhruv. I'm sorry for whatever happened and I know you need to be out of this college for the summers but I just need this. I really need this.'

'Why are you telling me this?'

'Because you should be prepared, Dhruv. Behind those doors, I'm a queen, and you're not going to beat me. This isn't Temple Run, this is real life and I'm prepared for it and you're not. Just because you studied for a month doesn't mean you have the wherewithal to beat me. I'm not being pompous, Dhruv, I'm being realistic. And you just saw Raghuvir walk in. Who do you think he will choose? Please don't have hopes from this internship. Find something else to do in these two months. Please. I don't want to feel guilty later. I want to tell myself I told you to not have any hopes from this.'

'You wouldn't have to feel guilty, Aranya,' said Dhruv and waved his hand like he didn't care. Aranya felt her heart slowly turn to mush and slip to her knees; she was already guilty.

'Take back your application, Dhruv. You're not going to win this and you're going to hate me for it.'

'I already hate you, Aranya. I don't think there's anything more I can do in that department.'

'No, you don't,' Aranya said.

Dhruv shrugged.

Aranya checked herself. If she were to continue the conversation, she would tell him that she loved him and that would be the end of her.

60

'Can I have a word with you?'

'Me?' asked Aranya. Raghuvir nodded. Dhruv rolled his eyes while the third student threw his hands in the air.

'This interview was clearly fixed,' whispered the third boy in Dhruv's ear.

Aranya got up, smoothed her skirt nervously, and left with Raghuvir, fully aware of Dhruv's eyes following her every move.

'What is it, Sir?' asked Aranya.

'Come with me,' said Raghuvir, reaching for her. Raghuvir led Aranya by her hand to the steps of the training and placement department. He sat exactly where he had the night of the Freshers' Party, the night they first met. Aranya kept standing, unsure and a little angry at the preferential treatment.

'Sit,' he said.

Aranya complied, sitting away at a comfortable distance. 'Sir, this is not correct. The rest of the students will think you have a partial attitude towards me. Is that why you never told me which company you had joined? Are you doing it out of pity for me, Sir?'

'How does that matter, Aranya?' A bunch of students walked past them, squinting, murmuring. Aranya looked away from them, pretending she was invisible. She waited for them to turn around the corner.

'It does. My win won't be warranted if it's not won with total honesty,' argued Aranya.

'And where has your honesty taken you, Aranya? This whole thing, this entire interview is dishonest,' confessed Raghuvir now catching her gaze. 'Interviewing first-year students for a paid internship was my idea from the very beginning. It's no secret to the college authorities why I have come here. I have come back for you. I'm turning over a new leaf.'

'But . . .'

'I kept thinking about you after you left that day. Frankly, at first, I wasn't confident about you or even me, that we can do this—you and me giving a shot at being together. But then I thought why not? The belief only got stronger when I told you I was trying to turn over a new leaf, and I was no longer looking for replacements for Smriti, and you stopped texting me. Not one text!'

'A new leaf? I thought you had moved on! That you had found somone!'

'Ha! No, I hadn't. And that's when I thought we might be meant to be together. We are both strong-willed, ambitious people, Aranya. And I have seen how difficult it is to find someone who gets you. So that's why I'm here. To turn over a new leaf and give it a shot.' Raghuvir took her sweaty hand into his. 'You and me, in a different city than this, away from the prying eyes of your parents. Who knows? Maybe you will find love?'

Words eluded Aranya. The last time she had strayed from her path hadn't ended well. What were the ramifications of this daring proposal? What would she tell her parents? Would she hide it? If not, what would they say? Would they burn her? Mutilate her? Or should she not tell them? Ever?

'I don't know what to say to this, Sir. You're asking me to lie to my parents again. I'm not sure I can do that.'

'I'm asking you no such thing. I am asking you to tell them everything.'

'You're joking, Sir. You don't—'

Aranya felt sick in the stomach just imagining the scenario. But then again, would it be so bad? Wouldn't her father be happy to offload his burden on someone else who was willing to carry the responsibility?

'I can't promise you much, Aranya, but I do promise that I will put all the work that's required to make this work. Persistence is one thing I have learnt from having spent years staring at unsolvable equations.'

'I'm not an equation, Sir.'

'You're not, but love's an equation. You put in the right variables and you win. Finally, your parents and you can breathe easy, mend your bridges; you can probably even show me off to your friends and cousins, that is if I'm not too old or nerdy,' Raghuvir chuckled. 'And we can work together on whichever project I work on. We will be a power couple in our field,' said Raghuvir, his eyes lighting up.

'I don't know what to say about it, Sir. I'm overwhelmed.'

'Did I say too much?'

'No—'

'I just thought you would be happy hearing this. Because that day . . .' His voice trailed off and his shoulders drooped. This was the sweetest thing anyone had ever done for her. Why was she being difficult?

'Of course I'm happy. I'm very happy,' said Aranya.

'Your face says something entirely different.'

'It's just that I'm overwhelmed at what you're doing for me. It's a lot to think about,' said Aranya, rummaging through a million thoughts clamouring in her mind. After all, Raghuvir did call love an equation which you can manipulate to get the best results. Love was always supposed to mean passion, happiness, disappointment, depression, exhilaration, but in Raghuvir's version of love, it meant comfort and convenience. Shouldn't Aranya be happy with just that? Beggars can't be choosers after all

'You can take your time,' said Raghuvir, and as if on cue he looked at his watch. 'I need to go now. Three more kids to interview. Best of luck, Aranya.'

'You too, Sir.'

'Raghuvir.'

Raghuvir patted Aranya, got up and left. Aranya felt all the questions drown out till just one of them bobbed to the surface, begging to be answered, the promise of acceptance and a new life, Raghuvir, with the uncertain possibility of love—Dhruv. In her heart, thinking about Raghuvir already meant betrayal of what she had begun to feel for Dhruv.

She got up and walked towards the room, the ferocity of her feelings for Dhruv, hatred or love, fully hitting her. She saw the third boy leave the room for his interview.

'Best of luck,' she whispered to the boy. The boy didn't answer and walked straight to the interview room.

Aranya turned to the door behind which Dhruv sat.

She would ask Dhruv, the only boy she now believed she had always been in love with, if he wanted her to stay with him or leave forever. It was time to see if the boy who fought for everything would fight for her. It was her last chance at the kind of love she wanted to experience.

It was time for Dhruv to stand to the test. If Dhruv failed, Aranya would have to relegate herself to a life where love's just another set of rules written on a paper, understandable, mediocre, compromised, dull . . .

61

Dhruv saw Aranya push the door open rather lazily after her conversation with Raghuvir, as if lost somewhere. To mask his concern he spat out angrily, 'So do you have the job yet or not? Finally your sycophancy seems to have paid off, Aranya. Congratulations! You didn't even have to interview.'

Aranya didn't answer. She walked slowly to her seat and sat down, her skirt crushed beneath her thighs. She fidgeted with her pen, opening the cap, closing it. Click. Click. Silence. Click. Click.

'The interview of that boy is taking long, isn't it?' asked Dhruv after ten minutes of piercing, irritating silence.

Aranya clenched her jaws and put on her poker face. She wouldn't react, she told herself. She would keep the facts and choices open in front of Dhruv and wait for his reaction. 'Raghuvir proposed to me. Sorta.'

'What?'

'He said we could try being in a relationship,' said Aranya, a little loudly, her voice still stripped of any expression, like a mean lawyer.

Dhruv felt his stomach grumble. 'You're kidding, right?' Dhruv was in half a mind to grab Aranya, tie her up, and take her away from anyone who might stake a claim on her.

'He said he would talk to my parents, make everything okay. He said he will be with me for good. I don't think he is going to kid about such a thing. He was very serious about it.'

'Are you out of your mind?' said Dhruv. 'You're talking nonsense right now. You're imagining things. He would never say that. You know his history with all those women. He's never leaving that for you.'

'He would. He's getting his act together. And if he has decided it, he will do it. Raghuvir will make everything all right for me,' she said and she looked at Dhruv. 'He said that. Quite a few times actually.'

'You're kidding.'

'I'm not, Dhruv. He said it to my face. He's mature enough to think before he says what he says. He's out there waiting for my reply and I'm still thinking what to say to him,' said Aranya. Her matter-of-fact tone angered Dhruv. Why the hell was she asking him? He was not going to be a part of her mathematics about whether she should choose him or not.

'So tell him what you want!'

'What do you think I should tell him?' asked Aranya, holding Dhruv's gaze, careful enough to keep her voice's interrogative tone alive.

'Whatever you feel like doing. Why are you asking me?'

'You have nothing to say about it? Nothing? No jokes? No wisecracks? Nothing to humiliate me? Where did all that hatred go? Because frankly, Dhruv, if I leave this room and tell him that I'm going to be with him for the rest of my life, I'm going to win our game of cat and mouse. You will lose. Are you ready for that?'

Dhruv hesitated. 'Okay, you want to know what I think about it? Well, I can't wait for you to leave and have little ugly, penguin babies with him!' Dhruv laughed nervously and looked away, not wanting to dwell in that thought.

Aranya slumped back into her chair, defeated. 'So you think I should say yes?'

Dhruv nodded reluctantly. 'Yes,' he said. Dhruv had to act right now. He had to tell her he loved her and keep her from going away. But the words dried up in his mouth. What could he possibly say?

'You're right, Dhruv. Probably this is the first time we concur on something. It's the right thing to do. My father would lovingly hand me over to him. After all, they thought I would die alone in some hole after putting them through the shame of having an unmarried daughter. Of course, this is the right thing to do. Thank you, Dhruv. Do you think this would be my last chance for a normal, happy life?'

'Why would you ask me that?' snapped Dhruv, flipping open a book, staring at random pages, his heart slowly breaking.

'Because you would know, Dhruv. You are the only one outside my family who has been capable of giving me indescribable pain. You're the only one who has destroyed my life—twice,' said Aranya, her eyes welling up.

Dhruv wanted to tell her he loved her, but how could he do that? He had lost every right to wrest her away from certain happiness. 'I think you're right. Raghuvir is your last chance at happiness. I think he might be a terrible choice of a man to be with but he's your chance at happiness.'

The door opened again. Aranya was called for the interview.

'Best of luck,' said Dhruv.

'I don't need it,' Aranya answered and left the room.

62

Dhruv sat staring at the ceiling, evaluating his options. There were a few more companies that offered internships, but none of them were paid. He could take one in a smaller city like Gwalior or Bhubaneswar and wait it out there for these two months.

His train of thought was broken when Sanchit came barging into his room, shouting. 'What the hell did you just do?'

Dhruv ignored his presence, instead fired up his laptop, and started to compare rentals of Gwalior.

Sanchit slapped the laptop down and asked him again. 'What did you do in the interview? I am asking you something.'

'I didn't take it,' said Dhruv, still not making eye contact. He picked up the sports magazine lying near the bed and flipped through it.

'I know that, Sherlock. WHY DIDN'T YOU?' asked Sanchit.

'There wasn't any point, okay?' snapped Dhruv, meeting Sanchit's eyes. 'Raghuvir was there. He wanted to take Aranya and that's why the company was picking first-year students. Got your answer? Now get out of the room and leave me the fuck alone. I need to masturbate.'

'So why are you getting so pissed off?'

'Because you're in my face right now!' shouted Dhruv. 'Get out!'

'Not before I tell you what I wanted to say. A) You're my most disappointing student and you're not getting that favour ever again and B) apparently, Aranya screwed up so bad in her interview that the other two interviewers sent placement coordinators looking all over for you.'

Dhruv closed the magazine. 'What are you talking about?'

'My highly placed sources tell me she froze in the interview. Not one answer came out of her! NOT ONE.'

'Okay.'

'Wonder why that would happen?' asked Sanchit.

'It must be the pressure,' dismissed Dhruv.

'Pressure? Aranya? That girl was born in a pressure cooker, dude. Pressure's a way of life for her. Don't you think for a moment that she did it intentionally? You watch a lot of soaps, don't you? Think? Hmmm?'

'Why would she do that?' asked Dhruv, the question directed towards himself rather than Sanchit.

'Maybe because if she did choose to take the internship, she would lose you forever? Maybe the girl is in love with you? Making sense?'

'That's bullshit,' snapped Dhruv.

'That's only my theory, Dhruv. You can choose not to believe it. I just want to know why you wouldn't believe the theory.'

'BECAUSE I CAN'T FUCKING GIVE HER WHAT RAGHUVIR CAN!' shouted Dhruv.

Sanchit pumped his fist, a creepy smile swept across his face. 'I knew it!'

'Huh?'

'I know you so well I think we should date.' He walked up to Dhruv and pulled up a chair. 'I understand, man. Dhruv, the eternal lover, backing down, sacrificing his love for a better life for the girl. So noble.'

'You think I should pursue her? What good would come out of that?' asked Dhruv, introspecting.

'For once, Dhruv, I think you're doing the right thing. The girl deserves a break. And no matter how much I love you, I think you make for an awful boyfriend. I don't think Aranya can take another failed relationship.'

'Glad to see your confidence in me.' Dhruv smiled weakly.

'Don't be gloomy,' said Sanchit and tapped his head. 'It's fucking brave what you're doing.'

'It's not brave. It's cowardly.'

'Two sides of the same coin, my friend. Love's like going to war, Dhruv. Those men with medals strapped to their chests aren't brave. They are afraid to get killed. So instead they kill. You're just saving collateral damage here. Taking a bullet for her. You should be proud of yourself.'

'Shouldn't you be advocating for me? Pushing me to go, get the girl who could be my only shot at love?'

Sanchit laughed heartily. 'If it would have been any girl other than her, I would have. But I love Aranya too. Don't forget that. And I would not see any harm come to her. And you, my best friend, are poison.'

'Fuck off.'

'As you say, Dhruv,' said Sanchit. He got up, saluted Dhruv, and left the room. 'But if Raghuvir is hanging up his boots at being the perpetual philanderer he must have thought it through. Goodnight.'

Dhruv pulled the blanket over himself and in the darkness he thought about how much, if at all, Aranya was in love with him.

63

Aranya sat on the bench outside the interview room, crying. Inside, she could hear Raghuvir arguing her case, pushing the two interviewers into hiring her even though Aranya hadn't answered a single question correctly. Raghuvir had prodded her, asked her to take a break, relax, have a glass of water, but nothing had helped.

She had been too distracted by the thought of the interview taking her life in a direction she hadn't had the time to think about. She couldn't think of anything else but Dhruv. What the hell was she doing? She was a pathetic, weak wreck.

It must have looked like she deliberately tanked it.

She held her head in her hands and cried. What did she want? Dhruv was a closed chapter. Didn't she already see that first-hand? Why was she still holding on to the thought inside? Life had thrown a great opportunity her way and she had spilled it.

The door opened and Raghuvir walked out looking for her. He stood tall in front of her, hands on his waist, angry but controlled.

'What happened in there, Aranya?'

'I don't know,' sobbed Aranya.

'Listen, Aranya, I dragged them all the way from Bangalore so that they could hire you and not only did you embarrass me inside, you ruined the chance of us being together. I NEED to know what happened inside,' muttered Raghuvir angrily, his eyes burning.

Raghuvir rolled his eyes, turned and slammed the wall with his palm. 'Damn it.' He breathed deeply to calm himself. 'Okay. There's nothing to worry. We can still make it. Dhruv didn't take the interview so you just need to beat that halfwit boy we interviewed before.' He sat on his haunches in front of Aranya and took her hand into his. 'We are going to be fine. I'm going to talk to them and we will take the interview again. Just stop crying. I will make it okay, all right?'

Aranya nodded, tears still flowing abundantly, and all she could think about was Dhruv and his running away from the interview. She stopped crying when she saw her phone ring. It was her father. Raghuvir prodded Aranya to take the call.

'Hello? Aranya? How did the interview go?' asked the father, without any pleasantries.

'I . . . I . . .'

'THINK BEFORE LYING TO ME, ARANYA. I'm warning you,' shouted the father, his deafening voice audible to Raghuvir.

'There's . . . another . . . round left,' stammered Aranya.

'Huh? Even after warning you, you're still lying to me. I talked to the dean. He told me you said nothing in the interview. NOTHING! Why? I want an answer, Aranya, or I will drag you home and never let you leave the house. I had warned you. No more chances.'

Raghuvir snatched the phone from Aranya. 'Hello, Sir. This is Prof. Raghuvir.'

'What do you want?'

'I'm the one interviewing your daughter. I also happen to be the professor with whom Aranya was caught on tape. I am talking to you to assure you that she did nothing wrong that day or even today,' said Raghuvir authoritatively.

'But—'

'I assure you that she will get the internship today. I will personally make sure she gets through the interview. We hit a snag during the interview process. We thought of her as a fourth-year student as opposed to a first-year student. Your daughter is very talented and will be an asset to the company. Aranya has never intentionally broken a rule or done anything in the college that would disgrace you or your family and would never do so in the future. She was a victim of circumstances and of college politics. If you ever have any doubts about her activities, you can call me. If you have any doubts about my credibility, I will have someone send over my qualifications and my body of work. If you still doubt my character or my intentions towards your daughter, I can share with you the contact numbers of my parents and you can have a word with them. They know about my friendship with your daughter. I bear no ill intention towards her. She's safe with me. And she would do nothing without your permission.'

There was no answer from the other side. Aranya, gobsmacked, thought the line was cut. But then her father spoke in a tone which wasn't angry or furious, just functional, 'Text me the number of your parents. And pass the phone to Aranya.'

'Gladly, Sir.'

Raghuvir gave the phone to a scared Aranya who put the phone to her ear. 'Hello?'

'Best of luck for the interview,' said her father.

Click.

Aranya looked at Raghuvir, not knowing how to thank him. This was the sweetest gesture she had ever seen from her father.

'What do you think he thought about me?' asked Raghuvir, smiling now, a far cry from his serious self moments ago.

'I think he found the person he can pass on the baggage to,' said Aranya, and smiled weakly, thinking of how pathetic and predictable her father was.

'Don't say that, Aranya.'

'I'm your responsibility now. He's sure to call your parents.'

'They know about you,' said Raghuvir.

'You keep surprising me, Sir.'

Raghuvir smiled. 'There's no surprise there, Aranya. Everything's got to fit in if we have to make this work. Okay, now you wait here. I need to convince them for another interview,' said Raghuvir and held her hand. 'Give it your best shot this time.'

'I don't seem to have a choice now, do I?' Aranya nodded, still thinking how Raghuvir always kept repeating the words 'compromise', 'let's make it work', 'hard work', like relationships were the most unnatural, forced things people got into.

64

This would be the exact moment when Dhruv would have been practising mind relaxation techniques if he knew any. Pacing around the room hadn't helped. Breaking the chair only resulted in a splinter lodging itself in his thumb, making him angrier. His laptop was too expensive to send flying out of the window.

Fuck noble. Because right now all he wanted to do was smash Raghuvir's face with a hammer and kidnap Aranya. Being sacrificial and doing the right thing wasn't quite working out for him.

There was a knock at the door.

'FUCK OFF, SANCHIT.'

'It's me,' said a girl's voice.

Dhruv rushed to open the door. It was Ritika in a sweatshirt and loose trackpants, looking sorry.

'What are you doing here?' barked Dhruv, ushering her inside the room, looking left and right to check if someone had seen her come in.

'I'm miserable without you,' said Ritika, her voice quivering, her fingers trembling like a drug addict's. 'I think we can build our relationship again. These two months might be exactly what we need.' She stepped closer and kept her hand on Dhruv's chest.

'You're patching up with me?'

'I think so,' said Ritika, her face hovering close to Dhruv's.

'The last time didn't end so well. I would rather not be dumped in full public view again,' said Dhruv, thinking what was the worst that could happen. He would lose the love of a girl he didn't really love. He had been through it before and it wasn't exactly painful. This could be the perfect rebound. Not that he would get over Aranya. Eight years hadn't changed anything. But then, two months couldn't hurt now, could it? he thought.

'Let's hope it doesn't come to that,' said Ritika and kissed Dhruv who kissed her back.

They stripped each other off their clothes. Dhruv pulled off the bed sheet, stained with month-old food gravies, man juice, alcohol, dried protein shakes, and pushed Ritika on to the mattress. He found the mind relaxation technique he had been looking for.

He fucked Ritika's brains out.

65

Raghuvir argued, fought, shouted, and got Aranya another crack at the interview. He left the room and found the bench empty.

Shit. He fetched his cellphone and frantically dialled her number.

On the other side of the campus, the phone rang in Aranya's trembling hand. She put it on silent and skipped up the stairs to reach the corridor where Dhruv's room was.

It was a leap of faith and made zero sense but she needed to tell him she loved him. He needed to know or she would forever be troubled by 'What If I Had Told Him?' She owed herself a better love story, an extraordinary love story rather than the one on offer. As she sprinted along the corridors she imagined Dhruv being shocked, then overwhelmed, going down on his knees, confessing his love for her, apologizing for everything he had done and would do, and then fight off Raghuvir, her tyrannical parents, her annoying brother and take her away and keep her for himself. She was smiling as she thought of this fantasy. Butterflies waged wars in her tummy. Could this actually happen? The more she neared Dhruv's room the more she started to believe in it. Why wouldn't it happen after all? This was going to change everything. Things would get messy, ugly, irreparable, but that's how love works, isn't it? She breathed deeply. She was ready for it.

She stood at the door of Dhruv's room and knocked.

'Go away,' shouted Dhruv.

She knocked again.

'GO AWAY!'

She knocked harder. She could hear shuffling inside. Her heart leapt. She would keep it short and simple.

The door was opened by Dhruv, shirtless, which distracted Aranya for a few seconds.

'Who's that? What's she doing here?' said a voice from behind.

Aranya, who had imagined the worst by now, peeked behind Dhruv's shoulder to see Ritika hiding her naked body behind a bed sheet. Damn. No. No. No. No. No. No. NO. NO. NO. NO.

Aranya ran as fast as her legs could take her. She was hurtling towards the training and placement department like a slingshot comet, trying not to cry when she became aware of Dhruv almost strolling and yet overtaking her.

'Just. Stop.'

'Get lost.'

'What were you doing there?' asked Dhruv, blocking her way.

'Dhruv, you need to get out of my way.'

'Fine,' said Dhruv and moved out of her way. Aranya walked past. 'GO! HAVE FUN WITH THE PROFESSOR!'

Aranya turned, furious, tears threatening to stream down her face. 'Fun? Me? And what was that that was happening back there? What were you doing, huh?'

'That was me and Ritika. I think I can allow myself that since you're running away with your knight in shining armour,' said Dhruv.

'Oh? You're blaming me? I'm at fault here because I'm trying to run away from my godforsaken life? Because I'm trying to corner the little bit of happiness that I can?'

'You took the easy way out, Aranya.'

'I took the easy way out? Me? DO YOU EVEN FUCKING KNOW WHAT I HAVE GONE THROUGH, DHRUV? Don't you dare say that I took the easy way out! I told you what Raghuvir had offered and I told you what I was thinking and you did nothing. NOTHING!' said Aranya and charged at Dhruv. She held him by the collar and shook him, a lone tear streaking down her flushed cheek. 'AND IT WAS ME WHO CAME TO YOUR ROOM RIGHT NOW TO TELL YOU I LOVED YOU! I ALWAYS HAVE! I was giving up the only shot at happiness to be with you. To give it a shot! Hoping you would leave your stupid girls behind, and be for me what you have been for them. Someone who would protect me. But what do I see? You in bed with a girl you don't even love, Dhruv. And you know what, maybe it's my fault. It's always the fault of the girl because she looks to the boy to love her, save her, protect her, and do everything she could do on her own. ENOUGH. No more, Dhruv. You have been in my head, screwing it for years, but this is enough. You're no longer a part of my life.' She let go of his collar. 'I will decide my own destiny, like I have always done. And you will rot with girls like her for the rest of your life. You're weak, Dhruv, you're fucking weak. And you're only going to get worse from here when you see me lead a perfect life! Bye, Dhruv. Hope to not see your face again. And if I do, I hope it's one of a defeated, broken man.'

She turned and started to walk away. Dhruv stood there, frozen. He gathered himself, and shouted, 'You're going to defeat me? You? Remember this moment you threatened me.'

She turned.

Dhruv continued. 'I am going to fucking crush you, Aranya. Because after all, you chose Raghuvir over me before I chose Ritika. You were taking that job up! What damn choice did I have?' The threat from Dhruv, unlike other times, seemed hollow and unconvincing, and even Dhruv didn't believe in it.

Aranya laughed like she had lost it. 'I love it how you conveniently pegged it down to a timeline. Who chose whom first? You know what, Dhruv? I feel bad about myself for having ever loved you. You know what's really funny? Or sad? Or pathetic? Right up till now, before you said you still want to crush me, I thought I would forgive you. I was telling myself that I will overlook how I saw you and Ritika right now, I would think of it as an outburst and move on. Dhruv, who fought for everything, if only you had fought for me even a little bit, even right now, I would have forgiven you. All I wanted to see was a little bit of that anger, that fight in you which you show for others! But yeah, I guess I have learned my lesson. Why on earth was I expecting anything from you? Thank you, Dhruv. Thank you for teaching me everything you have.' She shook her head and laughed at Dhruv like he was a pathetic loser.

Calming herself down, she caught his gaze, lifted her arm, and flashed her middle finger to Dhruv. 'I have never lost,' said Aranya and walked away.

Later that evening, the interviewer thanked Raghuvir for having bulldozed them into giving Aranya another chance; her performance was off the charts. She was handed the internship on a silver platter and she left for Bangalore three days later.

66

From: <aranyagupta@gmail.com>
   To: <royDhruv@gmail.com>
   Subject: To make you feel little and inconsequential
   Attached: 242WOOAR12
   242WOOAR13
   242WOOAR15
   242WOOAR16

Hi Dhruv,
   This mail is in reply to the threat you had isuued when I left. Your words were, 'You're going to defeat me? You?' Remember this moment . . . 'I'm going to fucking crush you, Aranya.'
   Since that clearly hasn't happened, I thought I would mail you and keep you updated on what has happened in the past one month and how badly you have failed in your pursuit.
   I hope you're in the worst of health. I sincerely imagine your insides to be rotting from the steroids you might have chosen to inject yourself with to maintain that useless body of yours.
   Oh, I digress.
   I'm not mailing to textually assault you. It's to make you feel little and inconsequential as the subject line of this mail says.
   As I sit on this really expensive recliner Raghuvir bought for me from Home Depot, I have to admit that at first I was sceptical whether moving on would be easy. But surprise, surprise! It was easier than the first calculus question I solved back in class nine.
   Though what remains is this lingering feeling of not having exacted my revenge yet and hence this mail.
   You can choose to stop reading this mail right now because what follows is a picture of my perfect life right now.

Raghuvir and I moved into two flats opposite to each other on the twenty-third floor of a building. I would add a celebratory wink after that sentence but you know where I'm going with it.

The flat is paid for by the company, which has taken an immense liking to me. I finally feel at home. My brains are respected here, feared, and everything else comes later. I have been doing great and I think I have a good shot at getting a job here and working under Raghuvir. Haha! Get the pun? Working under him? Get it? Get it?

Raghuvir is a man unlike you. He takes care of me. He's working on me with a welding flame and a sledgehammer, chipping away at the walls around me, trying to make me fall in love, making this relationship work. Soon, I think both of us will love the shit out of each other. Persistence, as he insists, is one of his strongest suits, and I think it's working.

Please also find attached with the mail a couple of pictures of us, Raghuvir and I, hugging, slightly drunk from the party Raghuvir hosted last Saturday where he showed me off as his girlfriend. GIRLFRIEND.

My parents seem to be extremely happy for me suddenly. My mother constantly tells my brother to type out recipes and send them to me so that Raghuvir remains impressed by my culinary skills. My mother thinks that food will keep Raghuvir ensnared.

I share those recipes with Raghuvir and he cooks them for me. Also sending two pictures of when he cooked elaborate meals for me. I haven't used filters on any of the pictures. He's a great cook and sometimes he cooks naked.

Until next time.

Bye!

Aranya

(The happiest girl in the world)

She hit the SEND button and shut down the laptop. It had been a month and Dhruv hadn't followed up on his counter-threat of '*I'm going to fucking crush you, Aranya.*' This had started to bother Aranya. Dhruv couldn't have so easily moved on with his life after wreaking havoc in hers. Things had to go her way, one way or the other.

It was time she made her move. She was not going to lose. She wasn't giving up on Dhruv so easily.

In the kitchen, Raghuvir was fastidiously trying to whip up something for their dinner that night.

'So what's on the menu today?' asked Aranya, smiling coyly. Raghuvir instinctively grabbed her by the waist and kissed her lightly on the lips. Even after a month from their first kiss, Aranya was taken by surprise every time. Why would Raghuvir kiss her after kissing so many women who were so much prettier than her?

Off late, things had moved beyond kissing. Three nights out of four, they would share a bed and sleep next to each other. And on some nights, they would have sex. She was yet to learn to enjoy it. Most of the times she would be too conscious, too aware of the mechanics of sex, the stripping of clothes, way too many limbs, hair, skin, sweat, and the glaring prospect of being disappointing, to indulge in the pleasure of it. But she would soon enjoy it, she was sure. She was just behind in the learning curve, that's all.

'The guys at the company are really excited at your work,' said Raghuvir. The palak paneer was ready and he served it for them. Off late, he had started to ration what Aranya was eating. She had already lost a couple of kilos.

Aranya smiled weakly, a forced smile, something that signified she wasn't too happy with what he had just said. Raghuvir, concerned, held her hand just like she knew he would. 'I'm still talking about it with my seniors.'

'You say the same thing every day, Raghuvir.'

'It's just been a month, Aranya. These things take time and you're just an intern right now.'

'I'm not pushing you, Raghuvir. I'm doing what I'm supposed to do. What you asked me to do. Not let go of my ambition. We are a team now. We have to work together to get to our dreams. I just expect support. I hope you know I'm being reasonable.'

'Of course you are. I wouldn't expect anything different.'

Aranya ate silently, not satisfied with the answer. For the last two weeks Aranya had been pushing Raghuvir to talk to his seniors about the possibility of a college transfer for Aranya.

The deal was simple.

AMTECH would pay the tuition fee for Aranya's engineering studies in a foreign university for the next three years. In return, Aranya would sign a ten-year bond with the company. And to get there, Aranya had been putting in nineteen-hour workdays. She was quite talked about among the senior management. But their decision about the college transfer was still pending.

'I trust you,' said Aranya.

'Though as I said I would rather not have you leave India. I wish you could stay back for a couple of years. We could shift together,' Raghuvir said.

'I know that. But two years isn't a long time, Raghuvir. And eventually, you will be there too. You have to know I just can't go back to my college. For the first time in my life I feel happy about this,' said Aranya, looking around the house. 'After another month of this, three years of that college will be hard for me to take. I want to be away from my family and those kids at college.'

Raghuvir nodded and ate in silence. After a while, he asked, 'It's about that boy, Dhruv, isn't it?'

It wasn't the first time Dhruv had come up in the conversations. Just a few days back, Raghuvir had caught Aranya Googling his name. 'I only harbour hatred for him. I want him to die,' Aranya had said, wrapping her arms around Raghuvir, who had gotten a little suspicious.

'I'm with you now and that's all I care about. I have had it with people like him. I don't want to be around him. I won't be able to take it, Raghuvir. It's too much negativity! Him, my parents, everything about that college and that city reminds me of my shortcomings. I want to feel normal for a while. I want a new life. And I want it with you.'

'Okay. I will talk to them tomorrow. You will not have to go to that place again.'

Aranya put her arms around Raghuvir and thanked him.

67

Aranya was in her bedroom that night, making last-minute changes to a presentation due the next day, when her phone beeped. Raghuvir stirred in his sleep. She put the phone on silent and waited for Raghuvir to reach REM sleep again.

DHRUV

That mail was probably the most juvenile thing ever.

ARANYA

Look who's talking.

And I was updating you about current events.

DHRUV

You're pathetic. It made me laugh. ☺

ARANYA

I know you better than that, Dhruv.

DHRUV

?

ARANYA

You were in love with me for eight years. You're not one who moves on so quickly.

DHRUV

Maybe I did. I found someone.

Aranya hesitated a little bit. It felt like someone had wrapped a barbed wire around her heart and was tightening it.

ARANYA

Please tell me the name you're going to take is Ritika.

DHRUV

?

ARANYA

Please?

DHRUV

It's Ritika.

ARANYA

LOL.

DHRUV

What the fuck?

ARANYA

LOL.

DHRUV

What's wrong with you?

ARANYA

You're not in love with her.

DHRUV

Of course I am.

ARANYA

And if you're trying to make me jealous, it's an epic fail.

DHRUV

Obviously, you're jealous.

ARANYA

LOL.

DHRUV

It's probably because I haven't told you how pretty she is. Also, just ONE colour. AND REALLY THIN.

Aranya wanted to scream at the phone, fling it against the wall and stomp on it. She felt herself drowning in anger. She closed her eyes, pressed down on the screen of the phone till it creaked, breathed heavily till she calmed down. Her brows furrowed. She texted.

ARANYA

That reminds me. I'm not a virgin anymore. ☺ *Raghuvir is quite good too.*

It worked. There was a time lag between the two texts. Dhruv was so predictable. Obviously. It had to hurt. Aranya could almost see Dhruv frown on the other end.

DHRUV

Good for you.

Aranya clicked a selfie of her leaning over a sleeping Raghuvir's body and sent it to him with a message.

ARANYA

1 image attached

I think I'm going to do it again.

DHRUV

You're still as ugly.

1 image attached

The picture Dhruv sent was of Ritika and Dhruv in the gym, flexing their biceps. Ritika wore tight yoga pants and a sports bra and she looked beyond fabulous.

ARANYA

I see two men in the picture.

DHRUV

Fuck you.

ARANYA

Fuck you.

DHRUV

And for a feminist you do make a big deal out of losing your virginity. No one cares.

ARANYA

No one except you. Goodnight.

68

Dhruv couldn't sleep for the rest of the night. He paced around the room, punched walls and nursed his knuckles, watched porn and masturbated unsuccessfully, went for a run, but sleep still evaded him.

Despite his threat, Dhruv hadn't contacted her for a month. It had taken all his will to not do so and be noble. But today, that ship had sailed. He had to send that text. It ended rather badly for him.

He was tired now, but whenever he closed his eyes he could clearly see Aranya pouncing on Raghuvir, stripping him, feasting on him, all the while looking straight into Dhruv's eyes and laughing. He would never get that image out of his head. He turned on his laptop.

From: <royDhruv@gmail.com>
To: <aranyagupta@gmail.com>
Subject: Regret, Sadness, Love

Hi Aranya,

You know how to play your cards. And so do I.

You knew that once you told me what you had done with Raghuvir I wouldn't ever be able to get it out of my head, didn't you? Obviously, you did. You know how shallow I am by now, don't you? Or have you always known?

It's time I accept defeat.

I love you.

Always have. Sometimes I have hated you more than anything else in my life, but I have always loved you as well.

I have half a mind to come barging into that bedroom of yours and fling Raghuvir outside the window and take what's mine. YOU. It's been a long time coming. You should have been mine since the time you were ten. We were meant to be together. Coincidences are God's way of telling us something.

You want to know why I didn't follow up on my threat? Because I think you deserve a good life, a life only Raghuvir can give you. Yes, I was being heroic. Cheers to that.

In the past month, I have come to realize that I would probably not fall in love with anyone else after being in love with you for years. And how can I? You're after all the only girl who shows me my place, who makes me feel like dirt, badgers my armour and other phrases that you will know better because of your untarnished kill record.

I have always been vain and superficial. That part of me is not going anywhere. I will always look at you and think—she could have been thinner and hotter. But I think that has more to do with what you did to me than anything else. I don't think I really care about how you look at all. Cursing you, telling you how ugly you are is just my coping mechanism, I think. You look fine to me and I say fuck you to the people to whom you don't.

And then there's this other part of me that's in love with you. I would use fancy words but I know none. It's like you're my corner of the world. I can come to you and feel safe. I can shed my masculinity, curl up next to you and feel sheltered. I can be the little Dhruv again. For all these years, I have hated myself for being in love with you, the girl who destroyed my only chance at love. And in the process I have hated you. But in that hatred, you have always been alive in my heart. You have always been there, Aranya. What wouldn't I give to be loved by you again, to love you, to protect you and be protected, to have my heart broken by you again, to feel alive!

I don't know where to go from here. Should I come crawling to you, beg mercy, and snatch you away from Raghuvir? I could do that. It's within my power, I think. You wouldn't have mailed me if that window was completely shut. Beneath all that hatred you have for me, I'm sure there's a little bit of love left yet, something I can exploit to my and our advantage.

But then, I find myself thinking, should I do that or not? Because what if you do find the love and the courage to be with me? Will we be great together? What if it all breaks down and goes to shit? Wouldn't that be a tragedy? Don't you think the current scheme of events works better for both of us?

You stay with Raghuvir and build a new life and I stay away from you and find it in my heart to hate you enough to not think about you any more.

I don't think I can do this to you, Aranya. Being right is a hard thing to do. But seems like it's what I'm going to do this time.

Best of luck for your life.

Regards

Dhruv

(Forever in love with you)

He was about to hit the SEND button but he felt weak. There was nothing other than humiliation to be gained out of sending the mail. Once he sent it, there was no looking back. Aranya and Raghuvir would read the mail together and laugh at him. He couldn't allow that.

Instead, he left the mail in the Drafts and slept restlessly for whatever was left of the night.

Every few days, a similar mail from Aranya would reach Dhruv's mailbox and he would spend the entire day reading it, furiously typing his confession of love, deleting it, and drinking the night away.

69

It was three at night. Aranya was returning home in a company cab after another nineteen-hour shift. Her body ached at places she didn't know existed. Thankfully, Raghuvir had bought her a treadmill desk, one which allowed her to walk while she tapped furiously on her laptop hence delaying the onslaught of spondylitis, spine problems and early death.

She was rudely woken up from her slumber when her phone rang. She sat up straight and wiped the drool off her face. She took the call. 'Hello?'

'WHAT'S UP!' shouted a voice from the other side. 'It's me, Sanchit! I'm shouting because I want to pretend this is a long distance trunk call.'

'What do you want?' asked Aranya, still groggy.

'What do I want? Can't a friend just call to ask how you are doing?'

'We are not friends.'

'That's not hurtful at all.'

'What do you want, Sanchit? I don't have time for this. I have to sleep. I have had a long day.'

'So are you going to sleep with Raghuvir or alone? Is he cooking today or are you going to order in? Is he going to paint your nails or you will massage his hair? Just asking because you have taken to updating Dhruv about your daily activities!'

'You have a problem with that?'

'Just the one. Why are you doing this? What would you get out of it? You already know he loves you and what you're doing is putting him through hell. Then why are you persisting?'

'Because I think he deserves it.'

'I think he has had enough, Aranya. I know you guys have a past and I wouldn't even try to imagine what damage he might have caused you then and now but it's time to call it quits.'

'Are you pleading on Dhruv's behalf?'

'No. I'm pleading on mine,' said Sanchit. 'He's never going to ask you to stop. But I can tell that it's killing him. He's draining bottles of alcohol like they're water. He's being all filmy and dramatic right now. You know how he is! So you need to stop before he self-destructs.'

Aranya laughed. 'Why? Isn't he too busy in love with Ritika? At least that's what he texted me.'

'What? No! Ritika went back home long back. He drove her away.'

'I know he lied. The picture he sent me was old; anyone could see that. He's a pathetic liar.'

'I always told him that. But that's not the point. The point is . . . just stop.'

'I won't stop till I get what I want. That's how I work, Sanchit.'

'AND WHAT THE HELL DO YOU WANT, ARANYA? HE'S ALREADY BROKEN,' said Sanchit.

'I don't need to answer your questions. And DARE you shout at me, Sanchit.'

The cab reached her apartment and she stepped out. She signed in the register and walked in.

'Fine, Aranya. Have it your way. I'm sending you a mail Dhruv wrote but never sent. Read it and hopefully you will have a change of mind. I'm just requesting you to leave him alone.'

'I will think about it,' said Aranya and disconnected the call.

She rang the bell and Raghuvir opened the door. He had waited up. There was a warm pizza waiting for her. She forgot it was pizza night. Of course. Right on schedule. Every Tuesday. Raghuvir had it marked on the calendar. That's how you make relationships function—schedule everything and follow it. What is love if not a routine? Raghuvir had totally nailed it. Together they could have written a self-help book on it.

'If you had taken one more minute, I would have dozed off,' said Raghuvir.

'Which movie are we watching today?' asked Aranya.

'I thought we would eat and do something more fun tonight,' answered Raghuvir and waved a wine bottle in Aranya's face.

Aranya smiled weakly. 'I will just go and change.' She left the room and locked herself in the washroom. She closed the seat of the toilet and sat on it. She waited for the mail. She refreshed her mailbox again. Inbox (1).

It was the same mail which had been lying in Dhruv's Drafts folder for a while now.

She read the mail twice. Her eyes welled up. Her phone beeped. It was Sanchit.

SANCHIT

?

SANCHIT

No reactions?

SANCHIT

Made of stone or what?

ARANYA

HAHAHAHAHAHAHAHAHAHAHAHAHAHAHA-HAHAHAHA.

I know why he didn't send the mail. ☺

SANCHIT

Why?

ARANYA

Because it's funny.LOL.

SANCHIT

Stop doing this to him.

ARANYA

You wish.

Aranya's phone rang. 'Hello, Sanchit,' she whispered into the phone. 'Why are you calling?'

'To hear your voice. I'm lonely tonight.'

'Stop wasting my time.'

'It's you who's wasting your time, Aranya. I called to see how convincingly you can lie and I know you can't. Stop taking me for a fool.'

'Lying?'

'I did think for a bit that all what you were doing was for revenge, or to make Dhruv feel bad about himself but it's much more than that, isn't it?'

'What are you talking about? It's just revenge!'

Aranya's breath stuck in her throat. Sanchit was on to her plan.

'Of course it's your plan. You are giving him reasons to fight for you. You want him to ball up and save you from a life without love, aren't you?'

'That's nonsense!'

'STOP LYING.'

'. . .'

'That's why you sent all those mails! Damn. To ensure he wakes up and smells the coffee.'

'. . .'

'I'm almost impressed!'

'I never agreed to what you're saying,' snapped Aranya, her secret now out.

'But if you want this plan to work, you need to hurt him a little more. You need to trust me on this, Aranya. I'm on your team and I will do anything to make the fucked-up love story of you guys work. I admit I was rooting for Raghuvir and you for a bit but seeing how desperate you guys are—you being all scheming and him being all mopey and depressed—it seems I made an error in judgement. And that's a first even for me!'

There was silence on the other side for a bit and then Aranya spoke, taking a leap of faith, hoping Sanchit could help her, scared if he would laugh at her. 'What do you have in mind?'

'Dhruv needs to hear or see or feel something that will crush him. These mails won't work. You have to do something bigger, something he would never forget, something very dire, something big.'

'Like?'

Sanchit thought for a little while and spoke with a great deal of excitement in his voice. 'Though it kills me to say this because I love Dhruv, have sex with Raghuvir and make him listen to every moan of yours,' said Sanchit as a matter of fact.

'What!'

'Trust me, it will work! It's the best plan ever.'

The door was knocked on again. 'Are you talking on the phone?' asked Raghuvir.

'No!' said Aranya and cut the call.

'Are you okay in there?' asked Raghuvir.

'I'm fine.'

Aranya washed her face, stared at her reflection in the mirror, sprayed herself with deodorant, pasted a smile on her face and stepped out of the washroom. Would it work? She found herself thinking about Sanchit's crazy idea.

Her phone beeped. It was Sanchit. *Go for it, trust me, it's going to work*, it said.

'There you are,' said Raghuvir, a slice of pizza hanging from his hand and his glass of wine half-empty. There was a light in his eyes. He poured Aranya a glass.

'What are we drinking?' asked Aranya and sat next to him.

'God knows. I just picked wine because it sounds more romantic, doesn't it?' said Raghuvir and chuckled. She picked up her glass of wine and started sipping from it. She had to get sufficiently drunk tonight to do what Sanchit had suggested. The plan seemed so crazy that it might work.

Half an hour later, the pizza was finished and Raghuvir led Aranya to the bedroom. He planted little kisses on her neck as they walked. Aranya felt a little woozy from the alcohol. As he dropped her on to the bed, she reached out for her cellphone in her pocket and dialled Dhruv's number. Then, she threw it on the carpeted floor. She could faintly hear Dhruv's 'hello' over Raghuvir's frantic breathing.

Raghuvir and she had sex, and she wished Dhruv heard it all. He would have to. This could work, she thought to herself the entire time she lay there.

The next morning, Aranya found her phone lying where she had dropped it, out of battery.

Aranya texted Sanchit.

I hope it works.

SANCHIT

It will. Trust me.

70

It had been a long time since the moaning incident. Dhruv hadn't texted, called or mailed her. She was freaking out. Maybe it was all for nothing. It had failed.

'Calm down,' said Sanchit. 'It's working.'

'How the hell do you know it's working? He didn't even text me! We were counting on his world coming to a standstill!'

'Trust me, it has. My closely placed sources, Ramadhir and Arshad, the hostel cleaners, tell me he has been drinking himself to death. So sooner or later he will put on his armour and come save you!'

'What if he just drinks himself to death? After all, it runs in the family.'

'Whoa. That's insensitive.'

'I'm just fucking tense, Sanchit,' snapped Aranya.

'Fine, if he doesn't make a move in the next few days, I will go pay him a visit and see what the hell is wrong with him,' said Sanchit.

'You'd better.'

'Hmmm.'

'Thank you, Sanchit.'

'But Aranya, have you thought about your exit strategy? How will you get rid of Raghuvir? Your parents love him! They will crucify you if—'

'Of course they love him. Their responsibility was over the day he came into the picture. They are even taking credit for it. After all they were the ones who had goaded me to study and ace every examination, something they think led me directly to the arms of Raghuvir.'

'. . .'

'I am still thinking about it. Leaving him will kill me with guilt. I have tried everything to wreck my relationship with him but nothing is working. Just like he said, he's working on this relationship like it's a fucking science project,' said Aranya.

Aranya felt strange even saying this because after all Raghuvir was proving to be quite the flawless boyfriend! He was all she had ever dreamt of in a guy.

But she could not get herself to be in love with Raghuvir. It's not to say she didn't have a galaxy-sized crush on him ever since she first knew of him. Meeting him in college and getting to know him was a dream come true. They didn't get to work together a lot but the time she spent with him in the laboratories was invaluable. She would cherish it for the rest of her life.

Then as if she had all the luck in the world, Raghuvir wanted to be with her. Why her? Was it because she was smart? Was it because finally he found someone intelligent? She always felt uncomfortable with these questions.

For the first few days that she was with him, she was quite suspicious, like a woman married to a star. But slowly, she started to feel at home with the knowledge of him just liking her. After all, he was a changed man. There were a trillion girls in AMTECH, Bangalore, but he had eyes only for her.

Raghuvir was proving to be the perfect ladder out of the pit Dhruv had pushed her into and not reached out for. But her goddamn luck!

She couldn't push the thought of Dhruv out of her head. Why did she need the thing she knew would destroy her? The choice was so simple. A second grader could have made it. But why? She had grappled with the question long and hard and hit a blank. There was no reason to love Dhruv and yet she did.

The guilt of being with Raghuvir and yet not being in love with him, free riding on him, trying to find the way out of the labyrinth using him, started to eat her up. The burden was too heavy to carry and she would have to carry it for the rest of her life.

But she had no other choice! Either it was Dhruv and his mad love or Raghuvir and the comfort of a routine life. She would have picked the former a million times over. But for that she had to get rid of Raghuvir somehow and not offend her parents for whom he was a living God.

It was easier said than done. Raghuvir was fucking perfect. She had to find a chink in Raghuvir's armour.

And that's when Sanchit came to her rescue and told her. 'Temptation! Raghuvir might be a saint but temptation can take any man down. Raghuvir has always been like that! People change but people don't *really* change. All you have to do is lay down the perfect trap, Aranya. If Raghuvir falters, that's your exit strategy. Neither him nor your parents would be able to blame you! Paraphrasing *Godfather*, give him a girl he can't refuse.'

'I don't think it will work. Raghuvir puts a lot into this relationship. He doesn't even look at other girls! He wouldn't be easy to mislead.'

'Yes, it won't be easy. But the only reason he doesn't look at other girls is because they aren't *perfect*. The girl we will create for Raghuvir will be perfect—a girl conforming to every standard every guy has in the world.'

'You mean Kim Kardashian.'

'Don't disappoint me, Aranya. We can do much better.'

'Like?' asked Aranya.

'I have some rough ideas,' said Sanchit.

71

Aranya knew she had only three weeks to pull this off. After that she would have to go back to college and live in the agony of owing her life to Raghuvir, the saint, while being in love with the bastard who didn't come for her, Dhruv.

To fool someone like Raghuvir she needed to be meticulous and pay attention to every small detail. She got down to the task. She, with Sanchit, created a perfect mistress for Raghuvir.

Step 1:

Decide whose identity you want to steal. Make sure that person isn't on Facebook because the chances of your profile being taken down increases dramatically. Find someone on Instagram instead. There will always be more pictures to choose from. Choose someone who's hot but not that hot. More in the range of cute. Someone approachable. Someone who looks shy but also has a naughty twinkle in her eye.

Aranya chose a girl named Swati Dhamija, an eighteen-year-old girl from Mumbai but now studying in the US. She didn't have a Facebook profile and was hot and cute in the right measures. She named the girl Farah Iqbal. Being diametrically opposite was a bonus.

Step 2:

Don't be lazy. Go the whole hog. Create an e-mail ID. A Twitter account. A Skype account. Even a Google Plus account and a blog. Link all of them together. Make sure all of these are locked because new profiles raise suspicion.

Farah Iqbal was now a real person on the Internet with accounts, blogs and pictures.

www.facebook.com/farahiqbal124

www.farahiqbaltalks1.bloigspot.com

www.twitter.com/farahiqbal1A124

Skype ID: FarahIqbal1A124

Step 3:

No cute girl in the universe is without friends. Choose a profile that you would use to establish contact with your target. Make yourself an active and a popular person on that profile.

Farah Iqbal got some friends. Aranya created twenty more fake profiles of a heterosexual friend group. All these profiles were locked except a profile picture. These twenty fake profiles commented on every picture of Farah Iqbal on Facebook. There were compliments, jibes and internal jokes. It was important to portray Farah as a demure, shy girl but not someone who lacked a sense of humour. The conversation on the third profile picture of Farah went something like this:

Amar: Great picture!

Smriti: I clicked it after all.:) You look great, Farah.

Farah: Thanks guys.

Ruhil: Such a poser.

Farah: At least I can pose. Your eyes look like dead fish.

Ruhil: Blah.
Kanika: HAHAHAHAHAHAHA.
Smriti: LOL.
Amar: Friday plans?
Farah: Ya? Anything yet?
Kanika: Check Whatsapp group people!
Ruhil: Okay.

Step 4:

Make sure you have common interests. Like the same pages— movies, bands, books—that your target has liked. If you do that there's less chance of running out of conversation when the time comes. But keep the girl interested in domains your target would know nothing about.

Aranya made Farah Iqbal like all major newspapers, blogs and science journals. Also a few movies that had roaring popularity amongst men—*Fight Club, Snatch*, the works. What men really want is a girl who acts like a man when it comes to lifestyle choices and like a woman when it comes to appearances. Farah Iqbal was now in final year law. She was not only a scholarship student but had already bagged a job at a reputed law firm as an intern. They put in a lot of pictures of books she intended to read. She was quite accomplished—just the way Raghuvir liked it. Aranya made Farah Iqbal a voracious reader and a yoga enthusiast. It helps if people can imagine their prospectives in yoga pants.

Step 5:

The most important step. Find something that they would bond over. A school? A common college? A city? No. You need something more. Yes. You're getting there. Yes! A relationship. If your target is someone who's in a relationship, you should be in one too. That's your common ground. That's how your target will feel safe. The conversation will be between two committed people, always safer than talking to someone who's single.

Farah Iqbal was in a relationship with a boy and they seemed to be in love but not that much in love. That final touch completed Farah Iqbal's profile. She was now a person. She may not have existed in the physical world, but ask yourself, did that even matter? We trust the Internet presence of a person more than his or her physical presence. Internet > Real life.

Farah Iqbal was now a real person. She was a promising lawyer who dabbled in fitness, read like a maniac, was into movies men liked, partied like a mad woman but was homely as well, an equal proportion of pictures in little dresses and salwar suits—the *perfect* girl.

The rest was easy. Farah Iqbal accidentally sent a friend request to Raghuvir. Raghuvir wasn't a big fan of social media so it was Aranya who 'accidentally' accepted the friend request on his phone. Raghuvir had rolled his eyes at that time but soon he started to visit Farah's profile.

It started slowly. A couple of likes here and there. Surprise from both ends at the accidental 'sending' and 'accepting' of the friend request. A couple of 'What's ups' thrown here and there, but slowly the conversations got longer.

They started to talk about his work and her college life, her impending internship, their ambitions and their dreams. It was working. They were physically separated thus making it even safer to pursue the conversation. Soon, they started talking about their relationship and Aranya found him faltering.

FARAH

So you're dating someone? Of course you are.

RAGHUVIR

Yes.

FARAH

Who's the girl?

RAGHUVIR
She used to be a student. Been dating for a while now.
FARAH
Umm! Student! Nice. ;)
RAGHUVIR
Why that wink?
FARAH
Because it's one of those things you always think about. Student–teacher. Doctor–patient. You know.
RAGHUVIR
Who are you dating?
FARAH
Just a normal guy. NOT a professor.
RAGHUVIR
Haha.
FARAH
Send me her picture.

There was a pause.

RAGHUVIR
Don't have any.
FARAH
Liar.

Of course, Raghuvir had pictures of Aranya. He was just embarrassed. Aranya felt hurt but this was evidence. She had to pursue this conversation to corner Raghuvir if and when the time came.

RAGHUVIR
We don't click a lot of pictures.
FARAH
You must have one.
RAGHUVIR
Fine. I found one. Sending.

Raghuvir was clearly embarrassed. In the picture, Aranya was behind a door, which hid around 25 kilograms of her weight, and peeping towards the camera. The pigmentation of her face was clearly visible.

FARAH

Okay. She seems nice.

RAGHUVIR

I'm not physically attracted to her. She's okay. But she's nice otherwise.

FARAH

Hmmm. There's something about her face though . . . in the picture?

RAGHUVIR

She has a condition. Vitiligo.

FARAH

Oh. I'm so sorry! I didn't know.

RAGHUVIR

It's okay.

The conversation meandered to an end. Aranya knew that she could make Farah seduce Raghuvir as and when the time came. Seduce might be a strong word, but Aranya knew she could make a fertile ground for a break-up if the need arose. But not before Raghuvir got her the deal—a college transfer, a tuition and a ten-year bond.

Aranya bought another cellphone. Farah and Raghuvir started talking over Facebook and Whatsapp for quite a few hours every day. Though Raghuvir hadn't cheated on Aranya yet, it now seemed like it could happen, if not immediately then sometime in the future.

This had only reaffirmed in her heart that the only person she could be in love with, even if it destroyed her, was Dhruv. For the first time, Sanchit and Aranya had concurred.

It was time for Sanchit to do his bit.

72

A couple of weeks had passed since Dhruv had heard Aranya and Raghuvir grunting over the phone and it still played in crystal-clear sounds in his ears.

That day Dhruv lay on the floor, his phone a few feet away, moaning with a hangover. Last night, like many nights before, he had had a little too much to drink. His head felt like it would implode. Being an alcoholic is tough in the mornings, he had realized that by now. He wondered how Dad did it day after day, year after year.

Every morning, like this one, he would promise himself to not drink again but as evening approached the pain would become too much and he would inevitably reach for the bottle. There was only so much time you could spend at the gym.

The emptiness of the hostel had started to get to him. The vacant walls were like a projector screen with a movie playing on it, one where Aranya and Raghuvir fucked each other like rabbits.

There were times, more often when he was drunk, when he gave in to the temptation. He would call Ritika and ask her to come over. She would say yes. But the next morning he would call her and ask her to stay put. This continued till she was irritated and tired of being played around with. Dhruv was now far gone. She knew that.

Dhruv's phone rang. It must be Sanchit again to ask if he was alive. He crawled towards the phone. It stopped ringing by the time he reached it.

Still on the floor, he opened the last few mails from Aranya and read them again.

From: aranyagupta@gmail.com
To: royDhruv@gmail.com
Subject: Oops.

Hi Dhruv,

Hope you're having a great morning. I know I am.

I'm really sorry for that little faux pas last night. I think I must have pocket dialled you. But what I fail to understand is why you wouldn't cut the call? You kept your ear pinned to the phone for 2:57:01 minutes? Why? But thank God you know how phenomenal Raghuvir is in bed!

I'm glad that now you have a first-hand account of how happy I am.

Also, Sanchit called me last evening. He was harping about how you're killing yourself. Going the exact same way your father went. He expected me to pity you and God knows I searched for it in the deep recesses of my heart and found nothing. All I found was hate.

It makes me so happy to see you like this. To aid your imagination, I'm sending you a few pictures from last night. The first one is of the pizza box and the empty wine bottle, the second one is of the unmade bed after we did it, and the third one is of me—smiling. Hope you never get this night out of your head and drink yourself to death.

Regards
Aranya
(The happiest girl in the world)

Tears flowed without restraint from his eyes. He opened the pictures again even though he didn't want to. It fucking helped him to recreate the scenario.

He opened another mail. By this time, he had reached for the half-filled bottle of Old Monk kept near the bedpost. He put it to his lips and took a large swig. His body revolted.

He read the mail.

From:aranyagupta@gmail.com
To:royDhruv@gmail.com
Subject: Are you dead yet?
Hi Dhruv,

I hope this mail finds you in the worst of health. I hope you're lonely and rotting in your hostel room.

It's been a week since I sent the last mail and I wouldn't have sent it if I didn't have anything to say to you which would make your life even worse.

Since I had realized that studying in India amongst certified losers like you wasn't my thing, I started to apply to colleges abroad and got accepted into many. Where would I get the money from? The company will pay for it! Raghuvir managed that for me. I told you—he's quite the man.

I AM SO HAPPY! I AM FINALLY LEAVING DELHI!

So as soon as this internship ends, I'm going to start the process to take that transfer. I will no longer be in that shithole where you will rot for three more years before you graduate or die, whichever comes earlier.

Raghuvir will soon be shifting with me to the US after he completes two years in Bangalore and I will wait for him! Because why shouldn't I? He gives me everything I want, is thoughtful and kind, and keeps me happy. And being with him ensures your defeat. So why not! ☺

I can't wait to see you in college and mock you. Do you have a paunch yet from all that drinking?

Regards
Aranya
(SO HAPPY!)

He threw the phone away from his reach before he had the urge to read any more mails and feel worse about it. He drank a little more and tried to sleep again but his head spun like a goddamn Ferris wheel and he vomited all over the floor.

Fuck.

He staggered to his feet and wobbled to the door and went out. He came back with a mop and a bucket of water and phenyl. He cleaned up his vomit even as his vision blurred, and mopped the entire room till it smelt like a hospital. He kept the bucket and the mop outside the room, and fell asleep like a log.

Dhruv woke up with a start. The throbbing in his head was back. He held his head but it didn't go away. He soon realized the throbbing came from the banging on the door.

'Who the fuck is it?' shouted Dhruv and he looked for his slippers. He found one beneath the bed and one on the study table. He put them on and walked to the door. The incessant banging had not stopped. 'COMING!' shouted Dhruv and opened the door.

He didn't even get a good look at who it was and felt a force pushing him to the ground. He fell headlong to the ground and was being kissed all over his face. He opened his eyes to see Sanchit sitting over him, smiling, his jaw open, like a Great Dane.

'Get the fuck off me,' snapped Dhruv and pushed him away. He crawled to the bed and hoisted himself up.

'You need to pick up my calls, Dhruv. I could have been in an accident! Or stuck on a conveyor belt slowly moving towards lasers that cut things in half.'

'I wish it were that,' said Dhruv and lay supine on the bed. 'Why are you here?'

'I'm here to say goodbye. My offer letter just came and I'm being posted to Belgium. I leave in ten days. And the way you're going, I don't think I will find you alive when I come back,' said Sanchit and joined Dhruv on the bed. 'So I thought we would have sex one last time.' He grabbed Dhruv's crotch. Dhruv slapped his hand away and got up.

'You're disgusting.'

'Says the boy whose room smells like a funeral home.'

'You're not staying here,' said Dhruv.

'Of course I am. I have nowhere else to go. And moreover, Aranya's internship gets over in a couple of days and she will be back. I want to see how you behave. I have a deep interest in orangutan's mating patterns.'

'I have nothing to do with her.'

'Of course you don't,' said Sanchit and smiled. 'Okay, now scoot, I need to sleep a little. The train journey was horrible and I had fat aunties breathing down my neck.'

Dhruv shifted and made space for Sanchit and they slept like little kids on a couch.

*

Sanchit woke up to see Dhruv walk in in his gym clothes.

'Dude. When did you wake up?' asked Sanchit.

'I couldn't sleep with you snoring like the damn Kraken,' said Dhruv. He took out a fresh change of clothes, bathed and came back to the room. He found Sanchit reading through Aranya's mails.

'It's nothing you haven't read before,' said Dhruv and slumped on the bed. He lit a cigarette.

'Quite a smoker you are now, aren't you?' asked Sanchit and pointed at the ashtray which was overflowing with cigarette butts. 'What do you want to do about these mails? About Aranya's perfect life with Raghuvir? What's your plan of action? Have you figured something out?'

'I will sit back and do nothing. That's the plan. Don't you agree with that? Being noble and heroic was the way to go? That Aranya deserved a better life? A life which only Raghuvir could give her? So my plan is to sit here and rot while she lives her perfect life. Any more questions?'

'If staying here and rotting is the game plan, why did you put in a three-hour cardio session to sculpt your abs?'

'So that she sees a happy Dhruv who doesn't give a fuck?'

Sanchit laughed. 'You're so juvenile, Dhruv. Of course you give a fuck, and she knows that.'

73

Aranya's last few mails had gone unanswered. So had the texts. She knew for sure that Dhruv was going through hell but it wasn't working out the way she had wanted it to. Dhruv had refrained from reacting and that was bad news for her.

'Have you packed all the bed sheets?' asked Raghuvir.

'Huh?'

'Where are you lost?' asked Raghuvir. He jumped over the open suitcases and walked up to her. 'There's nothing to worry. I have talked to the administration in your college. They will process your transfer application to California Tech in a week's time.'

'Thank you,' said Aranya. Raghuvir hugged her.

'C'mon now. We don't have time. Just go around the house and check if you have left something. I will go to my flat and check if I have missed something there. It's already six. You have to be at the airport at 10 p.m. max! The other interns are already waiting at the bar. We can't miss the party we planned!' said Raghuvir, kissing Aranya on the forehead before leaving.

Aranya stared back into her phone. She had been toying with the idea of texting Dhruv for a really long time now. Only twelve hours separated her and him, and she had no idea how she would hold up in front of him. Even the thought of Dhruv walking up to her, drunk and haggard, apologetic, brought tears to her eyes. But what if he didn't?

The reality had started to sink in for the past few days. All this while she thought she had everything under control, that the game was in her hands, but it seemed to be slipping away now.

She took out her cellphone and texted him.

ARANYA
Can't wait to see you again.

'You left all these clothes there,' said Raghuvir from behind a pile of clothes.

Aranya hid the phone just in time. 'I checked here. We have packed everything.'

Raghuvir dropped the pile of clothes over a suitcase. He caught Aranya's gaze. 'Are you crying? Oh shit. You're crying?' He stepped closer to Aranya, took her hands into his and kissed them, and said, 'I will miss you, too.'

Tears streaked down her cheeks. 'I will miss you, Raghuvir.' And she hugged him. And as she did, her phone beeped. It was a text from Dhruv.

74

'What the fuck did you just text her?' shouted Dhruv and chased after Sanchit. For a guy with skinny legs, Sanchit was quick on his feet. Sanchit gave Dhruv a good long chase across the football field, through the parking lot and the training and placement department, the mechanical and civil departments; Dhruv finally caught up with him, pinned him down in the lawns of the electrical engineering department and snatched his cellphone away from him.

Dhruv went into the text messages and saw the text Sanchit had sent Aranya.

DHRUV
Same here. We have to talk.

'Why the hell would you send that? I have nothing to say to her!'

'Oh yes, you do.'

The phone beeped. It was Aranya.

ARANYA
If by talking you mean I get to debase you further and push you down the slippery side of depression, then yes, we do.

Dhruv's face fell on reading it. Sanchit snatched the phone and read the text out aloud.

'She doesn't need to be mean all the time,' Dhruv grumbled.

'After what you did to her she has all the right to whip you for a lifetime.'

'Whose side are you on?'

'Aranya's obviously,' said Sanchit. 'I love her. Anyway, now reply to her.'

'I'm not replying to her any more. There's nothing to be gained out of this. I'm sure Raghuvir and Aranya laugh seeing these texts. I'm not falling into that trap.'

Sanchit lay down on the grass and soaked in the warmth. 'I'm not sure about Raghuvir but Aranya would surely laugh. The great Dhruv being reduced to a lowly, tongue-wagging, helpless puppy.'

'What the hell are you talking about? I thought you were with me on this,' said Dhruv.

'I was. But not any more. I didn't know you loved her enough to make a complete fool out of yourself. Look at yourself. You're pathetic, dude. I seriously thought this was another one of your obsessive streaks but it's not. Not going after her and letting her go and have a good life is probably the first selfless thing you might have ever done. For the first time you put someone else in the centre of the world. And I have to say I was impressed. I totally had a non-sexual boner. From being a scum you became a fucking knight. But enough is enough. Aranya is yours. She should be right here and indulging in some excruciating PDA with you. Dhruv, I think it's time you acted on this. What happened to the Dhruv who snatched what he wanted from the world?'

'Excuse me? That ship has sailed. I can't fight for her now. It's done. It's over. What is it that you want me to do? Nothing will change,' said Dhruv.

'All I'm saying is that if Aranya didn't want you in her life, she wouldn't text or mail you so much. That window where you sneak in, grab her, and leave is clearly still open. You just need to be up for it. She's still in love with you.'

'She's sleeping with Raghuvir. She's planning to move to the US. She's definitely *not* in love with me!'

'I was just saying. It's worth a try. Imagine a life without her and then you might think it would be worth it. I'm going to be really insensitive right now but you need to hear this. How are you different from your Dad if you don't fight for her?'

75

It was one in the night when Aranya signed in the hostel register and shifted back to her old room. It was to be her last five days in this college. After that she would never come back to this college, this city, her family . . . and Dhruv.

It was over.

She unlocked her room and dragged her suitcases inside. She texted Raghuvir to inform him that she had reached her hostel. Her parents would get to know the same from him.

She sighed at the irony. Theirs wouldn't be a love story that would end prettily. Her alter ego Farah could easily ensnare Raghuvir. If not Farah, someone else.

And the one she could imagine a life with was an impotent, powerless, selfish man revelling in self-pity and hollow heroism of letting her go.

She cradled her phone in her hands and almost dialled a number when there was a knock on her door. She opened it and Sanchit was standing there in a hoodie and pink pyjamas. She hurriedly ushered him in.

'I was just about to call you,' whispered Aranya.

'And now I'm here!'

'What the hell are you doing here? And that's the worst disguise EVER. Pink pyjamas? And which girl in this college is 6'4"? You look like a transvestite.'

'Hey! Hey! Transvestites have feelings too. And I'm 6'2",' said Sanchit and looked around the room. 'So cool! I'm finally in a girl's hostel room.' He picked up a pen and started scratching his name on the inside of the cupboard.

'I have been calling you since so long! Where have you been? You better not abandon me after pushing me so far into this. And what the hell is your friend doing? He has still not come around! You said he would!'

'Busy,' said Sanchit and kept on scratching at the paint of her cupboard.

'What the hell are you doing?' asked Aranya.

'Etching my name on your cupboard! What else? Oh. The look on your face says you want to know why I am doing it. It's quite simple, Aranya. You're going to leave this college and so am I. But after you scores of girls are going to come to this room and when they see "SANCHIT WAS HERE. MULTIPLE TIMES" inscribed on the cupboard, they would think of me as a real badass who used to walk in and out of the girls' hostel whenever he wanted to. Like Batman. Like a ninja Casanova.'

'Whatever,' said Aranya and slumped on the bed.

'Don't be sad now. He will come around. He's just taking some time.'

'He won't. If he wanted to, he would have done that by now. And you said he would! All this planning is going to come to naught if that bastard doesn't pull through,' said Aranya.

'I thought him listening to you making out with Raghuvir would break him. God knows why he didn't react to it,' said a puzzled Sanchit who had finished carving his name.

'This was a fuck-all plan from the very beginning. You made me believe that Dhruv was still in love with me and he would come around. Don't look at me like that. He's your friend. God! I feel like such a fool now.'

'I was just trying, Aranya! It's better than being relegated to a relationship without love. Look at what Raghuvir did. He talks for two hours with Farah every day and he hasn't even mentioned the name to you, Aranya. Sooner or later, he will slip and get back to his old ways.'

'You made me make that profile, Sanchit!'

'. . .'

'Okay, fine. I did. But you sowed the seed of doubt in me. YOU CALLED ME EVERY DAY TO PUT DHRUV'S CASE IN FRONT OF ME. I WAS HAPPY BEING ME. Or at least I was better than this mess,' grumbled Aranya.

'Me? You were the one who used to call me and cry for hours thinking about Dhruv. That wasn't me. That was always you.'

Aranya sighed. 'Yes. That was me. Stupid, stupid me. And now he's gone.' She started to cry a little.

Sanchit put his arms around her. 'There's still time.' Over the course of the past month, Sanchit and Aranya had gotten quite close.

'What do we do now?' asked a sobbing Aranya. 'I leave in another five days.'

'We will have to think of something,' said Sanchit. 'I better be leaving now. I can't think unless I'm drunk.'

Aranya nodded. Sanchit pulled his hood over his head and opened the door.

'Sanchit?'

'Yes?'

'At least I earned a friend in all this,' said Aranya and smiled.

'Umm . . . actually you got a lover and someone who fantasizes about you,' Sanchit said with a wink.

'You're gross.'

76

Dhruv had been dreading this moment ever since Aranya had walked into the college. He was in the queue three places behind her with a cheque and a registration form for the second year. She stood there, fidgeting with her transfer form, earplugs dug deep inside her ears, irritatingly unmindful of Dhruv's presence. She looked beautiful. He said that to himself, making sure no one heard it because that would be awful. Aranya? Beautiful? But surely, she was. The corners of her lips moved while she mouthed the song she was listening to, the twitching of the eyebrows, the gentle batting of the eyelids, the soft skin, were all quite hypnotic to him right now.

He moved out of the line and sat on one of the benches pretending he hadn't filled up his form. He waited for her to complete her formalities so that he could bump into her accidentally. The first ten seconds would be the key. He felt a cardiac arrest coming on. He saw them stamp her papers and tell her to come back in a couple of days to get her transcripts and the transfer letter. She looked a little sad when she should have been fucking happy to leave this shitty city, fly away and never come back.

'Hey?' said Dhruv as she crossed him, his tongue almost failing, flapping like a vestigial organ in his mouth. 'All set?'

She waved the stamped papers in his face. 'Yes.'

'Good for me,' said Dhruv.

'Good for you,' said Aranya.

Awkward silence. Like a soundproof wall had been erected between them.

'Are you going for a creative writing course? Just asking because you have taken a deep interest in writing letters and whatnot,' said Dhruv, trying to at least hate her if not be charming.

Aranya shook her head dismissively. 'That's your comeback? We have been away from each other for so many days and my arch nemesis welcomes me with this? Am I taking a creative writing course?'

'I would have talked about Raghuvir's small dick but I thought I would be nice to you since you're running away scared from this college.'

People in the queue turned and looked at them. The administration officer looked, too. Aranya and Dhruv slunk out of sight.

Aranya forced a smile on her face. They were out in the lawns of the electrical department and walking towards the canteen. 'Yes, I am. But at least I'm going after beating your ass. Look where we started and where we are now. You came in with all your swag, your big motorcycle, bloodied knuckles and all, and I came in hiding behind walls and people. And now I'm going to the US, have an insanely gorgeous boyfriend, and you're still here moping in the dirt. Oh, by the way, that lie about Ritika and you being together in college? I didn't buy it for one bit.'

'Because I didn't tell it convincingly.'

'Blah.'

'You forgot one thing though,' said Dhruv. 'The results of the first semester come out this evening, and I can bet anything in the world that you're going to be second for the first time in your life. And that will be my comeback.'

Aranya laughed hysterically. 'You? Dhruv? You're going to beat me? Are you out of your mind?'

Dhruv sat down on a bench and leaned back. He hoped she would sit next to him. 'No,' he said. He pointed to the board in front of him where the results would be displayed that evening. 'Here. In another six hours.'

Aranya smiled and sat next to him. 'Let's wait, then, to see who wins.'

'What's at stake?' asked Dhruv.

'Anything,' said Aranya and thrust her hand out.

'Everything.'

They shook hands on it.

77

An hour had passed and they were still sitting on that bench. Dhruv played Candy Crush, the phone held upside down, and Aranya stared blankly at the board. Time crawled at a dastardly pace.

'Did we decide to sit here and wait?' asked Aranya.

'We didn't but that's the beauty of it.'

'You're such a drama queen, Dhruv. If only you had been brought up on books rather than a diet of daily soaps there would have been a sliver of a chance of you beating me.'

'Says the girl who sent mails to see if it still bothered me,' said Dhruv.

'Of course I knew it bothered you. That was the whole point. To make you feel bad, which you did. See that little paunch peeking from over your belt. That's what I gave you.'

'So you're saying your effect on me is just a bit of bad cholesterol?' Dhruv laughed.

'You know what I mean. You still are head over heels in love with me and it crushes you to know that I'm with Raghuvir,' said Aranya.

A couple of more hours passed and Aranya dozed off on the bench. She woke up to find Dhruv drinking from a plastic bottle. It looked like Coke but going by Dhruv's crinkled face she was certain there were other miscible liquids in the bottle.

'What's that?' asked Aranya. Her face was imprinted with the pattern of the bench she had rested her face on. 'What are you looking at?'

'You look funny.'

'Tell me something new,' she said and snatched the bottle away from him and put it to her lips. Dhruv counted the seconds. Ten seconds. She gave it back to him. 'Alcohol makes everything better. Wonder what took me so long to warm up to it.'

'Your tyrannical parents perhaps?'

Aranya nodded and smiled weakly.

'Thirty minutes more to go. I will just go to the washroom and come. We will then start the countdown to your defeat,' said Dhruv.

Aranya waved her middle finger in his face and Dhruv left for the washroom.

*

'How's it going?' asked Sanchit, standing in front of the urinal, acting like he was peeing.

'She's not around, Sanchit! We can talk normally.'

'Shut up and move to the next urinal, Dhruv. And don't look at me while you're talking. If I have to play the double agent, I will do it well.'

Dhruv rolled his eyes and stood in the urinal next to Sanchit's.

'You better charm her today, Dhruv. Do whatever it takes. Seduce, emotionally manipulate, threaten, love, whatever!' said Sanchit.

'I'm doing my fucking best.'

'Keep that tone in control!'

'CONTROL?' thundered Dhruv. 'You asshole! You fucked me over, dude! You went on to her side and asked her to have sex with Raghuvir and make me hear all of it? And you have the balls to ask me to keep that tone in control?'

'Wait. Let's get the facts correct. She had already had sex with Raghuvir before. I just asked her to make you listen to her enjoy it, use it to rile you up so that you ball up and take what's yours!'

'Couldn't you just have fucking told me that and I would have done it?'

Sanchit winked. 'Where's the fun in that? And she wanted to see you fight! You needed to give her that. And moreover, I believe in true love and not deception. Had I told you, it would have been deception and no love story should start with that.'

'And what are you doing now, Sanchit? Changing sides and scheming with me to get her?' asked Dhruv.

'I realize that both of you are psychotic and I'm the only voice of reason. If it were up to both of you, this story would never end! But more than that tonight and the next two days are yours, Dhruv. Make her fall in love with you and fall in love with her and make sure you guys are forever . . .'

Dhruv rolled his eyes.

'Is that what I get for a good speech?'

'Fuck off.'

'Now go out. No one likes a boy who pees for so long,' said Sanchit. 'And remember: DON'T. LET. HER. GO.'

*

Other students had started milling about the lawns, counting time backwards, nervous about the impending results. A few closed their eyes and said little prayers. Others talked to their parents, and a few discussed the trend of marks in the last few years.

Dhruv and Aranya finished the bottle between them and were reasonably tipsy by the end of it. Enough to know that drinking more would get them drunk but it was probably too late to stop.

'Whoever loses buys the next bottle,' said Dhruv.

'You mean you. And I thought the stakes were higher, weren't they?' asked Aranya and giggled.

'Not funny at all.'

And just then, a few people from the administration department walked towards the notice boards with the rolled up result sheets under their arm. Dhruv and Aranya sat up. They were sober within a split second. They staggered towards the boards where the fates of 200 first-year students were stuck with little pins. A sea of people had descended near the area and swarmed it like locusts. Dhruv and Aranya were pushed to the back.

Dhruv's heart pounded and he crossed his fingers. He, too, said a little prayer. Students in front of them shrieked and lamented with equal intensity and then moved out of their way. After about five minutes, they reached the board. Dhruv noted Aranya's marks first and then his own. It was a close call from the look of things. They both started tapping their phones furiously, calculating the weighted average of their marks. A pall of gloom descended on Aranya's face, a brief smiled appeared on Dhruv's.

'What the—'

Dhruv interrupted. 'Looks like I won. Stop calculating it over and over again. It's 78.34 and 78.31. You have lost by a convincing 0.03.' Dhruv pumped his fist.

Aranya double-checked, still incredulous at her defeat at the hands of someone whom she was labelling as an ape a few moments earlier.

'What do you want?'

'Spend some time with me before you go,' said Dhruv and walked a few steps closer to her.

'That's all?'

'Yes,' said Dhruv, holding her hand and whispering in her ear. 'That's all.'

78

'What exactly are our plans?' asked Aranya as she climbed on to Dhruv's motorcycle.

'I'm not sure of it. But they will include chains, restraints, pliers and medieval instruments of torture.'

Dhruv tossed Aranya the helmet and revved up his motorcycle. He drove to the nearest booze shop and picked up a few bottles with varied alcohol percentages guaranteed to knock them out.

'Don't tell me that after all this, all you want to do is get me drunk,' shouted Aranya in Dhruv's ear. The bottles clanged near her legs in the black satchel.

'I want to celebrate our separation. Is that too much to ask for?' Dhruv shouted back.

Aranya shrugged. Dhruv parked his motorcycle at the far corner of the hostel parking and sneaked Aranya into his hostel room.

'WELCOME!' said Sanchit and hugged Aranya. 'I thought you were leaving without saying goodbye!' Dhruv closed the lid of his laptop. Sanchit had been watching fat women porn.

'This is the dirtiest room I have ever stepped into,' said Aranya.

'What's this?' asked Sanchit and took the bottles from her. His eyes lit up. 'PERFECT! Come, Aranya, we will show you the perfect place to drink this. The last night the three of us will ever spend together.'

'We are not friends,' echoed Dhruv and Aranya.

'And then you say you're not made for each other.'

Sanchit led them to the roof where they poured themselves large drinks. Dhruv noticed that Sanchit sit between him and Aranya like a parent. Dhruv was still a little high from the rum and the thundering victory over Aranya. He poured two shots down his throat. He found the anger, the animosity, years of hatred melting away and he wanted to wrap himself around Aranya, the cute, ugly girl.

'What will you miss the most?' asked Sanchit.

'Me?'

'Obviously, you. Why would I ask Dhruv? He's going to rot here for the rest of his life mourning you.'

'Fuck off,' said Dhruv and lay supine on the roof, facing the glaring emptiness that stared back at him.

'I would miss nothing, I think,' said Aranya.

'Alcohol is the closest thing we have to a truth serum. So I propose two more shots. What say, Dhruv?'

'She's a slave today. She will do anything I ask her to do,' said Dhruv.

'Anything and you asked her to drink with us? You're like the worst Delhi boy ever.'

Sanchit poured six shots for the three of them.

'Dhruv's my best friend, you know,' said Sanchit, cradling Dhruv's foot in his lap. 'The last of the men.'

Aranya laughed. 'You mean the last of the men who still think there's something inherently noble in being a species that has a flaccid piece of meat hanging between their legs.'

'What's so great in being a woman?' shot back Dhruv.

'We are always in control.'

Dhruv waved his middle finger at her.

'That's all you can do, Dhruv. Men and their abuses, their unnecessary display of power and perceived superiority—'

Dhruv interrupted Aranya. 'And the feminist rises to defeat all men, take them as slaves!'

'Ugh. It's so hard to talk to you. Do you even know what the term means?' Aranya shot back.

'Actually, I'm not interested. Are you, Sanchit?' asked Dhruv but Sanchit had already walked to the other end of the roof, a bottle dangling from his right hand, singing to himself.

Dhruv crawled and sat next to Aranya. Aranya looked away. Dhruv sat there quietly for a while and they passed the bottle between the two of them. Ideally, Dhruv wanted to cry at her feet and ask her to not leave but he knew just that wouldn't be enough after all that he had put her through. 'Remember the time we first met?' asked Dhruv.

'Clearly. You were standing at the door of our class. You were late and the teacher scolded you.'

'Before that. It was the day when I saw you near the ice cream cart. I know you saw me laughing at you and that you remembered that when you first talked to me.'

'. . .'

'You still talked to me. Why?'

Aranya sighed. She closed her eyes. 'I was lonely.'

'You didn't have to be nice to me. I laughed at you and ran,' said Dhruv, guiltily.

'It always helps to be kind. Humans are hardwired to be nasty, vengeful people and who would know better than the two of us. We are programmed to hate, to destroy, to be born pure and die evil. We are a mob. So I was just being nice . . . because it helps.'

'It's what I fell in love with, Aranya,' said Dhruv and shook his head. He reached out for the cigarette packet and found it empty. 'I will just get another from my room.' He waved the empty packet.

'I'll come with you,' said Aranya and they both walked towards his room. Aranya found the cigarette packet under a month-old pile of unwashed clothes generously sprayed over with a strong insecticide-smelling deodorant. She tossed it to Dhruv. He lit one and took a long, languorous drag.

'That's why it hurt so much when you threw me under the bus,' said Dhruv. 'I know, I know, you had your reasons but I was twelve and I had fallen in love for the first time. And the last.'

'I'm sorry, Dhruv,' said Aranya. She sat on the creaky chair and leaned back. 'Like you said, I really had no choice.'

She drank from the bottle till it was empty. She got up and kept it outside the room.

'This is all so fucked up. Can't you stay, Aranya?'

'I can't, Dhruv. There's nothing to stay for,' said Aranya and sat on the bed next to Dhruv. 'I will have a life there. And as you said, it's all fucked up here.' Aranya looked at Dhruv, her eyes glazed over.

'I'm here.'

Aranya laughed sadly. 'For now, you are, Dhruv. But what about tomorrow? Day after? Forever?'

'But you will never be happy with Raghuvir, will you?'

'You overestimate love, Dhruv.'

'No, I don't. I spent three months in love with you when I was twelve and the wretched thing has followed me ever since,' said Dhruv, grumbling.

'That's so sweet,' said Aranya and pulled his cheeks.

'I'm not a baby,' said Dhruv and looked at Aranya, her face hovering around his. Dhruv held her gaze and leaned forward.

'Don't do this,' said Aranya even as Dhruv's lips almost touched hers.

'Why not?'

They were kissing now. His lips were on hers. She sensed his eagerness and placed her hands on his shoulders to push him away but she couldn't. He pulled her closer to himself. She wanted to fight but she realized it was already a lost battle. Dhruv's kiss was more like an assault, an amateur kissing for the first time, and it almost took her by surprise as she struggled to make sense of the rapid and random movements of Dhruv's tongue and lips . . . and of what was happening.

You're a fucking dog, Dhruv could hear the words echo in his brain as he kissed Aranya in what would be the worst kiss in the world. He realized Aranya's helplessness and the disarray and slowed down a little. Slow. He told himself and went soft on her.

'We shouldn't be doing this,' said Aranya. She felt Dhruv backing off a bit. Maybe his education obtained from porn was giving way to what he had read in *Cosmopolitan* or something. Aranya felt like she should feel guilty but she didn't. Instead she thought of hypothetical situations involving mad, passionate sex between Raghuvir and Farah Iqbal. It became quite tough when she felt Dhruv's hand creep up inside her T-shirt. She felt more nervous, more conscious than she had felt with Raghuvir. She felt like a thousand cameras were trained on her and were relentlessly capturing every part of her.

'Lights,' she said.

Dhruv hopped off like an eager monkey and switched off the lights. He took off his T-shirt and walked towards her. She had to blink twice to make herself believe that those abs actually existed and were soon going to crash into the sea of fat that was her stomach.

'I'm not sure about this,' said Aranya as Dhruv stripped her, slowly yet dexterously.

'Obviously, you are,' said Dhruv and kissed her everywhere. Aranya froze in pleasure and embarrassment. How could Dhruv like kissing the girl he had called ugly all his life? She almost felt guilty for looking the way she did. Dhruv whispered in her ear, as he nibbled, 'Plus, I won the bet, didn't I?'

'Fine,' said Aranya and pushed Dhruv over. She sat on Dhruv, unmindful of how heavy she was, and dived into his neck. 'Just because we had a bet.'

'Fuck. You're hot,' murmured Dhruv as Aranya slobbered and sucked on his neck.

'Remember that tomorrow and for the rest of your life.'

They spent the next two days in Dhruv's bed, making out, reading newspapers, watching *Homeland*, *Vampire Diaries*, *Black Mirror*, mocking each other, kissing each other till their lips went dry, arguing about who was responsible for their doomed relationship, reading books they liked in the library, soaking in the afternoon sun, eating all the bad canteen food they had never tried, and not talking about what stared them right in the face.

Dhruv clicked a lot of pictures of them being in love. Because he was Dhruv and he wanted her for life.

79

'That's so sweet of you,' said Aranya as Dhruv got her breakfast for two days in a row. It was burnt toast and badly scrambled eggs. Since they drank and made out late into the night, they never got up in time for the breakfast at the hostel mess. 'But it ends today.'

'I know,' said Dhruv and placed the plate on the table.

'He's coming to college today. Raghuvir. The administration people called. The papers are ready. Raghuvir has the tickets booked. I will be in the US in a week, Dhruv.'

Dhruv nodded. He passed the little bottle of Coke to Aranya.

'I don't think you're listening, Dhruv. I'm leaving.'

'I heard that,' said Dhruv and clambered up on the bed. He sat next to her and hugged her. Aranya started to cry. 'We knew this was going to happen.'

'Still doesn't make it better,' said Aranya through her tears. 'I need to go. I need to pack my things before Raghuvir comes.'

'Stay.'

'I can't, Dhruv. The longer I stay the harder it will get for me.'

'At least have breakfast,' said Dhruv.

'That's the last thing I will be thinking about,' said Aranya and got off the bed. She put on her clothes. Dhruv looked on, forlorn. 'There could have been a thousand ways our relationship could have ended. And it ended in the worst of ways.'

'I will never forget you, Aranya.'

'I know you won't, Dhruv.'

'That's very pompous of you,' remarked Dhruv. 'Will you forget me?'

'I will try to.'

Dhruv sighed. Aranya collected her things from around the room and tidied it a little. It was time for her to go. Dhruv got up from the bed to bid her goodbye.

'You need your sleep. I will find my way,' said Aranya and closed the door behind her.

She walked out of the hostel and to the far end of the football field where she scrunched up in a little ball and cried for a few hours. Late afternoon, Raghuvir reached the college. She put on a fake smile, something she had to get used to, completed the formalities for the college transfer, packed her bags, and loaded them into Raghuvir's taxi.

Raghuvir was supposed to stay with her parents for the next three days. 'I hope your parents like me,' said Raghuvir. 'These three days will be the biggest examination I have ever taken.'

'They already do,' said Aranya.

She saw Dhruv, the spineless, adorable, scared little man she loved, staring through the iron grille of the college gate as the car drove away.

80

Aranya's bags were packed and were being hauled out of her apartment by her brother, father and Raghuvir. An Innova had been called by Raghuvir—he was certain they would need one. Shifting bases is a cumbersome process. Clothes, electronics, memories, all stuffed into polyacrylic suitcases. But much to Raghuvir's surprise, all her belongings fit into two average-sized suitcases.

'Check everything once again. Passport? Visa? Documents? Ticket?' asked Raghuvir like the responsible man he was. Over the past three days that he had been living with them he had floored her parents. He was the perfect prospective son-in-law. So much so that even her brother, she thought, got a little jealous from all the attention he enjoyed.

Though sometimes she could see the confusion writ large over her parents' face. Why would a seemingly perfect guy date their daughter?

Quite obviously, they didn't know that Farah Iqbal and Raghuvir were now steadily moving towards what could only be described as sexting. Raghuvir would go down for a smoke every night after everyone slept off and would talk to Farah till early morning. Aranya had now zero to no guilt about what had happened between Dhruv and her, only a crushing longing.

Everyone boarded the cab. Her parents were the happiest people. Aranya was happy, too. After all, her long-standing dream was coming true. Soon she would be miles away from the family which had failed her. No longer would she be concerned about what they felt about her moral or social takes. No longer would she have to depend on them for alms. She was finally going to be independent.

She rolled down the window and felt the Delhi smog run through her hair for the last time. Raghuvir held her hand. Aranya smiled weakly at him and wondered when her relationship would break down. She would have to stop pretending to be Farah Iqbal quite soon. It was too time consuming for her to be someone else. She had done it for far too long. But she knew it would happen sooner or later. Two years is a long time. Raghuvir would forget her, find a new muse, fall in love and leave her alone.

What really bothered her were the miles between Dhruv and her. Would she ever forget that boy? Would success and acceptance obliterate signs of his presence? It didn't feel like it would. The car stopped at a red light and suddenly she felt trapped. She wanted to run back to the hostel and hug him, handcuff herself to him and never leave. She found herself crying. Raghuvir put a loving hand around her.

About half an hour later, the cab reached the airport. Her luggage was loaded into a trolley and Raghuvir pushed it towards the gate. He bought visitor's tickets for all four of them. Aranya had never seen her mother cry before. Or her father not use his Aranya-specific tone at her. What was what? Was that a sense of sadness she saw on their faces? Aranya didn't feel it though. One moment of kindness can't erase the years of harshness she had been subjected to by her family. She maintained a stoic face as she played with her tickets, the forms, and rechecked her visa.

Her parents, her brother and Raghuvir waited in the lounge while Aranya stepped into the check-in line. Far in the distance she could see Raghuvir chatting up her family effortlessly. Now she felt like she could cry. Like always, she would be alone and lonely at a place far from here.

She took out her alternate phone and texted Raghuvir.

FARAH IQBAL

What's up?

She saw Raghuvir feign busyness while her parents talked amongst themselves.

RAGHUVIR

Dropping my girlfriend off. She's leaving today.

FARAH IQBAL

Oh! Party then! You must be happy. At least she would be! Into the land of handsome hunks.

RAGHUVIR

Umm . . .

FARAH IQBAL

By the way, I'm coming to Bangalore next week.

RAGHUVIR

That's awesome!

FARAH IQBAL

That's only if my friend doesn't ditch me. Then I won't have a place to stay.

RAGHUVIR

You can stay at my place.

FARAH IQBAL

I can't do that. My boyfriend won't let me.

RAGHUVIR

You don't have to tell him.

FARAH IQBAL

I'm guessing you won't tell your girlfriend either. ★wink★

RAGHUVIR

Obviously. ★wink★

Aranya had reached the counter by then. She gave the tickets and her virgin passport for inspection to the smiling ground staff of Emirates. Her baggage was checked in and she was given two boarding passes for her flight from Delhi to Dubai to San Fransisco. Her heart started to pound with nervousness and excitement. Her phone beeped again.

RAGHUVIR

Are you coming then?

FARAH IQBAL

Can't wait!

RAGHUVIR

Same here. ☺

FARAH IQBAL

Should I be a little scared?

RAGHUVIR

You should be. *wink*

FARAH IQBAL

**Heart starts to pound*

RAGHUVIR

**Can't wait to inspect it*

FARAH IQBAL

Didn't know you were into role play.

RAGHUVIR

If the patient's like you, why not?

FARAH IQBAL

That was cheesy.

RAGHUVIR

I intended it to be sexy.

FARAH IQBAL

You don't have to try. *wink*

Aranya laughed. Fucking men. She kept that phone inside and took out her other phone. There were still no messages from Dhruv. It was as if he didn't exist and had never cared. She dialled his number as she walked towards the visitors' lounge.

'Hello,' said Aranya, fighting her tears.

'Hey!' said Dhruv, almost cheerful.

'You seem to be happy.'

'And you don't? Why?' asked Dhruv, his jolly tone felt like death to her ears.

'Fuck you, Dhruv. You know why.'

'Oh, is it because you love me and I love you and we will ruin anyone else we will be with and that bothers you because you won't be able to be with anyone else and you will live a lonely life and die alone?'

'Are you out of your mind, Dhruv? Why would you say that?' said an angry Aranya into the phone. She was now only yards away from the visitors' lounge. 'You will always be the asshole I always thought you to be. And I said it's my fault I ever chose you.'

'Yes, it is. And you clearly don't know how big an asshole I am,' said Dhruv and disconnected the call.

Aranya tried his phone again but he kept disconnecting the call. This boy had single-handedly ruined her and yet she couldn't stop loving him. What the hell was wrong with her? She walked towards the visitors' lounge. Her parents were still there, chatting with Raghuvir when she was stopped by the guards. Apparently, passengers couldn't cross over to the lounge after they got their boarding passes. She pleaded a little bit and they let her go.

But as soon she looked at her family again, she saw them looking towards a boy who had joined them. He was looking at his Converse sneakers as he talked. Aranya gingerly walked towards them and saw Dhruv sitting right in front of them. The spineless, adorable, scared little man she loved had turned up.

Dhruv looked at a stumped Aranya and she thought he winked at her.

81

'I'm sorry for whatever happened in the past but you need to listen to me,' said Dhruv, his eyes stuck at his untied, dirty laces.

'What are you doing here?' Raghuvir grumbled.

'I'm talking to her parents,' said Dhruv. It wasn't the first time he had found himself in such a situation. His last victim was Satvika from not so long ago.

'Why are you here?' asked the father.

'Sir, I'm extremely sorry to bring this up now. I know I have put your family through immense pain before but this time it's not my fault. I lied that day in school and I have been sorry ever since but I am not lying today. I don't know if Aranya was exacting revenge on me for what I did to her earlier, but your daughter has cheated on me. She played with my feelings and she ran away with Raghuvir. I understand she has a better future than I have but she had no right to do what she did with me,' said Dhruv, his voice quivering. He was careful not to overdo it.

Sanchit had warned him against that. It was with him that he had planned this out.

Dhruv continued, 'We spent days together holed up in my hostel room. I really loved her.' Dhruv passed on his cellphone to Aranya's father and mother and they flicked through pictures of Aranya and him in college, the library, the mess, cute pictures of a couple who seem to be in safe, platonic love. It wasn't for nothing Dhruv was clicking those pictures. It was all a part of his and Sanchit's plan to take back what was his.

Raghuvir snatched the phone from him and went through the pictures. He looked at Aranya angrily, his gaze demanding an explanation for the series of pictures that looked like they had been clicked over a period of a month or two.

It was then that it hit Aranya. The nights and days that followed the announcement of the results had been carefully orchestrated by Sanchit and Dhruv. The drunk night, the passionate make-outs, the pictures taken by Dhruv to capture the moments they spent together were all leading up to this moment.

She was quite clueless to be frank. That ass, Sanchit! Devious Dhruv!

'And she left me,' said Dhruv. 'I did everything to please her. I even scored the highest marks in the first semester but to no avail. I'm sorry but I had to tell you this. You're the only ones who can make her realize that I really love her.'

Her father was unimpressed. He shot a glance towards Aranya. 'What the hell is this, Aranya?' he thundered.

Aranya looked down at her feet not knowing what to do.

'ANSWER YOUR FATHER,' said Raghuvir, clutching his head like it was about to burst.

'We are so sorry, Raghuvir,' her mother said in a pleading tone to Raghuvir who was now pacing around in little circles. 'I'm sure there's some mistake.'

Her father had now got up. Aranya and Dhruv both knew what was going to happen. 'Hold him,' her father instructed Aranya's brother. 'We will call the police. He tried making an MMS of my daughter. I'll get this bastard thrown in jail.' Her brother held Dhruv who allowed him to do so even though he could have flicked the boy away. People had started to look now.

Aranya's father charged towards Aranya but Dhruv shouted. 'Stop! It's not her fault. It's Raghuvir who misled her.'

'What are you saying?' Her father turned, his hand half raised. 'Shut your mouth, fucker.'

Dhruv saw a hand rushing to meet his face. It crashed against his nose, making it bleed.

'Check Raghuvir's phone. He's already seeing other women. He's playing with your daughter's life. Check his phone and you will know. DO IT!'

'What's he saying?' Aranya's father turned towards Raghuvir. Aranya was stumped.

'I . . . it's . . . nothing,' said Raghuvir and his hand reached his pocket.

'SHOW ME,' the father said and lunged towards Raghuvir. He grabbed him and pushed his hand into his pocket and pulled out his phone. Raghuvir tried fighting but her father was too strong.

Aranya's father frantically unlocked the phone and read the messages. His face bloated in anger. He passed the phone to Aranya's mother. Aranya looked on speechlessly. Aranya's mother squinted her eyes and read the messages slowly.'

'*Bhenchod! KAUN HAI YE FARAH!*' her father shouted and smacked Raghuvir who staggered backwards.

'Look, I can explain,' said Raghuvir and looked at Aranya.

'What's there to explain, Raghuvir?' said Aranya, fake tears streaming down her face.

'GET OUT OF HERE, GET OUT, BEFORE I BEAT YOU UP IN FRONT OF EVERYONE!' her father said to Raghuvir who tried to explain himself to Aranya and to Aranya's mother but none of them looked in his direction.

Raghuvir started to walk away from them towards the exit. 'I will call you,' he shouted.

'Don't,' said Aranya and sat next to her mother who cradled her.

'GET OUT!' her father shouted again and Raghuvir exited the visitors' lounge, confused at what had just hit him. He waited, took a few undecided steps, and left.

Aranya's father sat next to her mother and held his head in his palms. Her brother let go of Dhruv's arms and Dhruv sat down again.

He spoke. 'I think I should get going. I understand it all now. Aranya pretended to be in love with me so that she could punish me for what I had done years ago. I have learned my lesson.' Aranya's father nodded, only half listening to him, trying to make sense of all this. Dhruv continued, 'But I loved her truly.'

'Do your parents know?' asked Aranya's father.

'My father's dead. My mother knows,' said Dhruv. A sense of relief swept over Aranya's mother's face. She looked at Aranya for an explanation.

Aranya finally broke her silence, mumbling through little sobs. 'He hurt you. He hurt my family. I had no choice but to do what I did. I did this for you, my family.' She cried.

Dhruv was quite surprised to see her come back with an awesome improvisation on the situation and gave her a metaphorical Best Actress Oscar for it. It was her parents' turn to be shocked. Her mother cradled Aranya's face and kissed it.

'So you lied that day in school?' her father demanded. Dhruv nodded. 'We knew that,' he said in hindsight. 'My daughter would have never done what you said she did.' Dhruv almost anticipated another smack coming his way but it didn't.

'Thank you,' Aranya's mother said. 'Raghuvir looked like a really nice guy. We would have never known had you not told us.'

'Thank you,' said Aranya, shyly.

'But have you forgiven me?' asked Dhruv.

Aranya nodded. 'I'm sorry.' And just as she said that Aranya's flight was announced and all passengers were asked to get their immigration and security check done.

'I should be going,' said Aranya to her mother.

Her mother whispered in her ear. 'He's not that bad. Think about him. He really likes you.' Aranya nodded and stood up. She touched her father's feet; he hugged her and wished her the best of luck. In a surprising turn of events, her brother hugged her too.

She had just started to walk towards the gate again when Aranya's father tapped Dhruv's shoulder and said as a matter of fact, 'Go, drop her.'

'But—'

'We don't mind,' said her father and shot Aranya a look. Her father had already decided who they would shift the responsibility of Aranya on. Such pricks.

Dhruv walked shyly towards Aranya. Aranya acted like a coy newly wed bride.

'You're incorrigible,' muttered Aranya.

'Would you have me any other way?'

Aranya smiled. The guard stopped Dhruv at the gate but Aranya pleaded that she was going away for two years and she could really do with some extra time with her fiancé. The guard let them go.

Dhruv and Aranya walked towards Immigration.

'When did you plan this?' asked Aranya.

'Once Sanchit told me he was working with you and that I had disappointed you, failing almost everything you had put me through.'

'What if he hadn't told you?'

'We shouldn't be thinking about this right now, should we?' asked Dhruv.

'Are we still in the line of sight of my parents?' asked Aranya.

'No. Why?'

Without another word, Aranya turned and grabbed Dhruv by his collar and landed a rather savage kiss on his lips which

Dhruv reciprocated with equal ferocity. Several minutes and a lot of embarrassed passengers later, they separated.

'That was good,' said Dhruv.

'I know.'

'Pompous bitch.'

'Get used to it. And anyway, you have to wait for three years now. I hope you know that, Dhruv.'

'I waited for eight. Three years is nothing.'

They announced her flight again.

'Time to go.'

'Time to go,' repeated Dhruv.

'You're the most annoying, irritating, chauvinistic, vain man I have ever met but I love you.'

'You're—'

'Don't call me ugly or I'm already breaking up with you.'

'What makes you think I care? I'm in love with you. And how you look is the least of my concerns. You're going to a country where 58 per cent of its population is overweight and frankly I don't expect you to come back as a Victoria's Secret model. All I know is, I will love you even if you come back as a sperm whale.'

'Great to know that my first proper, proper boyfriend compares me to a whale,' said Aranya and threw her arms around him.

'Stop playing with words, you witch.'

'Fuck you.'

'Fuck you.'

'We are so fucked up.'

'That we are. And that's why we are meant to be.'

'I love you.'

'I love you.'